THE FRAGILE BLUE DOT
Stories from Our Imperiled Biosphere

Published by GladEye Press
Interior design: J.V. Bolkan
Cover design: Sharleen Nelson
Author image: Kristin Hiatt
ISBN-13: 978-1-951289-08-9
Library of Congress Control Number:

Printed in the United States of America.
10 9 8 7 6 5 4 3 2 1
The body text is presented in Jenson Pro 11 point for easy readibility.

Dedication

For Barbara. Without you there wouldn't be any stories to tell.

Table of Contents

The following stories have previously been published; each has been at least slightly modified for presentation in this volume.

"Boiling Alive" appeared in the anthology *Extinction Notice: Tales of a Warming Earth*, edited by David Harten Watson, Silver Sword Press, 2022.

"Downsizing" appeared in *Pangyrus* (March 2022).

"Cowabunga Sunset" appeared in *Sinking City* #11 (Autumn 2021).

"Chrysalis" appeared in *Litro* (October 2021).

"If Anything Changes" was selected as a winner of Defenestrationism.net's 2022 Short Story Contest.

"Ophelia's Understudy" appeared in *North Dakota Quarterly*, Volume 89, Numbers 1-2 (SpringSummer 2022).

"Plans" (as "The Omelet Maker") was selected as a finalist in Defenestrationism.net's 2020 Short Story Contest.

"The Fifty Faces of Albert Einstein" appeared in *Wisconsin Review*, Volume 55, No. 1 and was selected as a finalist in *EcoTheo Review*'s 2021 short story contest.

"The Real Manhattan" (as "My Big Break") appeared in *Blue Lake Review* (January 2022).

"Tool" appeared in *Lime Hawk*, Issue 13 (Winter 2021) and received Special Mention recognition in the Stories to Change the World 3 contest (2020).

"Untellable Tales, Chapter XXXVII" appeared in the *Santa Ana River Review* (April 2022).

Chrysalis

The roar of the engine filled the small cabin of SunVista's sleek propeller-driven airplane. My fingers rested on the window, and I watched puffy cotton-ball clouds drift past, well-spaced in a bright blue sky. I was barreling at great speed toward what I could only think of as my future.

After I had been assigned to gather data from the Rocas Caliente job site, Human Resources sent me a prep packet for the trip, full of tips about heat exhaustion and scorpions. I thought it might be a good idea to talk to Eddie Vanvactor, an engineer with a cubicle near mine at SunVista headquarters. He'd been on the original Pier Design Team and done onsite testing and specification work in the project's early days.

"What I can tell you, Lisa," he'd said, happy to share what he knew, "is that back then things were way different from what's out there now." With a few clicks on his keyboard, he brought up photos of what looked like a Wild West mining camp. "Those were our tents," he said, pointing to the screen. "Slept on cots, hot as hell. Now it's modular housing, AC, everything."

I wanted to do my field assignment as well as possible, and to me that included figuring out the who's-who and what's-what of a place. So I asked Vanvactor, "Anything about Rocas Caliente I ought to know? Any good dirt?" He stiffened and rotated his office chair back to his computer, closed the photo app, and said over his shoulder, "I have something I have to get done."

The airplane's engine noise changed; the cabin tilted downward. Once the tires touched the dirt runway, I didn't breathe until we rattled to a stop. Waiting for me when I got off the plane was a company man with a company SUV offering me a company swag bag.

"Richie Simms," he said, extending his hand for a shake. "Autonomous construction coordinator and welcoming committee."

"Lisa Contreras."

It was a big hand and he was a big friendly guy, a few years older than me but probably still under thirty. We got in the SUV and tore over dirt and gravel on the straight desert road, past miles of sagebrush, juniper, and cactus. Unable to resist, I dug into the bulging tote bag on my lap.

"Coffee cup, T-shirt, hat, water bottle, key chain, letter opener, binder, pen and pencil set." Richie spoke in a funny voice that sounded like he was hawking the stuff on QVC. "Each item emblazoned with SunVista's distinctive sunburst logo. As fine an assortment of corporate crap as you'll ever find—at least on this side of the landfill."

I laughed. "You'd never make it in public relations."

"I take that as a compliment."

"How did you end up out here?" I asked.

"Worked in robotics and autonomous machines for a couple of years at a start-up. When this job posted, I jumped on it. Thirty-six arrays in North America, each bigger than anything ever built—our own frickin' Manhattan Project."

"You don't mind the isolation?"

His face screwed up like, Are you crazy? He reached into the tote bag, pulled out a copy of *Engineering Weekly* and handed it to me. "Hot off the press." I opened it to the page marked with a yellow stickie note and read the headline: Rocas Caliente: They're Fabbing the Future. A grin on his face, his head rocked up and down like he was hearing a favorite song.

I saw my opening. "Did you ever know a guy named Vanvactor? Eddie Vanvactor—they sent him out from Palo Alto probably eighteen months ago."

"Just before my time. What about him?"

"Odd guy. When he talked about being out here, he acted kind of, I don't know . . . funny."

"No shortage of weird shit in this desert. Pardon my French."

A security checkpoint appeared up ahead, a small structure with a long yellow barricade arm extended from its side to block the road.

"You'll need your ID," Richie said. "It's in with the trinkets."

I found the laminated tag and slipped its lanyard around my neck as we came to a stop. A uniformed guard wearing mirrored sunglasses and a US Department of Energy patch on his shirt approached Richie's window. They exchanged a few words and the guard looked my way. I smiled and held out the plastic badge.

He touched two fingers to his brow. "Welcome to Rocas Caliente, ma'am."

Up went the barricade and in we drove. After a mile or so, the left side of the road changed abruptly from a wild rugged wasteland into SunVista's manicured, state-of-the-art solar energy installation. Thousands of sturdy, precisely spaced concrete piers rose up twenty feet tall, each topped with one of our dual-axis heliotrackers, an advanced photovoltaic panel the size of half a tennis court.

The structures were identical, every panel angled toward the sun at exactly the same inclination. Row after row after row, like some alien robot army standing at attention.

As suddenly as the desert had bloomed into a well-tended solar farm, the farm now gave way to several acres of messy chaos where gigantic construction machines roared and clanked and belched black smoke. Bulldozers, graders, excavators, pile borers—and not a single human operator in sight.

"They're finishing up Phase I," Richie said. "Next week we start in on the south side of the road."

"All fully autonomous?"

"Run 'em 24/7—or until something breaks."

We sped past the machines and were now back alongside more elevated PV panels that we skirted all the way to the base of the eastern hills. The road ascended the slope, hugging the twisting contours up the rimrock. When we'd gained a good deal of elevation, we pulled to a stop at a turnabout.

"It's not far," Richie said, getting out of the SUV and leading the way to a trail that disappeared behind a bulky outcrop. "Keep your eye out for snakes."

I followed him closely. The badge around my neck swung back and forth with each step up the steep rocky staircase. Heat radiated from boulders and sheer walls baking in the late afternoon sun. I wondered how much farther and if maybe we should have brought water. We rounded a corner and the trail broadened onto a flat overlook.

Richie walked to the edge of the high cliff, sweat blotching the back of his shirt. "This is the best view," he said.

Breathing hard from the climb, I stood next to him, and we stared out over the vast frying pan of the desert, a broad valley extending to a range of hills in the west. Bisecting our view was the thin line of the only road in sight. On the south side of this incongruous geometry, a barren wilderness that seemed as if it hadn't changed since time began; to the north, the solar towers, an architect's vision imposed on the landscape with the precise angularity of a chessboard. The rows of gleaming heliotrackers receded toward the horizon in converging perspective lines.

"See over there," Richie said, pointing at the construction site we'd passed where twenty or so bright yellow earthmoving machines crawled with the coordinated industry of ants.

I took in the whole of the project, one of three hundred being constructed around the world as part of the UN's Comprehensive Climate Emergency Initiative. We were finally taking responsibility for our impact on the planet, finally repairing rather than destroying. I remembered the joy I felt when I learned I had landed the job with SunVista, how proud I was when I told my parents.

"Four months ago I was in grad school," I said to Richie, trying to keep my voice steady. "Now I'm part of this."

He nodded like he understood. "For so long it was all this gloom and doom shit. The planet's dying! The planet's dying! But nobody was doing dick about it. Pardon my French." He reached down and picked up a rock, hauled back, chucked it. "Those days are gone." The rock sailed in a long, lazy arc and landed far below with a little puff of dust. "Well, if you've seen enough . . . the VIP tour will conclude with a visit to the Cantina del Mar for a tall cold one." He flashed a quitting-time smile.

We drove ten miles to a crossroads, the four corners occupied by a cantina, a minimart, a gas station, and a boarded-up Quonset hut, each in its own way losing the battle with dust and dilapidation.

The bar was half full and quietly murmuring. Three workmen in yellow reflector vests with SunVista logos were sharing a pitcher and watching a baseball game on the big screen TV.

"Hey Rich," one of them called out.

Richie bobbed his chin. "Hey Stan. Guys."

We settled into seats at one of the tables and a grizzled waiter with a Willie Nelson ponytail and a faded Metallica T-shirt came our way, rising and falling on uneven steps. He took our order and limped off.

The walls were adorned with fishing nets and starfish, a captain's wheel, life preservers, a pair of crossed oars, a velvet tapestry of Noah's ark with animal pairs lined up to get on board, and, arched above the liquor bottles behind the bar, a stuffed marlin.

Richie noticed me checking out the décor. "What's up with the nautical theme, huh?"

"They know their geology," I said. "A hundred million years ago this desert was under half a mile of saltwater."

The waiter brought two pints. After our hike the cold beer tasted good and went down easy. Setting his glass on the table, Richie leaned toward me and in a low voice said, "See that guy over there?" He made a slight nod, his eyes pointing the way behind my left shoulder. With a stealthy turn of my head I spied an older man slumped alone at a table for four—rumpled shirt, dirty pants, dusty worn boots, and a week's worth of gray stubble.

"Looks like my crazy uncle," I said.

"Professor Carlton Maddox, the world's expert on the desert pygmy blue dot butterfly."

"Okay . . . and?"

"He's a big deal out here—or was. People wanted to build a wind farm in this valley since back in the nineties and he fought it." Richie let out a little laugh. "He was stubborn as a mule and fiercely anti-windmill—which got him the nickname Donkey Hotey."

I smiled and sipped my beer. "He stopped the windmills?"

"For decades."

"But Rocas Caliente?"

"Maddox and his Sierra Club buddies used the Endangered Species Act—installing the windmill towers would destroy butterfly habitat. But then along came the Clean Earth Act with its 'emergency superseding authority' clause and poof, with those three magic words, everything changed."

"So, what's up with the butterflies now?"

I wasn't sure if Richie heard my question. He rose suddenly from his seat, said, "Excuse me," and walked to the restroom. Passing the bar, he caught the waiter's eye and gestured for another round. One would have been fine with me, but apparently that isn't how they roll at Rocas Caliente.

I thought of the Clean Earth Act and remembered the famous video clip we'd all seen a hundred times—the senator from Mississippi pounding her fist on the podium as she delivered her impassioned speech in a heavy Southern drawl—If we don't pass this Act to protect the Earth, there isn't going to be any Earth left for us to protect.

I finished off what was left of my beer. Richie's exit had been so sudden—maybe he had heard my question. His behavior brought to mind Eddie Vanvactor and how he froze up when I asked about his experiences out here.

It's better not to turn over rocks—I recalled my mother's voice from when I was a five or six. She was a woman who liked things tidy and always avoided trouble; but as a little kid I took the phrase literally and, being a smarty-pants, started turning over every rock I could find. Under most of them wriggled a freaky menagerie of creepy-crawlies, my very own circus of tiny dinosaurs.

The waiter brought over our pints. Richie wasn't far behind. He sat, sipped, and brushed a finger across his lips. "As far as the butterflies are concerned," he said, picking up the conversation as if he'd never left, "we're operating in full compliance with all applicable regulations and controlling legal authorities."

Huh? Did he get a law degree from one of those little machines in the bathroom?

"How does that play out?" I asked. "I mean, specifically?"

"Full compliance." He shrugged like, What else can I say? "Everything's by the book."

"That sounds pretty corporate." I knew immediately it was the wrong thing to say.

His face flushed. "You want to know about the butterflies," he said, strangling his glass with both hands, "specifically?"

I didn't want to seem pushy, but yes, I did want to know. I raised my eyebrows and gave him an unthreatening nod and my sweetest smile.

He blinked his eyes and made little huffing sounds. I could almost hear him counting to ten. The tension left his fingers first, then his face. "Okay, screw it," he said and shifted his weight in the chair. "When the dozers grade the lots for the panels, it's kind of like . . . well, byebye habitat."

"You mean at the site, right—just here in the valley?"

He cleared his throat. "This is the only place they breed."

I stared, waiting for the rest of the story, eager to hear the clever way the problem had been solved. But he just sat there, a sheepish look on his face.

"There's gotta be more to it than that."

He shook his head. "All I can say is we're in full compliance. All the Ts are crossed." Not satisfactory. Not at all.

I glanced over my shoulder and saw that professor Maddox was still there. "I want to talk to him."

Richie made a face and ran his hand over the back of his head. "He can be a little . . . prickly."

"I'm a good talker," I said with the confidence that comes when I drink. I took up my beer, rose, and marched to Maddox's table, planting myself opposite him.

With his gray eyes fixed on his glass, he said in a deep voice, "What do you want?"

"I heard about your work. I'm interested—"

"I don't have any work," he snapped. He hoisted his beer and drained it. "Not anymore." He slammed the glass hard against the tabletop twice. The waiter looked over and Maddox raised a finger for another pint.

Richie walked up as I tried again. "The butterflies—"

"Who told you about me?"

"He did. He works—"

"Oh, I know him." Maddox cocked an eyebrow and squinted at Richie. "The exterminating angel." He turned his gaze back to me. "But who are you?"

The waiter lumbered up, removed the empty glass, and set a frothy pint on the table.

"Lisa. I do geology, geoengineering—the dynamics of foundation piers and soil substrates. My team is tasked with—"

"Oh Christ." He snatched the glass and drank. "Sit down. Sit down." He swept his free hand toward the unoccupied chairs. "At least while you're here you aren't killing anything."

As we sat, Maddox's eyes were daggers trained on Richie. "You and your damn machines." He drank and then worked his lips like he wanted to spit.

"The fact is, professor," Richie said, "what me and my damn machines are doing is part of the solution, the global solution—in case you missed the news flash."

"You're right, you're right," Maddox answered, slathering on the mock contrition. "In all their infinite wisdom, Congress hath declared your work to be more important than mine. Has more val-ue." He lifted his pint, took two great swallows, and dragged the back of his hand across his lips. "With a stroke of a pen." He growled like an angry dog. "'Emergency circumstances.' 'Extraordinary necessity.' Just like when we locked up the Japanese during the war." He sank lower in his chair and rubbed at his forehead. "Stroke of a goddamn pen."

"But isn't there some provision in the Act," I said, "some exception, some way to challenge—"

Maddox snorted. "No, young lady, there is no such provision. The pendulum has swung. As pendula will. The day the Clean Earth Act passed, the whole country celebrated with marches and parades. You know what I did? I sat right here, right at this table, and I got drunk. Drunk, drunk, duh-runk. I saw the handwriting."

"There are always going to be trade-offs," Richie said. "That's how things work. In a perfect world—"

"Of course, of course. You're saving the planet. I get it, really, I do." Maddox said in a conciliatory tone that disappeared when he thundered, "All hail the great god Sus-tain-ability! In whose name no wrong can be done." He made a sloppy sign of the cross and threw down the last of his beer. "But this glorious new world of yours, it's not a place I want to live." He shook his head, burped. "So, over and out, adios amigos."

I looked to Richie, who put his hands on the arms of his chair and gave a little jerk of his head toward our table.

It couldn't end like this; I couldn't let it. "Show us one," I blurted. "Show us one of your butterflies. One of the blue dots—in the wild. I want to see one. Right now. Will you?"

He considered this for a moment, then his bony body shook with a weary little laugh. "Off limits, I'm afraid. Roadblocks and drones, and that gentleman in the guard shack—he might not understand."

I grabbed the ID hanging around my neck and thrust it toward him. "We have credentials."

Maddox eyed the badge, blinked several times, then rolled his head toward Richie. "What do you say, boss?"

Richie picked at a callus on his hand.

"C'mon," Maddox pleaded. "I worked with those butterflies thirty-six years."

Richie ignored Maddox and said to me, "You really want to do this?"

"We could be the last people ever to see them alive."

We paid our tabs and went to the car. Maddox had his keys out, but Richie shook his head. "I'm driving."

No one spoke all the way to the security checkpoint. The guard with the mirrored sunglasses recognized us. When he saw the passenger, he made a circling motion with his finger and Maddox rolled down the back window. The guard bent down and gave Maddox a careful once-over.

"He's with you?" he said to Richie without turning his head.

"That's right."

The guard shifted his jaw back and forth. He leaned in a little farther, sniffed, and recoiled. Noticing the safety belt dangling unused, he hooked his finger around the nylon strap and gave a tug. "You ought to be wearing this." Maddox made a show of pulling the harness across his chest and clicking the buckle.

The barricade arm swung up and we eased forward.

"Up there on the right there's a turnout," Maddox said, unfastening the buckle and flinging the restraint aside. "The blue dots are stubbornly resistant to transplantation," he said like the bio professor he was. "There's something that allows them to thrive on this plain, at this elevation—some micronutrient, some symbiotic relationship we have yet to identify. As soon as the plans for your project were announced, we focused all our attention on answering this question, but . . ."

"You ran out of time," I said.

"When the feds tell you, 'Restricted area, do not enter,' it's generally a good idea to listen." He sighed. "I passed the lab to my post-doc, retired, moved to the cabin I always kept out here." A sullen shadow darkened his face—maybe sadness, maybe shame. "I tell people I'm writing a book."

The high wall of solar towers rose on our left. Maddox gawked up at them, curious and horrified, as if glimpsing in broad daylight the monsters that haunted his nightmares.

"There's the turn," he said. Richie steered us onto two pitted tracks, and we slowly bounced through gullies and washouts.

Maddox craned his neck at the landscape, getting his bearings. "At my old lab they maintain a temperature- and humidity-controlled propagation chamber. But that's only a stopgap, hardly adequate."

The rough trail became no trail at all. Richie braked to a stop and cut the motor. "End of the line."

We stepped from the air-conditioned SUV into the hot, still air. The sun was halfway below the line of western hills and colored our harsh surroundings in mellow orange light.

Maddox meandered with unsure steps first one way then another, his eyes sweeping the terrain.

"Is this the right place?" Richie asked.

Maddox ambled in an aimless arc. "Without studying them in situ," he said, his words trailed off—something had his attention. "There!"

He thrashed through the brush and trudged up a rise topped with jagged rocks and spindly plants. I followed, thorns grabbing at my pantlegs.

"We pass idiot legislation like the Clean Earth Act, rushing forward before counting the costs," he groused, carefully scanning the low hilltop. "Humanity's great cycle: saving the world from the last joker's effort to save the world." He stopped and listened, panning his head slowly left then right. "Collateral damage, acceptable losses." He turned to stare Richie in the face. "Trade-offs, as you people so delicately put it. Oh, the sublime hubris of the exculpatory euphemism."

"Look," Richie said, chest out, hands dug in his back pockets, "I'm not seeing a whole bunch of butterflies, doc. Fact is, I'm not seeing a damn one."

Maddox glared at Richie and Richie glared right back.

When I had asked to see the blue dots, I'd imagined a happy little field trip to a big green bush shimmering with a hundred bright butterflies. Instead, here we were, in the middle of the desert, traipsing after a drunk Donkey Hotey through a thicket of nettles going nowhere.

"Let's get out of here," Richie said.

"Shhh," Maddox held up his hand. He listened, swiveled his head, listened some more while looking hard into the scraggy brush. He whistled a bird call, whit-whit-whit and stood motionless. Whit-whit-whit . . . whit-whit-whit.

A small brown bird appeared and landed on a boulder. Its head twitched side to side.

Maddox whispered, "Don't move."

The bird hopped to the ground and pecked at the sand. It pushed a twig with its beak and clawed at a small rock. Spooked by something, it flew off.

Richie and I relaxed, but Maddox held up his hand for us to remain still. He whistled again, whit-whit-whit . . . whit-whit-whit. The bird glided back onto the same boulder. It flitted to a small cactus and from there to the ground near a low leafy vine with a white trumpeting flower. The bird glanced left and right then hopped closer to the vine and after glancing nervously around once more, ducked under a large flat leaf. The leaf quivered as the bird pecked at it from below.

"Byah!" Maddox called out, clapping his hands to shoo the bird away. He dropped to his knees beside the plant. "That little fellow likes a gnat that lives on some of these vines—but only some of these vines." He turned over one leaf after another, searching along midribs and veins.

"There's an association between those gnats and where the butterflies prefer—" He bent closer.

"Aha!" With a pinch of his fingers, he removed a bit of the leaf, stood, and walked toward us, his discovery held before him. Dangling from the green swatch by the thinnest of threads was a tiny pod the size and color of a coffee bean.

"Put out your hand," Maddox said, his face aglow.

He placed the chrysalis on my outstretched palm and our three heads moved in close.

"Behold," he said, "Brephidium bolanderii."

It weighed at most a gram or two. But what if this fragile little thing was, after millions of years of evolution, the species terminus, the blue dot's last incarnation, its last hope?

"Put that in a jar, outside, in the shade. Punch some holes in the lid," Maddox said. "If you're lucky, you'll be there to watch it emerge."

We climbed back into the SUV. Richie executed a series of maneuvers and got us back on the road. He accelerated, and we traveled alongside the PV panels. From ahead of us came the beep-beep-beep of the machines' warning horns, soon joined by the noise of clanking treads and gunning engines. The sound rose to a crescendo as we passed the behemoth earthmovers, hydraulic shovels, and dump trucks carving relentlessly into the soil—driverless, guided by some invisible plan. As we left the construction site and the din faded, I heard soft snores coming from the back seat.

I looked down at my hand, open, palm up. On it, the bean.

If Anything Changes

When the front desk clerk at the Reykjavik Manor Hotel eyed Kat's dusty duffle bags and asked if she needed any help carrying them to her room, she said she could handle it just fine by herself. She lugged the bags into the elevator and pushed the button for the twelfth floor. The whir of the machinery reminded her of the whooshing sound of meltwater reflecting off the smooth rounded contours of the ice caves she had been exploring all week . . . sunlight filtering through the glacial ice, tunnel walls glowing an otherworldly blue. She piled the bags on the bed in her room, dug her phone from her rucksack, and checked it for the first time since getting back within cell coverage. The message was there: a voicemail from the dean. She listened—the committee had made its decision, please give a call. The dean's voice was cheery. He had left both his home and office numbers. Kat pumped her fist and danced around the room. The university would be offering her the position.

She found a tiny bottle of champagne in the minibar, poured it in a plastic glass from the bathroom, and held it high, reciprocating a toast from a room full of admirers.

It was evening, a little late to return the dean's call—but not too late. First though, she needed to calm down. In the shower, she bounced on the balls of her feet, arms hugging her torso, water falling on her like hot rain. The tenure-track position would open doors she would run through—to Patagonia, Greenland, Antarctica. Plum gigs on *National Geographic* expeditions. And more books, definitely more books. Another TED Talk. Maybe a special science advisor appointment. What incredible luck to be in a field so flush with opportunity. She recalled Reuben's joke—The really great news for glaciologists is that global warming will be frying the planet for decades to come.

Toweling her straw-blonde hair, she considered how the job would require a move to North Carolina—at least for her. Reuben didn't want to leave Seattle. They could keep their house there. He could keep his job. But she couldn't possibly turn this down. Maybe she would commute.

Pacing around the room in the hotel's white terrycloth robe, she tossed down the last of the champagne and phoned the dean. They chatted and laughed; he talked enthusiastically about the Center for the Study of Women, Science, and Society. The phone to her ear, Kat walked to the window, rested her free hand on its smooth cold surface, and gazed down on Reykjavik spreading to the harbor, the ocean extending to the horizon. Her eyes filled with tears. She accepted the position.

Kat called Reuben, told him the university had made the offer. No, of course she hadn't accepted it—not without talking with him. They could discuss it when they met up in Alaska.

She suddenly felt very tired and slid between the cool sheets of the bed with a relaxed sigh. Her last thought before sleep was of flying between Seattle and Raleigh-Durham . . . east then west then east again . . . striding down the long airport concourse, her wheelie suitcase rolling smoothly behind, errrr-errrr-errrr. It wouldn't be a problem.

✺

Turning the key in the front door lock, Reuben frowned. Could the timing be any worse? Not an hour ago he'd signed-off on the Halloween campaign for the ad agency's biggest client; now home to pack and fly off early tomorrow for a vacation in Alaska that would leave the restaurant chain's Thanksgiving campaign in the hands of ... Well, nothing he could do about that now. Plans were plans.

He set his briefcase, keys, and phone on the kitchen table and poured himself a Scotch. After a first sip, he decided to take one more look, just to be sure. The news of Kat's job offer had left him preoccupied all day; he could easily have missed something important. He opened the briefcase and paged through a folder of the approved artwork for the Halloween menu, print and online ads of various sizes, in-store posters, on-table placards, and take-out bags promoting this year's Freaky Five: Scary Cherry Shake, Frankenstein Fries, Double Deluxe Dracula Drumsticks, Zombie Pastrami, and Fear-o Hero. He scanned each page for color mismatches, registration errors, bad spacing, text mistakes, anything. He slipped the files back into the case, snapped the latches shut, rubbed his tired eyes. Let it go.

After dinner, Reuben packed, emptied the fridge of food that would go bad, took out the trash. The last item on his list was taking care of the cacti. Carrying an eyedropper and a juice glass of fertilized water, he moved from windowsill to windowsill where his dozens of species of prickly and spineless cactus lived in their little clay pots. He cooed words of encouragement to them while squeezing the dropper's bulb to give each plant what it would need in his absence.

A second Scotch in hand, he took a seat at his computer. Best not to surprise her up in Alaska. She'll need time to think it over. He opened a new email message and typed.

Dear Kat,
Love you. Miss you. Congratulations, again, on getting the
offer! What an honor! You rock!!!

He sipped and pondered how to begin.

I've been doing a lot of thinking since we talked last night.
Mostly I've thought about where we want to be in five, ten,
twenty years, and what we do to get there. It seems we've
come to the point of making some decisions—and not just
to accept or not accept the UNC offer.

Did he want her to take the job? Did it even matter what he
thought? She wanted it and she'd take it. She hadn't always been
so driven—or maybe she had been, maybe he just hadn't noticed.
Everything suddenly feels so serious.

He took off his glasses and rubbed his eyes until the words
came to him.

Most of all, I want us to be together and I'm willing to do
anything to make that happen. I thought back on all our not-
very-specific talks over the years about having kids. Remember
when we used to dream about kids and getting a Jack Russell
terrier? I want us to have those kids, to have that life.

You've listened to me bitch for years about how much I hate
being Management, and all my half-baked fantasies about
going back to being a production artist or quitting and setting
up my own studio.

But here's what I'm thinking now. My salary is enough so you could keep building your career in Seattle, doing all the fieldwork you want AND we could have a family. For that, I'd be willing to do anything, including change how I feel about my job.

No, I'm not being a martyr. I would, in fact, be really, truly, genuinely, honestly happy and grateful to do this. I know we can work it out one way or another. What I want is for us to be together always. Everything else is just . . . everything else.

All my love, my dearest one. See you soon,
Roobie

PS: You're still on flight 374 (Reykjavik/SF/Juneau) arriving at 8:45, yes? Call if anything changes.

He read the note and read it again. She wouldn't want to hear this, wouldn't want the pressure. If she took it wrong, it would be a week of her scorn and dagger eyes in Alaska. Still, it had to be said, their future depended on it. He tapped the send key. In her court now.

The *Adventure Quest* churned northward through the frigid waters of Alaska's Inland Passage. The shoreline was blanketed with evergreen forests and, farther off, a range of sawtooth mountains white with snow. Their first evening on the water, the hundred Eco Tours Expedition passengers gathered in the ship's dining room. Kat and Reuben took seats next to one another at an unoccupied table for four and ordered a bottle of wine.

She glanced at Reuben while he read the menu. It was there in his pinched lip, the tension in his brow—he was thinking he'd written his thoughts in the email, and now it was up to her to respond. But not yet, not here. Put it off a while. Tell him more about Iceland—the three minke whales breaching off Húsavík. No, they had said they would talk, they should talk. But where to start? She sipped her wine, read the menu again.

"Well, hello there," a voice chirped from nearby. Kat and Reuben looked up to see a petite woman with perm-curly hair standing beside a lanky balding man. The woman extended her hand, "Cynthia and Robert Grossmeyer."

"This is Kat. I'm Reuben."

They shook and the Grossmeyers sat, with Cynthia explaining in a flurry that they were from Peoria, that Rob was an optometrist and she, an avid birdwatcher and gardener—it was absolutely breaking her heart to leave her vegetables at this time of year—was active in the PTA and the Beautify Peoria Parks Campaign in the few scant moments she wasn't busy raising their fifteen-year-old fraternal twins currently at summer camp—sort of a dude ranch, really—in Montana.

"What about you guys?" Rob asked.

"We've met some of the most interesting people while cruising, haven't we Rob?" Cynthia said. "I mean, really, really interesting people. From all over. We just love it." Rob nodded.

After giving their orders to the waiter, Kat and Reuben shared about living in Seattle, his job at the ad agency, how this was his first cruise and first time in Alaska, how her aunt and uncle lived not far from Peoria. They tiptoed around mention of Kat's work, fully aware of what would happen once the

Grossmeyers learned she was one of those interesting people they were just dying to meet.

Reuben tilted the wine bottle toward Kat. She raised her eyebrows, yes, and he topped off their glasses. Cynthia fixed Kat in the stare of her perky bright-blue eyes. "So, tell us about *you*."

As soon as they finished the baked Alaska and decaf, they exchanged a glance, and Kat told the Grossmeyers how nice it had been to meet and how, tomorrow being a big day, they were turning in early.

Descending the stairs to their cabin's deck, Reuben chuckled and imitated Cynthia's voice, "It's not like I don't have a life of my own or anything, but gawd, Kat, you are just so interesting. Isn't she, Rob?"

"Our new best friends, the Grossmeyers," Kat said with a mock shudder and a roll of her green eyes. Reuben held open the cabin door for her. She entered, switched on the bedside lamp, and stood in the stillness and soft light watching him kick off his shoes.

"So," she said, "your email."

He settled onto the bed, propped against the headboard, arms wrapped around a pillow on his chest. She pulled up a chair and sat.

"I keep thinking back to how things were when we first moved in together," he said.

"The apartment with the lovely sloping floors."

"And the crazy drummer dude always pounding away next door." He smiled at the memory then continued, choosing his words with care. "I was working and you were going back to school

so you could get a job you wanted … and then we'd have a family."
He looked at her. "That was it, that was our plan, wasn't it?"

"And we've done pretty well making it happen."

"We have, and I'm not taking anything away from that. At
the same time, what I want is to be with you. And I want—"

"Aren't we here right now?"

He shot her an annoyed glance. Her heartbeat quickened.
She always cut him off when they talked like this. It wasn't how
she wanted to be, but it was what she did.

"And when we dock," he said, "we fly back home and in two
days you're off to … I don't even remember where."

"New York, to meet with—"

"Your agent. Right." He took off his glasses and rubbed his
face. "I can't tell you how big the hole is when you're gone."

She wasn't sure what to say. Yes, she was away a lot. But—

"Everything's coming your way—and that's great," he said.
"But if we put things off much longer … "

"You want kids—with your family, all your cousins, I get it.
I guess I get it now in a way that I didn't when it was more …
theoretical. So yes, a family, okay. But I don't know, maybe more
like … later." He stiffened.

"When something big comes along, you can't ignore it," she
said. "You win the lottery, get cancer, it changes everything. It
doesn't make sense to pretend it's not happening."

"You want us to put everything else on hold?"

She leaned toward him, her eyes pleading. "I never thought
I'd have so little time."

"How long do you want to wait?" His voice was brittle. He
was tensing up; the discussion would soon become an argument.
But this was worth fighting for. And it didn't have to be a fight,

just give and take. Lay out a position, make a stand—if he doesn't like it, he can come up with something different.

"I don't know," she said. "A while."

He slumped forward, his face contorted by some mix of emotions—disappointment, resentment, anger. His head shook slowly back and forth—maybe working himself into a rage. "I did have one other idea," she said. "Sort of a compromise."

He turned to meet her gaze.

"I'd still be traveling a lot, but you could stay home, get all the family time you want." He swallowed, his eyes wide, expectant.

"If we moved to North Carolina, you could quit the agency and," she paused, nodding her head several times, "we could adopt."

He stared and blinked. His lips opened, about to speak, but he hesitated and turned away.

"You could freelance or work part-time, work from home—whatever feels right. We could get a nanny." He wasn't listening, was withering before her eyes. "Your mom could come visit." What had she done? "I'll have great insurance."

They held one another in the dark for a long time, spoke not a word. Then their bodies entwined and writhed and thrashed with an intensity unusual in their lovemaking.

Their panting subsided, they lay side by side holding hands. Her mind raced—she was horrible, selfish and horrible. Yes, they had planned. Yes, she had agreed. And now it was, oh, hey, sorry, new plan. When she had said adopt, she had crushed him. She hadn't intended to. It wasn't like an ultimatum or anything. Just an idea. A wrong, bad, stupid idea that she should have never said.

He stared at a small red light on the smoke alarm. After a while her breathing quieted and then became regular with sleep. He took his hand away from hers and rolled onto his side facing the wall. A tear pooled in the corner of his eye and slid down toward his ear. Another ran to the end of his nose, hung there, dropped onto the pillow.

The *Adventure Quest* floated in Solstice Bay, anchored a quarter mile from the sheer towering ice wall that marked the terminus of Alaska's second largest glacier. The air was still, the water like a mirror. Many of the ship's passengers had signed up for either a nature photography class or a workshop on boreal ecology and ice-core sampling. Others had already departed in motorized Zodiac boats to view wildlife and hike on a nearby island. Reuben and Kat stood on the open deck near the ship's bow in a group of twenty who had chosen to kayak among the bay's icebergs. They listened to one of the tour's naturalists, Megan, a tall, square-shouldered woman about thirty. Her Eco Tours parka glowed a vivid orange against the lapis sky and the blinding whiteness of the ice sheet's face.

"You're looking at ground zero for global warming," she said. "The glacier is shrinking; sea level is inching ever higher. Scientists predict rising water will flood hundreds of millions of people out of their homes." She turned to the shore, staring at the ice long enough for the group to consider the fragility of something so large and seemingly indestructible.

"Okay, enough with the gloom and doom," she said, facing them again. "What you are looking at is a river of frozen water flowing slowly into the sea. When the forces of fracturing exceed the forces of cohesion, pieces of the glacier body break off, or calve. Sometimes it's only a small avalanche, a few hundred pounds of ice. But keep your cameras ready," she said, flashing a playful smile. "On a glacier of this size you just might see fifty million pounds of ice do a belly flop."

Kat and Reuben wriggled into their dry suits, gloves, and neoprene booties. They donned personal flotation devices and loaded their cameras, dry bags, and water bottles into sleek canary-yellow kayaks.

Once all the boats were in the water, Megan called out, "Everybody pull in close." A tight flotilla formed, with Kat and Reuben bobbing beside one another. "We have two special rules on this bay. Numero uno: stay within sight of each other. And numero dos: never get any closer to the glacier than I do. Got it?" Heads nodded.

"Okay, let's head on over to bergville." Her kayak sliced forward; the others fell in behind.

Reuben's shoulders warmed with the exertion of pulling his boat through patches of slush and past refrigerator-sized blocks of ice. He stroked around larger and larger obstacles until the group reached the gallery of ice sculptures jutting from the water.

He stopped alongside a gargantuan berg and peered down into the water. The submarine ice descended ever farther, ever fainter, until it disappeared in the dark depths.

Kat eased her boat next to his. Her short blonde braids peeked out from under a knitted Icelandic wool cap. "Is this awesome or what?" she said, cheeks aglow and green eyes merry. Taking his gloved hand in hers, she squeezed. "Did you see that one?" She bobbed her chin toward what looked like a giant glass mushroom. "I gotta get a picture."

She dug her paddle into the water and cut a sharp turn while thinking how happy he looked and how she loved it when he was happy. Roobie-doobie. No way she could hurt him. Close to the mushroom, she stopped her boat and stared for a long time at the strangely shaped berg. What if they had the kids? People do it all the time. It wouldn't be the end of the world. The university would accommodate.

Megan found a high archway between two large ice masses and led the procession of kayakers through it. The first boater following her let out a gleeful yee-haw as he passed beneath the bridge, and each one that followed let loose as well. Reuben belted a whoo-hoo and thought of the many times Kat had shown him pictures she'd taken from berg-filled bays like this around the world—nearly every time mentioning how the beauty took her breath away. Now he understood.

The group followed Megan into a narrow canyon winding between tall walls of smooth glistening ice. The curvy surfaces reminded Reuben of whitest alabaster carved into the form of a voluptuous human body. He let the others pass by, turned his boat, and aimed his camera back at the canyon. The angle was right, the light unbelievable. He took shot after shot. Would he ever see anything so beautiful again?

He steered toward the other kayaks now far ahead, but his strokes had little force as he gawked left and right. Each berg, each weirdly weathered formation was as staggeringly gorgeous and inspiring as the canyon and the arch. It was all perfect. The elemental purity of ice, water, sun, and sky; the extreme white, the piercing blue. The salty granite smell of the thick cold air, each breath alive in his lungs. The gloop-gloop of the eddies swirling around his paddle blade, the sound of each splashed drop plopping back into the water. He and Kat, too, he suddenly saw with great clarity, were perfect. What they had, perfect. It wouldn't matter so much what they did. No one right way. Every path its own song.

He sat still and drifted in the current. She had to take the offer. He couldn't keep her from what she loved. If he was willing to sacrifice ... quit his job, move ... she'd feel connected if the kids were her own ... it would work ... somehow. If they wanted it badly enough, it would work.

The other boats disappeared around the corner of a bulky ice outcrop leaving Reuben alone among the bergs. Overwhelmed by the expansive solitude, he closed his eyes and raised his paddle high above his head. As if weightless, as if hurtling untethered through space, he felt free.

When he opened his eyes, he noticed the current had taken him to the right, nearer the glacier. Its vertical face now loomed much taller. The vast ice sheet's incomprehensible mass, the glowing blue-white color, the shush of ripples lapping gently at its base. He aimed the kayak toward it and paddled slowly closer.

Distant voices called out behind him—Kat, Megan, others—a singsong chorus echoing off the ice, like they were searching for a lost child.

"I'm here," Reuben hollered over his shoulder. He began making a turn to rejoin the group when from the top of the glacial cliff came a sound like twisting metal girders. Looking up, he saw a hunk of ice the size of a house tremble then lurch downward until it smacked into the water sending a splash shooting high into the air. A wave rushed toward him. Two quick strokes pointed the bow into the swell just as it arrived, the boat bucked up and over.

A jolt of adrenaline surged through his body. He craned his neck—had the others seen the calving? He heard another sound, only on a far grander scale, as crisp and sharp as a harsh crack of thunder. His eyes snapped back to the cliff where a whole huge section of the wall shuttered and fractured from the glacier. As if in slow motion, it tilted into the void, fell, and slapped the bay in a titanic explosion.

Water and ice rained down on Reuben. He made himself small in the boat's cockpit and raised his arms in front of his face. A jagged chunk of ice as heavy as a block of concrete slammed into his head. He folded to the left, nearly tipping the boat. The mountain of a berg bobbed in the water like a colossal polar bear; a tall collapse wave rolled outward and, meeting the kayak, capsized it. Reuben spilled from the cockpit and floated face down.

The others raced toward him, Kat paddling furiously, paddling faster than anyone.

Cowabunga Sunset

The salty beach air was filled with the lazy calls of sea gulls. The crowds of people who'd come to spend the day at Cowabunga! were having their fun, playing on the sand and in the water.

I got a resupply pack from the Maintenance & Repair Shop and lugged it out to the floating wooden dock next to the kayak rental booth. After opening the pack and taking out the electronic controller, I punched in the command. A harbor seal stuck its head out of the water and with a few kicks of its powerful tail propelled itself up onto the dock next to me. Another command launched the seal into its rollover routine that brought it to a rest propped up on one flipper, underbelly exposed. I inserted the special wrench and opened the door in the seal's chest. Out popped the old toaster-sized battery unit. I slid in its replacement, snapped the door shut, and tapped the done button on the controller. The seal barked, scooted across the dock, and dove back into the water.

That afternoon I worked a lifeguard shift at Tower 2. When it ended, the owner of Cowabunga!, Greg Becker, was standing there waiting. He was forty-five or so, shaggy-haired and a little chunky, wearing a Hawaiian shirt and a pair of dude shorts.

"Hey man," he said. "You're Jacob, right? How about if you and me take a little walk." I'd only been on the job three days, mostly in the repair shop—had I already messed something up?

We went down to the busy waterline, past some kids building an impressive sandcastle. "I like to meet the people who work here," he said.

"Cool."

"We've got almost a mile of beach," Greg said, grinning and slapping his belly. "Boogie boarding, snorkeling, volleyball, pipeline surfing—you name it."

He pointed at the dark blue sky streaked with a pair of clouds shaped like white feathers. "The Sky-Tron dome covers the whole park—gives us a completely programmable environment. Those sailboats on the horizon and those surfers out there riding the reef break, all holograms. What you feel is the artificial sun's infrared heat."

"Awesome."

He laughed. "That's just the word I like to use." He picked up a shell and chucked it into the surf. "So why do you think all these people come here?"

I didn't want to say the wrong thing. All I could think of was, "To have fun?"

"Exactly," he said. "For fun and to get away from the crazy stuff outside the park. Half the world's starting to look like freakin' Mad Max. Drought, starvation, water wars. Even in this country, things are getting a little gnarly. So, it's important we give our visitors a vacation from all the doom and gloom. Make sense?"

"Totally."

Greg stopped walking and looked me right in the eye, dead serious. "You and the rest of the staff make that vacation happen. You are the Cowabunga! vibe." He talked to me like an adult— very different from any of the teachers and coaches and bosses I'd ever had. "People are suffering," he said. "This place is a hospital.

The beach is our medicine. And you, my friend," he tapped a finger against my chest, "you are Doctor Feelgood. Can you dig it?"

It was like he'd knighted me or something, like all of a sudden I knew what I was supposed to be doing. I felt ten feet tall, ready for anything. Oh yeah, Greg, I could definitely dig it.

In high school I had mostly played water polo and hung out with the guys on the team—guys who had girlfriends and were always telling stories. But I was shy and didn't have much free time between practices and games, school, and the two part-time jobs I worked to help Mom with the bills. The guys used to razz me pretty hard about my lack of experience in the female department. Cowabunga! changed all that.

A few days after Greg dubbed me Doctor Feelgood, I was up on lifeguard Tower 4 when I looked up the beach and there she was—wearing a staff T-shirt and gym shorts, walking barefoot on the dry sand. Flipflops dangled from one of her hands, the other brushed aside a wavy strand of chestnut hair. Never had I seen anyone so beautiful.

I asked around and found out her name was Mary. Just hired. The next week our shift supervisor assigned the two of us to pair up later that afternoon doing Special Needs Aquatic Support. I couldn't believe my luck and bounced through my morning duties grinning, whistling, and feeling all kinds of stupid goofy happy.

Mary and I met in the parking lot just as the van arrived from the state children's hospital.

The driver, a nurse named Roberto, had brought us one tiny and very shy little girl about five named Jeannie. The Special Needs intake form had a note in the Additional Information box.

"Uses wheelchair. Eleven surgeries. Hospitalized more than half her life."

We made our introductions and got Jeannie into a floatation jacket then wheeled her down the access ramp into the water. Her face scrunched up with fear. We stopped, the water just lapping over her thighs. Mary bent in close, stroked one of her little stick-like arms.

"Can I tell you a secret?"

With tears about to spill out of her eyes, Jeannie gave a shaky nod and a quivering, "Yeah."

"Jacob here is about the best swimmer in the whole wide world. Did you know that?" Jeannie shook her head.

"See that island way way out there?" Mary pointed at the man-made atoll we called Gilligan's Island, a quarter mile offshore. "He can swim all the way out there and back." Mary rested her hand on my chest. It felt so good, my thinking went a little blurry. "Isn't that right, Jacob?"

"Uh, yeah, done it a hundred times." I smiled and gave the kid's cheek a brush with the backside of my finger, something that used to help when I babysat my cousins and they were headed for a meltdown. It didn't work any great miracles with Jeannie, whose hands remained clamped on the armrests of her chair while we rolled her farther down the ramp. The water came up around her and the flotation jacket lifted her out of the wheelchair. Mary and I held her, one on each side, but even so Jeannie was panicky, straining her mouth upward and gulping down breaths like a hungry baby bird.

Every time the water came up close to her mouth, we made sure she bobbed right back up. After a while she calmed down. She made a few tentative strokes and seemed surprised by how the water supported her, how easy it was to move her frail body. She was getting the hang of floating and paddling and kicking. It wasn't long before she was flinging herself back and forth between Mary and me.

"I'm flying," she squealed. She was a little giggling motorboat, spinning around and around, slapping the water to make big splashes.

Jeannie swam and we played until Roberto honked the van's horn and waved his arm.

"I don't wanna go," she cried.

We rolled her out of the water and got her all bunched up in a towel.

She pushed her fists into her cheeks. "Don't. Wanna. Go!"

"You can always come back," Mary said.

Her face lit up. "Promise?"

I took her hand and gave it a squeeze and a little shake. "Promise."

Roberto got Jeannie and her chair strapped into the van. She bounced happily up and down, talking to us through the glass, saying words we couldn't hear. When the van turned out of the parking lot, she waved and blew us a kiss.

I waved back. "What a cutie."

"Hope she comes back," Mary said.

We just stood there in the parking lot like neither of us wanted to leave. Mary loosened the hair she had pinned up. It fell halfway down her back, and she pulled it into a ponytail.

"So how did you know I've been out to Gilligan's?" I asked.

The corner of her mouth curled up in a sneaky little smile and she aimed her green-greengreen eyes at me. "I've been watching you."

I froze.

"See you tomorrow," she said and walked off toward the Operations Center. I couldn't take my eyes off her—the graceful way she moved, her swimmer's shoulders, how her ponytail swayed.

When I showed up for my shift the next day, Greg was waiting for me at my locker.

"You were real good with that little girl yesterday," he said, surprising me. "I saw your whole session through a telescope from upstairs. Couldn't hear what you said but didn't need to."

He was close enough that I could smell alcohol on his breath. Maybe I should have been paying attention to that—there were rumors—but right then I was just happy to hear him say I'd done a good job.

"I got kind of a special project coming up. Could use a little help," he said. "Thought you might be the guy."

I shrugged like, sure, I'm up for it.

"Come on then, I'll fill you in."

We walked along the water chitchatting like we did it all the time. Me and the big dog. Far down the beach he turned away from the water, crossed the dry sand, and took a path that sloped up through clumps of beach grass to a small bluff. I knew it was the place he stayed when he was in the park, but I'd never gotten a good look.

When we made it to the top of the bluff I saw a hammock slung between two stout palm trees next to a lanai shaded by a canopy of bamboo stilts covered over with palm fronds. Under the canopy were a couple of little tables and some wicker chairs—including a big one obviously for Greg. The hut itself was like something a castaway would bang together—weathered boards and bamboo. Looked like it wouldn't stand up to a strong wind.

We went inside—it was a regular modern apartment. Greg rattled ice into a blender, unscrewed the caps from different bottles, splashed in a couple of glugs from each one, squeezed a lime over the top, and let it rip. When the clattering roar stopped, he reached into the cupboard to get glasses and over his shoulder said, "You and Mary Yeager seem to be hitting it off."

My face got hot in like two seconds. He handed me a glass filled to the brim with the icy margarita. "She seems like a real fine young lady," he said with a wink and a smile.

I sipped the sweet, strong drink and hoped he wasn't going to say anything more on the subject.

"So here's the deal," he said. "Some people are coming to look over the park in a few weeks. It's an annual inspection—required by the bank that loaned me the construction money."

I gave him a nod, like I knew all about borrowing a gazillion dollars. "During their visit, I'll want someone with me, for support, in case I need anything. Sound like something you could do?"

"No prob."

"Alright," he said, laughing as we bumped fists. "Welcome to the inner circle."

"Cool."

"Today we've got something to celebrate." Greg handed me a piece of paper he said had just arrived—some news about his loan. One paragraph was circled. "I read it once, but I'd kinda like to hear it again. Would you mind reading it?"

"Out loud?"

"Yeah, I'm—" he waved his hand back and forth. "It's a kind of dyslexia."

"Okay, yeah, sure." I cleared my throat and read:

The intensifying global emergency of catastrophic climate change (including the worldwide disappearance of beaches resulting from rising sea levels) is forcing governments to enact unprecedented draconian restrictions, eliminating freedoms of activity and expression. Constrained consumers are increasingly resentful of these imposed austerities; their compensatory desires thus stimulated, they crave respite and distraction as never before. One year of not only positive but accelerating bottom-line revenues substantiates the value proposition offered by Cowabunga! Ocean Park.

I looked up from the paper. "Is that supposed to mean something?"

"It means," Greg said with a big smile, "we're making enough money to stay afloat." He held out his glass and I clinked it with mine. "And the visit from the bankers ought to be smooth sailing."

Nights were super popular at Cowabunga! We had bonfires and weenie roasts and smores, full moon surfing, couples taking romantic walks along the sand. But about a week after Mary and I worked together in Aquatics Support, the park closed

37

early—the staff swept all guests off the beach and out the doors
well before the Sky-Tron kicked into its sunset routine. A
maintenance crew was coming from the wave machine company
to do their quarterly checkup on the hydraulics. My job was
to let them in, keep an eye on them, and make sure they had
whatever they needed.

With the crowd and the staff gone and the crew not yet
arrived, I was the only guy in the whole huge park. Very peaceful.
I went for a walk on the deserted beach and stopped at one of
the concrete fire rings that held a pile of ashes and charred wood
left from the previous night's luau. I found it amazing that in the
middle of a global climate train wreck we could have open fires
on the beach. Outside in the real world just about anything that
released even a puff of greenhouse gas was regulated seventeen
different ways by six different government agencies. Not to
mention the EcoGuardian vigilantes that would go after "Earth
killers" by burning down their businesses, cars, and homes. But
Greg wasn't about to have a beach without campfires, so he
purchased ten times more carbon offsets than were required and
ended up winning a Green Hero award. Smart guy.

My phone rang. The maintenance crew leader said one of
their trucks had broken down and they'd have to reschedule for
another night. Before we even finished the conversation I was
already thinking about Mary and working up the courage to
ask her if maybe she might want to come hang out and go for a
swim.

"Love to," she said when I called. "I'll be right over."

I went into the Tech Room, opened the Sky-Tron control
panel, and nudged up the intensity of the sunset routine a couple
notches. I paced around and looked at the clock about five times,

then went back to the Sky-Tron and, what the heck, cranked all the inputs to the max.

When Mary arrived, we ran to the beach, laid out our towels, and dove in. Soon we were beyond the breakers, moving in the open water as easy and happy as a couple of otters. As the sun dipped lower, the western half of the dome throbbed with ever more intense neon colors— orange, red, gold, green, purple. I told her what I had done.

"You made us a tie-dye sky," she said, a big grin on her face. She slapped water at me and dove. I felt her gliding smoothly past my calf.

We swam back to shore and toweled off in the fading light of the greatest sunset in the history of the world. I lit a fire while Mary opened a bottle of red wine. We sat and drank and laughed, watching the flames of the crackling fire. We drank some more and got a little buzzed.

"Oh my god," she giggled, looking at the eastern horizon. "What is that?"

The full moon I'd programmed on the Sky-Tron was rising. It wasn't a normal full moon—no, this thing was gigantic, twenty, maybe thirty times regular size, with the Man in the Moon gazing down on us, quite pleased to be setting the mood for what was to come.

We met the visiting bankers, Melinda Lanz and Lou Jordan, at the Operations Center. Greg introduced me as his assistant.

"We're glad for an excuse to get out of the office," Melinda said with a nice smile. She was about forty, kind of pasty looking in her shorts and sandals, but in good shape.

Greg toured them through the high-tech, climate-controlled building, showed them how everything was state-of-the-art and blah, blah, blah. They asked one incredibly technical question after another. Greg had all the answers, no hesitation, a side of him I'd never seen before. When they ran out of things to ask, he led the way to the double doors that faced west.

"Now you've seen the infrastructure," he said, "but this is the real Cowabunga!" He flung open the doors, and we stepped out into the bright sunshine and the bustling scene of sunbathers, Frisbee tossers, joggers, inner-tubers, kayakers, body surfers, picnicking families, roaming clumps of kids, and an old couple fishing with long poles out on the jetty.

Melinda shaded her eyes with her hand, took it all in. "Wow," she said, slipping out of her sandals. "Oh, the warm sand feels so good on my feet."

Lou stared at the water where a pod of gray whales was playing near the surface, spouting and showing their flukes as they dove. The head and fins of one of the whales rose into the air and splashed back into the water. People on the beach cheered.

"Animatronic," Greg said, clapping his hands together. "Every afternoon at three."

"But those are real," Lou said. He pointed at a group of surfers floating on their boards waiting for waves while two riders cut up and down the face of a perfectly formed six-foot curl.

"Must be one hell of a wave machine."

"Built by the Swiss, oddly enough," Greg said with a chuckle. "We won six different awards for the lattice supports that hold up the dome. Graphene nanotubes and positive air pressure—the architects and engineers went nuts." He craned his neck from horizon to horizon smiling and shaking his head as if he could hardly believe what he had created.

"When I was a kid, I lived at the beach. Never felt more alive." His face turned solemn. "Then a while back they started talking about beaches around the world disappearing. I said to myself, Hey man, this is a bigass problem. In fifty years or maybe a hundred we'll get ocean levels under control and natural beaches will come back—that's the hope, anyway—but in the meantime, my job, my sacred duty, is to keep the flame of the beach vibe alive."

"Sacred," Melinda said, "that's a strong word."

"Global warming is just bummer after bummer after bummer. A soul killer," Greg said. "People need a break—a way to recharge. We're Homo ludens, man—Homo playful. We need to have fun. And we can't afford to bum out and give up. The stakes are way too high." He opened his arms to take in all that surrounded us. "We need surfers and slackers, parrotheads and pirates, a place where lovers can rub lotion on each other and lie in the sun, where kids can chase each other into the surf."

He was on a roll and would probably have continued but something behind Lou caught his attention. The rest of us turned around and saw a tall white-haired man in a funeral-black suit lumbering across the sand toward us, a thick envelope in his hand. When he arrived, he adjusted the hang of his still buttoned coat and said, "Gregory Becker?"

Greg nodded.

"I'm with the Office of Cultural and Historical Disambiguation," the man said, passing the envelope to Greg. "You have ten days to comply with this order and cease all operations." The undertaker turned and walked off.

Nobody moved. Greg just stared at the envelope in his hands like he was holding a dead cat. Then they all started looking at each other, even at me, as if I had any idea what just happened.

Lou ran his hand through his hair. "I, uh, guess that just about wraps things up," he said with a sympathetic shrug. Melinda patted Greg on the shoulder and said something about it being up to the lawyers now and please keep her informed of developments. The bankers shook hands with Greg and off they went.

He plodded down the beach in the other direction. I caught up with him and asked if he wanted me to come along. He made a grunt that could have been a yes and I followed his silent, hunched form all the way to his hut.

Once inside, he went straight for the blender and dumped in ice cubes and what seemed like a ton of booze. When he hit the button, the ice made a hellacious racket. He slopped the chunky slush into two big tumblers and handed me one. He took the other glass and the pitcher and fell heavily into a chair. I felt sorry for him and figured I'd stick around to help however I could. But nothing was happening—he just sat there brooding, staring off with a blank look on his face, sipping his drink. When he drained the pitcher, he made another batch.

The clock on my phone said 4:19. In three hours I'd be with Mary. She and I had been spending every spare minute together, and after work we were going to have a little celebration—one month since our first night together on the beach. We'd be at her apartment. Alone.

He slapped the fat envelope on his thigh, his breath suddenly faster and louder, his chest rising and falling in short, sharp spasms. He tossed the envelope at me.

"Read it," he said.

I opened the packet and read aloud the cover sheet that explained what was inside, a list of what sounded mostly like legal documents.

"Also included for purposes of overall context is an initial assessment taken by the OCHD in response to—"

"That's the one. Read that," Greg said, thrusting his finger toward the papers I held.

I flipped through the pages until I found it then read aloud.

To: Office of Cultural and Historical Disambiguation

From: Delilah Mallet-Grimshaw, Assistant Director, Office of Narrative Compliance

Subject: Progress Report, Case No. 1307

Background

In accordance with the Accuracy in Historical Representations and Communications Act (AHRCA 8.3.26b), I am reporting progress related to actions taken by this office.

On April 19 it was reported that a commercial enterprise—Cowabunga! Ocean Park (hereafter referred to as "the replica beach")—was operating in violation of numerous provisions of AHRCA.

Field investigators were dispatched. Upon confirmation that the replica beach promoted and/or portrayed inaccurate historical representations, an Action Team was formed for further investigation and electronic surveillance warrants obtained. Formal analysis, assessment, and response preparation activities ensued.

Objectionable Representations

Numerous violations of Class 1 restrictions were identified including, but not limited to:

Romanticized and unhistorical representations (as set forth in AHRCA subsection 1.1.4: "No description of an historical time, place, situation, etc., may be shown/presented inconsistent with the full and accurate context of the historical dynamics of anthropogenic geodegradation.").

Denial of basic tenets of science-backed consensus on mechanisms of climatic change and associated impacts.

103 specific infractions of the Code of Observance (see Appendix G for full list).

Greg snorted. He tried to rise out of his chair, stumbled, caught himself. He went to the kitchen and got ice from the freezer. "Continue with the execution," he called out, slurring the words while he emptied a bottle of booze into the pitcher.

I read on.

Action Plan

Sole proprietor of replica beach, Gregory L. Becker, to be served with a Letter of Finding enumerating violations of the AHRCA and demanding cessation of operations. Letter will inform recipient that failure to comply will render the proprietor subject to the full extent of the Act's punitive remedies (17.1–67).

Replica beach operations to be suspended. Historical Reconciliation improvements to begin under auspices of the Office of Cultural and Historical Disambiguation, Office of Narrative Compliance.

Anticipated Outcomes

Successful removal/remediation of offensive, unhistorical, and dangerous misrepresentations of significant natural and cultural activity associated with ecological dynamics/degradation/dysfunction.

The blender screamed like it was mixing gravel. Standing right next to it, Greg didn't seem to notice. Sweat shined on his forehead, his eyes twitched from side to side. He looked like he could do with some fresh air.

When the racket stopped, I said, "You got a nice-looking hammock outside—how about if we go out there and I give it a try?"

This seemed to catch him off guard, but he was agreeable, and glass in one hand, pitcher in the other, he wove his way to the door. I followed close behind, ready to grab hold if he started to fall.

Once I had rolled into the hammock, I made a big show of rocking back and forth. "This is awesome," I said.

He wasn't listening. He thrashed around the lanai, mad, mumbling. "Pissy little pissant bureaucrats . . . high on pissant power." He scowled and kicked over one of the little tables, then thrust his flushed face close to mine and growled, "Beware the man," he paused, burped, "who knows only one book."

He went on raging, but it wasn't aimed at me. I figured he needed somebody to vent to, so I just swayed in the hammock and listened to him rant about people being blind and stupid, about there being many paths to the top of the mountain. Eventually the booze caught up with him. He settled into his chair and passed out.

Something big was up—definitely—but I didn't really grasp what all this government blah-blah meant. And anyway, in a couple of hours I'd be with Mary in her bed—next to that, what else could possibly matter.

When the government lowered the boom, everything went down the crapper fast. Greg fought with every ounce of his strength, his lawyers made appeal after appeal—and they lost every time. He showed up at the Operations Center less and less. Mostly he spent his time alone in his hut drinking and smoking weed.

I was among the people who were lucky enough to keep their jobs. Over the next eleven months we watched as Cowabunga! got completely overhauled and changed into the Beach Museum—the BM, as we called it. The transformation was slow and painful, like watching a beautiful animal die. It was without doubt the worst year of my life.

I had the most seniority of almost anybody left on the staff and one of my jobs was to break in the new hires. This kept me pretty busy—morale was so bad we had a hard time keeping people on the payroll.

My latest trainee was Randall, a chubby, baby-faced guy just a couple of years younger than me. Like almost all the hires since the swimming requirement had been eliminated, he was in terrible shape. I took him to the employee dressing rooms and got him squared away with a locker and a set of work clothes to match the ones I already had on.

He awkwardly wiggled into his pea-green rubberized rain suit and the knee-high rubber boots. The bosses said this gear was designed to protect us from contact toxins and environmental pathogens—what it was really good for was making us sweat like pigs.

I unscrewed the cap from a tube of zinc oxide cream and squeezed a thick white gob onto my finger.

"Really?" Randall said, narrowing his eyes.

"Don't worry," I said, "it's just sunblock with an SPF of like ten thousand." I applied the white goo to his nose, cheekbones, and forehead in kind of a starburst pattern. "The dome filters out all the UV radiation, but the Narrative Control Team decided this stuff emphasizes the E.D.N.'s section on the resurgent ozone hole and skin cancer."

"What's the E.D.N.?"

"Environmental Degradation Narrative," I said, looking in the dressing room mirror and gooping the white stuff onto my own face. "It's our bible, the document that controls everything we do." I wiped the excess cream on a paper towel. "Time for the tour."

We trudged up a sand dune on the way to the beach. Randall ran the back of his wrist across his sweating forehead.

"A little warm, huh?" He fanned his face with his hand.

"The temperature is set for 93 degrees with 95 percent humidity under an always overcast sky."

We crested the dune and saw the beach, strewn with its array of E.D.N.-mandated improvements—cigarette butts, random plastic crap, crude oil and beach tar, dead fish and rotting bird carcasses, a soiled diaper, and a condom. Not far offshore, a one-tenth-scale cruise ship was anchored in a vast gyre of floating plastic trash—from a bilge pipe in its stern plopped chunky gray-brown sludge.

"Right over there used to be our number-one surfing area," I said, bobbing my chin toward a patch of flat water.

He squinted to see through the non-greenhouse smoke rising from a pile of simulated burning tires. "Surfers? Here? Are you kidding?"

"The wave machine's still out there—it's just turned off. The accountants say it saves a ton of money. And why not? With the E.D.N., the water's so filthy it would be like surfing in a toilet."

He looked like he'd just taken a mouthful of sour milk. "Didn't this place used to be like a resort?"

I told him how the government brought in the Narrative Compliance Team to transform the place—artistic director, experience designers, code writers, a crew of construction workers, and the main man, the Story Czar who, with his one droopy eye, oversaw the whole project.

"The Czar," I said, "was big on living-history dioramas—his vision was for schoolkids on field trips to have the experience of learning about global warming by talking to real people: a lifeboat full of climate refugees, island people whose village was submerged, an environmental scientist in a lab coat, a UN delegate working on global policies.

"Sounds pretty good. Do the kids go for it?"

I laughed. "At first. Some of the laid-off Cowabunga! staff got rehired to put on costumes and be actors in these dioramas, but they got laid off again when the Czar replaced the living dioramas with holograms—much more cost-effective.

"So what we do now," I said, "is march kids through the museum's fourteen Info Stations where they get lectured at by holograms about another glacier melted, another forest burned, another species gone extinct."

I picked up the pace, and we made our way onto a tongue of beach that jutted out into the sea. "Just out here is something pretty cool," I told him. We arrived at a child-sized body lying face down on the sand, wavelets lapping around its lifeless form.

"The Experience Designers went through a bunch of different models before they settled on this one. The first version was too stiff—like a statue. Then there were a few that were too loosey-goosey, sort of jiggly like water balloons. Technically this guy is the CMBC-6, the sixth version of the Climate Migrant Beach Corpse. We call him Ricky."

"My god," Randall said. "That's disgusting."

"Narrative Compliance says it really hammers home the tragedy. The schoolkids are totally grossed out, but it's the only thing in the park they actually pay attention to."

Randall looked at me, trying hard, as I hoped he would, to understand what the Beach Museum was really all about.

Heading back toward the parking lot, we saw a grimy yellow school bus pulling to a stop, the noise of high-spirited kids pouring from its open windows.

Randall's face brightened. "I'm planning to become a teacher. The ad for the job said I'd get to work with kids. Good for my résumé, you know."

I wanted to tell him how, by Info Station 4, the squirmy kids from this bus would be turned into yawning, glassy-eyed zombies. But that would have been cruel. Just then I remembered Jeannie, the little girl in the wheelchair. I had promised her we'd always be here for her. We weren't. That must have broken her heart.

"Class field trips now make up ninety-six percent of our visitors," I said, my voice sounding as lifeless as one of the holograms. "That's the business model. We don't make squat on gate receipts anymore. Everything's subsidized by the government." Next to the bus, the teachers herded the boisterous kids into a line.

Randall and I came to lifeguard Tower 1, the place where I'd last seen Mary. She too had kept her job during the transition to the BM, but she saw where things were headed. She was smart that way, a lot smarter than me. We were standing right by the tower in our knee boots and our dorky rubber rain suits. "This place is the shits," she'd said. Staying was crushing her spirit.

We both knew she had to go. She said she wanted to find somewhere that was more like what Cowabunga! used to be.

"You could come with me," she said, but not with much hope—we'd talked about going off together many times and each time it came back to me needing to stick around to help my mom financially and wanting to help take care of Greg.

"I just can't stay here anymore," she said. "I'm so sorry."

"It's okay." I didn't need to make it any harder on her than it already was.

"When I find a good place, I'll call," she said, brushing a tear from my cheek. "Maybe Greg will be okay by then."

"Every time my phone rings," I said, "I'll be praying it's you."

She gave me her warmest, twinkliest smile, then took my head in her hands, looked into my eyes for a long time like she wanted to remember, then kissed me soft and slow.

"Be brave," she said.

She turned and walked down the beach. I felt twenty different emotions all at once and just stood there watching her get smaller and smaller and then she was gone. Randall said something I didn't hear. "Sorry, what?"

"Is that the end of the tour?" he repeated.

"Yeah," I said. "That pretty much gets you up to speed."

After I got off work that night, I walked up the beach to see Greg at his hut. I found him on the lanai, slumped in his big chair, looking to be in even worse shape than he'd been the night before. His squinty face bloated, his skin so red it looked sunburned, the beard he'd grown was wet with spilled drinks. He waved the half-full pitcher at me. I nodded. He poured me a tall one then collapsed back into the chair, exhausted from the effort.

"Should I get the book?" I asked. He raised a finger, let it fall.

I found the fat biography of Brian Wilson of the Beach Boys. We were at the part where the creepy manipulating psychiatrist had taken control of every aspect of Brian's drugged, damaged life. I knew the story, knew Brian was about to escape and get his life back, and I thought maybe it would give Greg some hope. I read for only a few minutes before I heard raspy rhythmic breathing. His eyes were closed. Gone for the night. I wondered how long he'd last.

Another week? Probably not a month. I covered him up with a beach towel.

It was a moonless black night. The lanai was softly lit by a couple of strands of little Christmas lights strung in lazy arcs. They gave off a friendly warm glow, like a campfire in a dark wilderness. I sat, sipped my drink, and thought of Mary. I imagined, like I imagined a hundred times every day, she was off the grid someplace in Peru or Thailand or maybe New Zealand, doing whatever it was she needed to do. She hadn't called yet, but she would. I was sure of that. She'd call and tell me she'd found a place. And I'd go to her, wherever she was, anywhere on earth, and everything would be like it was before.

Plans

I flew to London to deliver a TED Talk, part of the campaign to promote my newest book. Truth be told, the book wasn't really new, but an updated, thirtieth anniversary rerelease of *Europe on the Half-Shell*, the travel guide that launched my career. The contract for the talk included a first-class flight and a suite at the newly constructed Savoy Westminster, a towering 1,000-room hotel overlooking the Thames. I found my lodging modern, efficient, crammed with every imaginable amenity—and completely devoid of anything even vaguely resembling a soul.

When the time for my talk came, I took the concert hall stage and shared with the audience some of what I've learned over the years, ending with this:

In all I do at Half Shell Adventures—the guidebooks, the special tours, the radio and television programs—I try to keep in mind the experience of the first-time traveler. Perhaps a little nervous, perhaps unfamiliar with the local money, food, language, or culture. I try to help that person overcome their resistance, their hesitancy, because I know that waiting on the other side of their fear is a whole new world of adventure. Thank you.

After a cab ride back to the Savoy Westminster, I was too keyed up for sleep, so I rode the elevator to the hotel's top-floor lounge. Quiet and largely empty, it offered an impressive view of London's twinkling lights. Halfway through my ridiculously priced glass of Brunello, a woman in her mid-thirties sat beside me at the bar. She wore large round tortoise-shell glasses that had the effect of making her lively green eyes seem unusually large.

She ordered a glass of wine, bantering back and forth with the barman in a Dubliner's pleasing lilt. She noticed me and said, "You're Colin Parsons, aren't you?"

I get recognized all the time—along with requests for photos, autographs, and tips on good nearby restaurants. "That's me," I said, never good at a clever response in one of these chance meetings.

She smiled awkwardly, which was somehow comforting, as if she felt as ill at ease as I did.

"I listened to your talk today," she said. "In fact, it was to see you I got myself to this conference."

Our random encounter suddenly felt a great deal more complicated. "Oh?"

"Deirdre O'Fallon," she said, extending her hand which was small, soft, and warm. "I'm doing doctoral research at the London School of Economics on tourism and its global impacts."

Ah, that explained it. Sooner or later she'd likely get around to asking me for something—an interview or, if she had ambitions of turning her thesis into a bestseller, maybe a letter to a potential publisher or a promise to write a blurb for the dust jacket.

Happy to have her company and eager to hear more of her lovely musical voice, I said, "Interesting work?"

She took the opening and with a remarkable clarity laid out the essence of her research:

100,000 flights each day, billions of passengers per year—
each jet emitting so many tons of greenhouse gasses, melting so
many cubic feet of polar ice, raising sea levels just a little more.
She pulled her laptop from her bag, opened it on the bar, and
brought up articles from scientific journals, graphs, projections,
trend lines. In a half an hour's time she'd taken me through a
semester's graduate seminar.

"And all this destruction, Colin," she said, pointing to a graph
with a line sloping upward at a stark and dispiriting angle, "in
twenty years it doubles." Deirdre looked at me, her eyes as sincere
as any I had ever seen. "The time's now come for all of us to do
what we can."

Her expectant gaze made it clear that by "all of us" she very
pointedly meant me.

The barman asked if we'd like another round. I looked at
Deirdre, who shook her head. I paid the tab and, feeling drawn
to everything about her, thought I might ask her to come back to
my room. She must have seen it in my face and smiled in a way
that seemed to acknowledge the possibility, but then, clutching
her laptop to her chest, said, "I'll leave you now to dream on the
future." She leaned toward me, placed a quick kiss on my cheek,
and was off.

Riding the elevator to my suite, I smiled at how quickly and
strongly I felt attracted to everything about her. I missed being
close with someone—it had been such a long time. I blamed it
on all the traveling, all the work.

In bed, I stared at the ceiling, hearing Deirdre's voice, the
facts she'd worked so hard to gather, wanted so much for me to
hear. Some of it I already knew, but only in bits and pieces—
ones I had never taken the time to fit together into the coherent
picture she so deftly drew.

I repositioned the pillow under my head.

If we shifted our focus from Europe to North America . . . all those transatlantic flights not taken, all that jet fuel saved . . . and if we reached tens of thousands of people . . . year after year.

The pillow still wasn't right. I fluffed it.

Half Shell Adventures had gotten so large and complicated— so many employees depended on me. European travel was what we knew.

I rolled onto my side.

How simple it had been—highlighting Florence, Barcelona, Paris. But Provo, Kalamazoo, Bangor? Would people buy those guidebooks or watch those TV programs?

I kicked the blanket off my legs.

It didn't matter. We needed to do our part. It was, as Deirdre had made so clear, the right thing to do.

Immediately upon my return to Oregon, I called a special meeting of Half Shell's board of directors. I so wanted them to share the same eye-opening experience I'd had in London that I invited Deirdre to join us remotely and make her presentation. The group of eleven board members plus top company executives sat around the big table in the conference room watching the large monitor on which Deirdre clicked through her slide deck and made her forceful points.

When she finished, I summed up my new vision for reinventing the company. "We will adopt a new vision, a new ethos, a new way to help people see the world—without destroying it."

I scanned the room looking over the faces of my closest colleagues, people with whom I'd worked side by side for decades building what we jokingly referred to as the Half Shell empire. And each one of them stared back at me as if I had lost my mind.

Six weeks later I returned from filming in Scandinavia and got a call from Board Chairman Kitt Jordan. He asked me to join him and President Mindy Maxwell for what I thought was going to be an update on plans to transform the company into Half Shell Adventures 2.0. We met around an oak table in Mindy's ninth-floor corner office, surrounded by all-glass walls and panoramic views of Portland's skyline and the Willamette River.

"Let's get right to the point," Kitt said with the same no-nonsense tone I'd heard him use with cowboys on his Wyoming ranch. "The board can't make any decisions about changing the mission of HSA without solid data. So we instructed Mindy to prepare a comprehensive analysis." He turned to her and nodded.

"I'll highlight our key findings," Mindy said as she handed each of us a thick document. "First off, barring force majeure, we're locked into the television contract for the next twenty-one months. That leaves us with a potential perception problem: taking a public stance against transcontinental air travel while de facto endorsing—"

"You'd catch holy hell," Kitt cut in. "Critics would scream bloody murder—call you a hypocrite."

"The Book Division is where we project the biggest hit," Mindy continued. "The printed travel guides currently account for 82 percent of non-television top-line revenue. All our titles are on a two-year refresh cycle. If we followed your direction to stop updating the content, the books would rather quickly become . . . stale."

"We'd be handing the market to the competition," Kitt said. "And as for replacing those revenues with American guidebooks—that's more pipe dream than long shot."

It went on like this. Our little gathering turned into one of those interventions where family members step in to get the wayward drug addict or alcoholic back on the straight and narrow. Mindy and Kitt looked at me kindly and spoke with compassion while dishing out tough love in the form of facts and figures and charts with all arrows pointing in a downhill direction.

Half Shell 2.0, they explained, was so misguided it threatened the company's very existence. "We won't be the same old Half Shell," I said. "We'll be smaller, less profitable, have fewer employees. But we'll be making a difference."

They looked at one another. Kitt raised an eyebrow. Mindy saw the signal and paged to the end of the report.

"In Appendix One you'll see that we hired MetriQuant to run some numbers. According to their assessment, full implementation of HSA 2.0 would decimate the company. Revised mission and implementation would yield an overall impact on global travel sustainability that they categorized as," she paused, "negligible."

We exchanged uneasy glances. "But listen to this," Kitt said. "We've worked up a modified plan that splits the difference between a perfect world and brass tacks." The old horse-trader was doing his best to sweeten a sour deal. "In the long run, it may be our best shot."

As they described it, the new plan would rebrand HSA as a sustainability innovator leading the transformation of the American travel industry. I would become the spokesperson for a wholesale rethinking of how we vacation: fewer but longer transcontinental trips, more train use, eco-friendly cruises, biofuels, carbon offsets, donating a portion of our profits to protecting rainforests, anything and everything that would lessen ecological impacts.

"We also like the idea of you writing a book—a sort of manifesto," Mindy said cheerily.

"It would put you and your ideas squarely in the spotlight."

"And a whole new television series," Kitt added. "Sustainable Travel with Colin Parsons."

"If we succeed in starting a trend, there's a real chance we could move the needle," Mindy said.

"What's the timeline?" I asked.

"We'd roll her out in stages," Kitt said. "Stepwise, over the next three to five years—faster or slower as needed."

I rose and walked to the window. Out on the river a motorboat sped upstream, slapping over the choppy water, the white chevron of its wake spreading behind. I thought about their plan, about how hard they were trying to find a way, about all that melting glacial ice.

"It's not enough." They stared with blank faces. "What we need," I explained, "is big and bold and now."

They had no response, which surprised me as I'd never seen either of them at a loss for words. Finally, Kitt cleared his throat. "I'm afraid the chips aren't gonna fall that way, partner. We can't sacrifice the company just because you got religion."

"What's that supposed to mean?"

"It means—and this is not where I wanted this conversation to go—but it means that if push comes to shove, well, you're the one's gonna end up on his backside."

I looked to Mindy for some sort of support, some sanity, anything. "I'm sorry Colin," she said. "Our fiduciary responsibility is to the shareholders."

A tense silence filled the room as we looked at one another, looked away. "I need to think," I said, heading for the door. "I'll be back in a little while."

I went to my office and phoned Deirdre. After apologizing for the lateness of the call, I told her about the meeting.

"Are they genuine in their support for this revised plan, or are they just coddling ya?"

"Very real, I think, both of them. You should have seen Mindy's eyes light up when she used the phrase 'initiating the process of disruption.'"

"She's got the gift of the boardroom tongue, that one," Deirdre said, and we both laughed.

Soon we were talking about the nature of change, compromise versus ideals, the many paths up the same mountain. She was so bright, such a pleasure to talk with, her voice such pretty music—and as long as we kept talking, I didn't have to deal with Kitt and Mindy.

"Aren't we getting a tipsy bit philosophical here?" Deirdre teased. She was right, and we got down to a more practical discussion of my options. "Don't you think that what matters, Colin, is staying in the game?" she asked. "The planet won't be saved or lost in a drizzly weekend."

It made perfect sense. Seize the opportunity. Do what we can. Hope for the best. I returned to Mindy's office and declared my full support for their plan.

Never had the staff at HSA worked as hard as they did in the following months—all hands on deck, lots of overtime, the office as busy on weekends as during the week. We set the unveiling for the Wednesday before Memorial Day, the start of the summer vacation season and the peak of media interest in anything related to travel. Our PR director orchestrated a campaign that would begin in New York with me appearing on Good Morning America followed by three nonstop days of interviews and speaking engagements, cable news shows, meetings with newspaper editorial boards, and on and on.

I was in a cab from LaGuardia to a hotel in Manhattan when I got the call from Mindy. "There's been a leak," she said.

"What?"

"An anonymous employee passed internal company documents to a reporter at the *Times*: emails, HSA 2.0, the MetriQuant documents, everything. The reporter called, wanting a response. She said the story will be posted online at midnight and run in tomorrow's print edition."

All the publicity events were cancelled; I flew back to Portland. By early the next morning, the magnitude of the crisis was becoming clear. The *Times* ran the story under the headline "Leak Reveals Greenwashing at Half Shell Adventures," along with a blistering editorial, "Half Shell Sells Out."

The editorial included this dagger: . . . after calculating that the proposed eco-conscious actions would cost HSA millions of dollars, the company chose not to do the right thing. Instead, they ginned up a marketing and PR campaign to position itself as a global sustainability leader while doing virtually nothing of real substance. HSA has joined the rogue's gallery of corporations publicly touting a concern for all things green, while behind closed doors pursuing only one thing of that color, the dollar.

I had never given much thought to the term media frenzy, but now reporters were behaving like crazed sharks ripping the flesh off some bleeding animal—and I was that hapless beast. Social media took whatever passed as reporting and twisted it, coated it with venom and crushed glass, disseminated it further. I was the chief conspirator, the money-crazed, megalomaniacal spawn of Satan. Vicious memes and sanctimonious petitions circulated

THE FRAGILE BLUE DOT

online along with calls to boycott our products and programs.
I was disinvited to speaking engagements, tours were cancelled,
our book sales fell off a cliff.

Damage control became our fulltime occupation. We worked
around the clock in the HSA conference room, the bunker
where we devised increasingly desperate strategies to protect our
crumbling empire.

On the third day of the siege Mindy said she had something
she needed to discuss. We entered her office where Kitt was
already seated at the oak table. He started out with some phrases
about my contributions to the company—a uncharacteristically
frothy preamble that had me bracing for bad news. And it came
when he delivered the fateful words, "For the good of HSA, we
propose a complete severing of all ties with Colin Parsons."

While the company couldn't function without our eighty
employees, the fact was that as far as the outside world was
concerned, I was Half Shell. Something in me said fight, fight
with every ounce of strength. But when I looked at Kitt and
Mindy I saw in their faces that they would do what they had to
do, it was their obligation. Yes, I could resist; we could lacerate
one another with years of bitter litigation, become enemies. And
for what? They were right. Getting rid of its tainted leader was
now the only hope for saving the company.

A flurry of meetings with lawyers and more lawyers took
place. I signed stacks of papers. I didn't argue, didn't negotiate.
While walking out of one of these somber sessions, I asked
Mindy if she had found the source of the leak.

She nodded and made a face. "Of course, we can't lift a finger."

"Certainly not," I said. "But I want to talk with him."

She got me the employment file on Jude Fitch-Efferson. He'd
worked in HSA's accounting department for a little over two

years. He was twenty-nine, had a degree from an online college I'd never heard of, and claimed no dependents on his W-4. He'd been written up once by his supervisor for using work time and his office computer for personal business, which the reprimand cryptically described as being "of a political nature."

I called him and asked if we could meet. His voice sounded like he had a head cold. "Sure," he said. "Who cares."

We agreed to meet during the lunch hour, not far from the HSA offices at one of the concrete chess tables in Willamette Park, a green belt along the river.

As I approached, I saw that he was thin with pale blotchy skin and a haircut that wasn't doing him any favors. He'd flattened a brown paper sack on the table's black and white tile squares and on it had arranged his sandwich, a baggie of carrot sticks, and an apple.

"You must be Jude," I said, extending my hand. We shook, his grip was limp, thin-boned, and moist.

I sat down. "One thing I'd like to know is, what caused you to . . . do what you did? I mean, I very consciously built this company on my values—that everyone counts, that we're all in it together. Did we fail you in some way, or—"

"Or fail the whole world?" He sneered—surely counseled by his lawyer about the lawsuit they could bring if we retaliated in any way.

"The documents you gave to the *Times*, how did you . . . come across them?"

He took a generous bite of his sandwich and spoke while he chewed. "I was assigned a project—gave me special access on the server." He swallowed. "I'm a curious guy." I smelled peanut butter on his breath and saw a speck of purple jelly at the corner of his mouth. "What I found was like, whoa, smoking gun." He ran his tongue over his teeth. "People need to see how corporate wheels turn."

I took a breath and another to make sure I was in control of my emotions. "And you were certain that what we did was wrong?"

He shrugged. "My contribution was to liberate the documents." He popped a piece of carrot into his mouth and crunched it. "I really had no idea it was going to blow up so big. But you're all famous, right, so it's like IMAX. God bless America."

"What about, I don't know, context, extenuating circumstances?"

"Not my problem."

"And if the company tanks, if you and half the people you work with get laid off?"

A mischievous smile curled on his lips. "In the grand scheme of things." He completed the thought with another shrug. "Look, you got rich flying around the world writing your little guidebooks to help other rich people fly around the world and consume and pollute. Like there's no tomorrow. But there is. And if it isn't going to totally suck, things have to change. So some people get laid off. Boo-hoo. Nobody cares if you write another book or do another TV show—nobody but you and the parasites that depend on you."

"How do you think we should create this better future—the one that doesn't suck?"

His face brightened. "We replace the whole cultural narrative. Recode all economic and political models—radically, from the ground up."

"A revolution?"

He smirked. "Utopia on the half shell."

"Will people get on board with you?"

"We start with the kids—early, before society dumbs them down into idiot muggles. Old people and their oppressive ideas die off. The tipping point kicks in."

"And if a few eggs have to be cracked to make the omelet?"

He looked at me quizzically, as if he'd never heard the expression. "Sure, if that's what it takes."

How was it possible that this guy was destroying a company it took me and a whole lot of very smart, very hardworking people thirty years to build? All it had taken was a thumb drive and a call to a reporter and he'd altered history, wiped out everything we were trying to do, prevented all the good that might have come from it.

He sank his teeth into the flesh of his apple and ripped off a mouthful. "Do you?" he insisted, rousing me from my thoughts.

"Do I what?"

"Do you really think we can save the world without eating the rich?" I'd had enough. I stood and walked across the grass toward the river, leaving him to his carrots, peanut butter, and moralizing.

"What's the matter, can't take the truth?" he called after me. "It's people like you, man—you think you got it all figured out."

What I had figured out was that Jude was scared about the future, believed he could change things, make things better, felt an obligation to do so. It didn't matter that his act had unintended consequences. Not his problem.

He kept yammering until the distance between us increased to the point where his plaintive whine was replaced by the happy hubbub of a dozen five-year-olds chasing one other and a soccer ball. They scurried one way and then the other with unbridled energy in coordinated movements like a school of fish or a flock of birds. I watched, listened to their gleeful shouts.

Suddenly, it was as if a fog lifted; I saw my situation with a sudden clarity. Jude and the mob he'd unleashed had won. I was banished. Persona non grata. Contracts cancelled. Off the airwaves. I'd had my run and now it was over.

Deirdre's words came back to me: The planet won't be saved or lost in a drizzly weekend. Her clear and calm voice, how happy it made me every time I heard it.

I walked along the bike path parallel to the river, a soft warm breeze, my mind wandering. I'd been attracted to her from the second we met—her confidence, the softness of her presence, her devotion to her work, the sparkle in those green eyes.

It felt good to let myself think about what I hadn't put into words, what had only been a warm spot in my heart. I took a deep breath, expansive, joyous—the first time I'd felt alive in the eight days since the leak.

She'd once let slip she wasn't seeing anyone. Maybe? How good we'd be together. A flat. Rainy afternoons. Doing London arm in arm. She'd have conferences to go to—Oslo, Geneva, Trieste—I could do the planning, take her places she'd love.

She was younger than me. Quite a bit. Maybe that would be a problem for her. If she felt anything like I felt, it wouldn't matter. I laughed and did a little dance step right there on the bike path. All I could do was try.

Downsizing

In a perfect world I'd be painting from scaffolding—nice stable scaffolding—but no budget for that and no time. I take a sip of instant coffee from a paper cup, look up, and scan the clearstory, the seven rectangular windows that run the length of the great room just below the eighteen-foot ceiling. If all goes as planned, I'll be up there sometime this afternoon, dipping and dabbing, two hundred and forty pounds of brush monkey on a borrowed extension ladder.

The young couple who bought the house loved the kitchen island and they were definitely impressed with the unattached three-car garage, but when they looked up at the great room's high ceiling and the soft light filtering in through the clearstory, that's when I knew they'd be making an offer.

I aim my boom box toward the kitchen. Something sets off Spud out in the back yard.

ARK-ARK-ARK, ARK-ARK-ARK. He's a good boy. Pammy needs him. I switch on the radio and crank it up. "—and it's gonna be another scorcher in the Oldies 97 listening area," the jacked-up morning DJ announces. "Temps rocketing up to one—oh—six." On comes Elton John's "Rocket Man." Hardy har har, very funny. Spud is still going crazy out back. ARK-ARK, ARK-ARK-ARKARK. He's a good boy. Pammy needs him.

She's in the TV room down the hall, giving Dad his morning
pain pill and getting him situated in the recliner with cushions
under his leg. Coming out the doorway, she stops and looks
back in at him. "When the medicine kicks in you can do your
exercises. Your little PT cutie comes tomorrow." She says this
so easy, sweet as a peach. What I'm thinking is—They call it
elective surgery, Dad, as in, you can schedule it for when it's
convenient. If only I had a tenth of her patience.

We get to work—Pammy packing up her crafts room and me
in the kitchen, taping off the windows, wrestling the stove and
fridge away from the walls, draping tarps. Going through all her
scrapbooks—I hope nothing sets her off.

"Johnny B. Goode" plays on the radio, then "Born to Run."
I'm bending and squatting and stretching. Somebody should
start an exercise class—Painting the Pounds Away. The buttery
yellow paint comes off the roller easy—nothing quite like that
smell, almost sweet. "The City of New Orleans." What a totally
great song—in my all-time top ten. "You Can't Always Get What
You Want." The saleslady ringing me up at the paint store telling
me, You can't paint in this heat. I just take back my credit card
and smile, and what I'm thinking is, Really lady? I heard about
this crazy new invention—they call it air conditioning. "The
Boys Are Back in Town." Oh my gawd, Mattress King is having a
Fourth of July blowout sale!

My cell phone rings and I answer. "That's right," I say. "Yup,
still available." Pammy sticks her head around the corner to see
who's calling—she seems good. I wiggle my eyebrows and give
her a thumbs up.

"No, not really. Like the ad says, thirteen five—that's firm.
Includes all the accessories, plus the trailer too."

When I hang up, Pammy asks, "Well?"

"Says he wants to look her over." She holds up her hand, fingers crossed.

When I first ran the ad I got three calls. Not a single one wanted to come look. This guy sounded interested . . . but he was angling for a bargain—No, I'm not thinking about giving a little on the price. Jeez. A boat like that, perfect condition, with those motors, and all the extras . . . hell yes, thirteen five. Definitely.

When I kneel to paint around the electrical outlet under the bay window, my knees go snap, crackle, pop and I think of those kids who bought the house . . . knew they had a buyer's market, really stuck it to us with their lowball offer. Two pages of nit-picky repairs. And the capper, Sale contingent on us moving out in thirty days. Whoever even heard of that? And they're like, take it or leave it.

"Me and Bobby McGee" comes on as I'm using the small brush to cut in around the kitchen cabinets. Telling Pammy how doing the painting ourselves was the only way to go—she just stood there, hands on her hips, glaring at me like I'm crazy. Paint it? We'll be lucky if getting everything else done in a month doesn't kill us. Had to open my big stupid mouth—Look, you just don't understand. No job, no money.

Definitely could have handled that better—should have put a cork in the dork. The DJ repeats the same news he's been giving all morning about the ten-car pile-up out on the interstate and how we're headed for a record fourteenth straight day over 100. "Oh, Pretty Woman." "Don't Stand so Close to Me." Come on down to Mattress King, Set you up with the real thing. Lamest jingle ever. I'll be fine driving the U-Haul . . . but Pammy and Dad stuck together in her little car . . . for two days . . .

I finish the kitchen and move on to the great room, switching roller heads and laying down broad swaths of what Sherwin-

Williams calls Igloo White in push-pull strokes to the thudding baseline of Stevie Wonder's "Superstition."

Pammy comes out, a little flush in her cheeks, and says, "Okay, all boxed up and ready to go." I nod and ask if she has any ideas about lunch.

"I could run get something."

"Bucket?"

She finds her purse under the tarp covering the kitchen counter and is out the door. I hear the clunk and grind of the electric garage door opener and from the front window watch her back out of the driveway. When she makes the left onto Armstrong I go to the fridge and crack a cold one. Two quick gulps make a good dent, two more finish the job. I bury the can in the bottom of the paper grocery sack we're using for trash and do a little shimmy to Tina Turner singing "Proud Mary."

I step into Pammy's craft room, which is empty except for her office chair, a couple of large folding tables, and a small mountain of cardboard boxes and big plastic bins, each labeled with an oversized yellow stickie note. I lift two of the boxes and lug them through the kitchen and out the back door. Spud comes bolting out of his doghouse and races at me with his full weight and momentum until he reaches the end of his run line and the choke chain jerks him backwards. ARK-ARK-ARK-ARK. He's a good boy—a horrible barking maniac is what he is . . . no, he's a good boy. And Pammy needs him.

I cross the patio between the house and garage and free a hand for the doorknob. Through the flaps of the top box, I see one of her scrapbooks, on its spine the word CANADA.

Niagara Falls roaring like a jet plane right in front of us— Pammy beaming, her hair matted down from all that billowing mist, standing at the front of the tour boat in a neon-pink plastic poncho. She was just starting to show with Dusty.

Inside the garage it's shady but the air hangs hot and stuffy, thick with an overpowering smell of tires, motor oil, and mowed grass. I set the boxes down and push the buttons to open the second and third overhead doors. While they rumble and swing up and let in more light, I look over all we've packed up in the last few weeks.

Every inch of what used to be my truck's parking spot is now stacked to the high rafters, like in a warehouse. Tables and chairs and headboards and rugs and lamps and framed pictures and the rest of it, but mostly boxes. Our whole life in cardboard. Definitely two loads in the U-Haul.

Again and again, I circle from garage to craft room and back, hefting boxes and bins. Her and her scrapbooks. All that work. Remember the good times, she always says. Remember the good and fend off the bad. Two and a half years since we lost him.

I get a beer from the mini fridge, sip, sip again. The light flooding into the garage shows off the boat's clean white curves. Spick and span. My baby. Can't forget to tell the guy about the two cleat screws being stripped. Knocking back another swallow, I close my eyes and we're cutting across the lake's glinting water . . . a cool breeze . . . Pammy's hair blowing back . . . days that were never gonna end.

I kill the beer and walk out to my pickup parked along the cul-de-sac's rounded curb. Backing the truck up the driveway, I check my mirrors on both sides, inching toward the trailer. If I can't sell her, then what? Towing a 19-foot boat behind a 26-foot U-Haul six hundred miles and over a mountain pass? No can do. I get out and position the trailer so the hitch is above the truck's tow ball and couple them with the crank jack.

Easing the truck forward and positioning the boat on the driveway, I start thinking about the ice chest, my big, beautiful Yeti. I carry out the box of spare parts and the heavy gas can and buck them into the boat and head back into the garage and run my hand over the top of Yeti—Pammy all smiles, watching me unwrap it on my birthday. I didn't list it in the ad, and it tears at my heart to give it up, but . . . you gotta do what you gotta do. Into the boat it goes. I'm breathing hard, my shirt's sticking to my back and chest and gut. Twenty pounds since the layoff. Maybe start some kind of diet after we get moved.

Whack-whack-whack—Dad smacking the metal wastebasket with his cane. The sound rattles Spud. ARK-ARK, ARK-ARK-ARK-ARK-ARK. He's a good boy. She needs him.

When I enter the kitchen, Dad's bellowing for his pill. I jiggle one from the plastic bottle and take it to him. He snatches it from my hand and washes it down with iced tea. Wheel of Fortune is blaring on the big-screen TV.

"Ever hear of the July effect?" he asks but doesn't wait for an answer. "They hire these kid doctors fresh out of med school every July and their patients die like flies. On the news just now." His mouth forms a tight line across his face. "What if they screwed up and I get gangrene and they have to cut my leg off?" he says. "What about that?"

"Your operation was in June and your surgeon was at least fifty," I tell him. "I think you'll be okay. Want some more ice in your tea?" "What?" he says, his eyes fixed on the game show.

I repeat the offer a little louder. "I gotta drink or I'll die in this heat," he says, shaking his head. "But then I have to pee every ten minutes and it hurts like hell to walk."

Thirteen five—too much?

"Does that make any sense to you? Huh?" He slaps the leather arm of the recliner.

"Hey, I'm not deaf."

"Do we have enough of my pills? Do we need to get more?"

"We have what your doctor prescribed." The contestant on the TV spins the big wheel and when it comes to a stop, she jumps up and down, flapping her hands in the air. She reminds me of Pammy's sister gushing on Zoom when she talked us into moving. It's sooo cheap living down here. You could get yourselves a sweet little house for next to nothing. And there's plentiful work. She kept saying that—plentiful work. How plentiful, Nicole? Plentiful enough for a fifty five-year-old supervisor whose only ever worked one job?

"I gotta pee," Dad says, his frown now pinched at a slightly different angle.

I help him up and get him balanced on the walker and hover close, ready to catch him if he falls. He wobbles to the bathroom, wincing every time he puts pressure on his new knee. If they just hadn't closed the plant. Standing at the toilet and unzipped, he calls back over his shoulder, "I wish you had handrails in here. Could we get some handrails?"

"I told you, we're leaving in a few days."

"I just think you should have some handrails."

Over the sound of the toilet flushing, I hear Pammy out in the kitchen. "I'm home," she calls. Thank god.

She's spreading out three paper plates and loading them up with chicken, coleslaw, and biscuits with little plastic packets of honey. I open the fridge and get what she'll be counting as my first, then scarf down a home run—leg, thigh, breast, and wing. Cold beer and hot chicken.

We get back at it. Pammy's brushing a coat of glossy latex on the trim around the kitchen windows while I use the roller to turn the lower part of the walls in the great room into an igloo. The DJ says the temperature just ticked up another four degrees, those ten cars are still piled up on the interstate, and one after another the hits just keep on coming. "Sitting on the Dock of the Bay." "Twist and Shout." "Watching the Detectives." "Rock the Casbah." And no, I don't want to buy a damn mattress!

Not long after Pammy drives to the paint store for another can of latex, I hear a horn honking outside, a tinny MEEP-MEEP-MEEP. I wipe my hands on a rag and step out the front door into a wall of shimmering heat so hot it feels like standing between the boilers at the plant. Parked in front of my truck is one of those two-seater super-microcompacts, its exterior an almost incandescent metal-flake orange. Unfolding himself out of this thing is wiry guy in shorts, sandals, and a billowy white T-shirt—forty or so, veiny arms, sunglasses. He puts on a widebrimmed sun hat, its dangling chinstrap swings back and forth as he ambles up the driveway.

"Howdy. I'm Loren," I say, maybe a bit too cheery.

"Skip." He bobs his chin toward the boat. "That it, huh?" he says this like he's got a migraine coming on.

"A real beauty," I say, and hearing how dumb it sounds, wish I hadn't.

He takes his time making a shopper's slow circle around the boat, climbing up on the housings over the trailer tires and leaning in here and there, inspecting the gauges on the instrument panel, pawing through the spare parts box, giving

73

a feel to the cloth of the folded-up mooring cover, running his hand over the curved surface of the big Mercury outboard.

"That fish finder was Bass Master's Product of the Year," I tell him. "Ship to shore radio. GPS. Temp and depth gauge. The trolling motor is almost brand new. Got all the original manuals and paperwork." It's like he's not even hearing me. I wipe the back of my wrist across the sweat on my brow. "I'm even throwing in the Yeti. Top-of-the-line, heck of a cooler."

Skip makes his way back around to my side of the boat and eyeballs me from face to boots and back up. "Doing some painting, huh?"

I think of my streaked and spattered pants and make a little laugh. "Couldn't have picked a nicer day, could I."

Skip looks away, over toward the garage, and digs his hands into his pockets. "I suppose you got life jackets?" I nod. "Can I see 'em?"

Huh? "They're just regular lifejackets. Orange." He looks at me like I'm the doofus.

"Okay, sure, I'll go get you one." I start toward the garage, annoyed, then notice the lifejackets, hanging on their hooks, perfectly visible in his line of sight. He follows right behind me all the way inside, but when I get one of the jackets and hold it out for him, his head is turned and he's sizing up the stacked boxes.

I tap his shoulder with the vest. "Here you go."

He refocuses, takes the vest, and glances at one side and then the other as if he's interested. I'm wondering what's going on—is this guy a thief or something? No, dumbass, he's putting two and two together. Skip hands the vest back, nodding with a fakey-do smile.

He returns to the boat and squats down, resting a hand on one of the trailer tires and bending over to check the underside of the hull.

"Those chrome wheels," I say, "I wouldn't've put the money into them myself, but that's how the trailer came. They polish up good. Look real sharp."

Not even glancing at the wheels, Skip stands, takes a paper from his back pocket, unfolds and studies it. "Your Craigslist ad's been up for, uh . . . quite a while." He looks up at me through his dark glasses. "Nobody much buying," he says, slowly fanning himself with the paper. "Maybe all the layoffs at the power plant, huh?"

I shrug like, who knows, and ask if he's ever fished for silver stripes up at Fall Lake. "Good-eatin' fish. They really go for the cheese bait."

Skip scratches the back of his neck. "So how much you say you're asking?"

Forget how to read? It's right there in the ad. I keep my voice steady. "Thirteen five."

"Huh." He pushes up the brim of his hat then pinches his earlobe and makes a sour face. "Seems a little . . . high."

"Lot of boat for the money."

He carefully folds up the paper and slips it into his hip pocket. "I was thinking more like . . . ten."

This stabs me, but I keep a poker face. "You can shop around," I say. "I looked online, checked the Blue Book. That's what they're going for—what they're worth."

He scans the boat, stem to stern. "Well," he says, shoving his hands deep into his front pockets, his bony shoulders riding up, "I'll have to give that a think over."

"Sure. Not a problem." I force a smile. The cleat screws pop into my mind, but no, not now—not with him playing games. "Course, I can't promise how long she'll be available. Got another guy coming by in a while."

Old Skipper cracks a smile. "Ain't that the way," he says, clicking his tongue and nodding his head. "Always another guy coming by." He reaches over, gives the boat a gentle pat, and walks away. When he drives off in his dinky little clown car, I see the bumper sticker: there are no jobs on a dead planet.

Asshole! I stomp toward the house and slam the door behind me. Spud goes nuts—ARK-ARK-ARK-ARK-ARK-ARK-ARK. Will you shut the fuck up! I clamp down my jaw and remember what the grief counselor told me to say. He's a good dog. Pammy needs him.

I guzzle a beer. Dead planet my ass. How much electricity can you generate? Ever use a lightbulb? We got flue scrubbers, low-sulfur coal. Never burned so clean. "Bye, Bye, Miss American Pie" echoes through the empty house—helter-skelter rhyming with summer swelter. Halfway through the next beer I'm even more steamed. I'll have to give that a think over. Yeah, you do that, bucko. And good luck finding a better price. Cuz you won't. Cuz that's exactly what she's worth.

"Hotel California" comes on. Gotta get back to work. No time to waste. The big ladder is awkward and I struggle to get it vertical and balanced then pull its rope to force the extension section upward—thirteen, fourteen, fifteen feet— screeching with that god-awful sound of aluminum rasping across aluminum. I tilt it against the wall opposite the clearstory windows, figuring I'll roll the ceiling first, then do the trickier brushwork around the glass. All this painting because of those damn nitpicky buyers—we're touring room to room and the guy starts bragging about his job with GaleForce. We operate the wind turbine arrays you've probably seen in the hills west of town. Yeah, you smug twerp, I've seen your eyesore. How many birds did your turbine blades chop up today?

Down goes the rest of the beer, crush goes the can under my boot, and like a frisbee it flies into the corner. I climb several rungs up the ladder to check the slope. Too steep. I move the base farther away from the wall and test its stability with a shake—Pammy should be here to hold it steady. The roller handle screws easily onto the six-foot extension wand. I dip it in the paint pan on the floor tarp and roll the load even and climb up the ladder's many rungs holding the wand upright in my left hand like a torch. A fair price isn't good enough for ol' Skip.

Diddling me just to diddle me.

I strain to run the roller back and forth across the ceiling while using the other hand to keep a death grip on the quivering ladder. The muscles in my abdomen squawk and burn, but I hold the position until the brush rolls dry. Back down the ladder, slowly, one careful step at a time. Wind power, yeah, that's really gonna fix everything. Except for the battery problem and not matching peak demand worth a crap.

Instead of going all the way down to the bottom, I stop on the third rung, bend and extend the wand down to the paint pan. The roller sinks deep into the puddle and loads up heavy on one side with a big wet gob. I try to roll it up the pan's incline to even the load and remove the excess. No go. I try and try again and still I can't get it to roll. The wand's getting heavier by the second, the blood pressure's building in my face. I rest the rod against the ladder, straighten my aching back, try to catch my breath. I see Skippy, in my boat, high-throttling across the lake and cackling like a madman—Ten! The stupid fuck took ten! Wha-ha-ha!

"Sweet Home Alabama."

I bend back over, grab the rod, and try again, applying more force and less force, tilting it so the friction's all on one side, anything—but it's like pushing a broom. A bead of sweat runs into my eye and burns. I clench my jaw—I am not climbing down. I lose balance, start to fall, and reflexively bend my knee, ramming my shin hard into a rung—a jolt of pain shoots all the way to my teeth. Nothing ever fucking works, so sure, why not, why not go all the goddam way down the goddam ladder to the goddam ground. I yank on the rod to hoist and gummed-up, fucked-up roller so I can get a better grip on it, and when it's at a forty-five-degree angle a fat string of paint gloops off. It falls through the air like a comet with a long tail and splats on the tarp. I jerk the rod with a sharp twisting motion to keep the rest of the paint on the brush head and the whole roller handle unscrews from the rod and drops to the ground, landing with a soupy plop.

For a second everything is still—until I yell and fling the piece of shit extension rod across the room. It bounces into a collapsed step ladder leaning against the wall, sending it sliding to the floor, knocking into a gallon can of paint, tipping it over. I stare, holding my breath. The lid stays on the can—one, two, three—then gives way, a slow-moving wave of Igloo White spreads over the tarp.

ARK-ARK, ARK-ARK-ARK-ARK, ARK-ARK-ARK.

Late in the evening I'm slumped on the recliner in front of the TV, arms and thighs sticking to its leather, a scab and a bruise on my shin. I drink and seethe, seethe and drink. When the beer's

gone I switch to Jack. Dad finally goes to bed. For about the
fourth time Pammy asks What's the matter and for just as many
times I tell her I don't even want to go into it. She thinks this is a
good time to start in on me about how much I've been drinking
since the layoff and I tell her to leave me the hell alone and she
says All right, if you're going to be that way and clomps upstairs.

I stare at the TV, show after show, nodding in and out,
drinking more and either thinking or dreaming about the plant
manager addressing the whole shift gathered on the loading
dock—You all have done nothing but an outstanding job, and
if it was up to me, we'd be burning clean coal for the next five
hundred years.

I open my eyes and squint to clear the heavy fog in my head.
The nature program about the extinction of the white rhino isn't
on anymore—now a red-haired infomercial announcer with a
loud shirt and a pinky ring is staring at me and asking, "Are you
sick and tired of being trapped in a timeshare?"

I rub my face and look at the clock, its glowing red digits
read 3:20, the two dots blinking on-off, on-off. Twenty-one is my
lucky number, so I sit there like an idiot, waiting. And then out
of nowhere it hits me—There is a way out. Even if a buyer won't
pay the thirteen five, the insurance will. The zero turns to one.

I turn off the television and listen to the house sounds—
nothing to indicate anyone is still awake. I go into the unlit
kitchen, stop at the sink, and look out the window—all black,
Spud's asleep in his doghouse. There will be questions—Who do
you think might have done this? Probably kids up to mischief.
Or, I don't know, maybe Skip—he got real upset about the price
I was asking. Drove off in a huff. No sir, I don't know his last
name, but he called, his number will be in my phone.

Out the back door, quiet as I can be, I pause on the landing. Still hot. No wind. I slip across the patio and through the back door of the garage. Moving through the pitch black, my hand brushing along the side of Pammy's car, I get to just inside the open overhead door and have a look. No movement on the cul-de-sac or out on Armstrong. All the houses dark, shut down for the night, just a dim porch light here and there. I go to my workbench and feel around until I find the matchbook, then, hunched down, creep out to the side of the boat away from the street. I reach over the gunwale, unscrew the cap on the gas can and ease it onto its side, glug, glug, glug. I stand back, strike one match, and use it to light the pack—it flares, and I flick it onto the aft deck. There's a deep, breathy whoosh and a fireball. I dash up the walkway and into the house. ARK-ARK-ARK, ARK-ARK-ARK-ARK-ARK.

Peeking back out through the cracked door, I see bright yellow flames rising from the boat dancing straight up into the air. My heart's pounding and I'm wondering if the trailer's gonna burn and what that'll mean for the insurance settlement, when BANG, something explodes—an arc of fire shoots up and out of the boat toward the garage. ARK-ARK, ARK-ARK, ARK-ARK-ARK, ARK.

I run outside to where I can see that flames have splashed across the garage floor and are shimmering right up against the stacked boxes. I scramble to the garden hose and twist open the spigot valve as far as it will go, then see the pistol-grip spray nozzle, grab it, try to screw it on the spewing hose—water jets out and sprays everywhere, my face, T-shirt, all down my legs. Twisting the nozzle tight, I look up and see the flames are spreading fast, covering the boxes and licking up toward the bare-wood rafters. Holding one hand in front of my face to shield the heat, I get as close as I can and shoot a stream of water onto the burning cardboard, melting plastic bins, and furniture that's now alight. No effect.

Pammy's at the front door. "I called 911," she cries. "I'll get Dad."

The workbench is burning—oil, paint thinner, propane, bug spray. My eyes dart up to the whisps of gray smoke rising from the roof shingles. I look across the patio to the house, wondering if the flames could jump the gap. The garage roof suddenly erupts into a sheet of fire—the intense heat pushes me backwards and I spin away and aim the jet of water at the house—the roof, the eaves, the door, the siding. My calves feel like bacon sputtering in a frying pan. I listen for sirens but hear only the roaring whoosh and crackle of the raging inferno.

I spray and spray and spray, and time slows to a crawl. Minutes seem to pass between each of my breaths. Our whole life is going up in flames—all our stuff, the photos, her scrapbooks. All of it, everything on fire—turning to sparks. Sparks skittering upward into the black sky. Thousands and thousands of them, rising ever higher with such lively energy, then so quickly winking out. Gone.

Each and every one.

Gone forever.

Nobody even left to remember what could and could not be controlled.

Ophelia's Understudy

Here I am, standing in my go-to bookstore's romance aisle, which I like to think of as the Romance Isle, an exotic place where in just a few pages I can be transported somewhere faraway and glamorous. For me, a big Saturday night is taking a romance novel to my favorite chair over in the store's fantasy section and reading the whole thing in one sitting, for free.

I hear some commotion over in the little-kids' play area where authors sometimes come to read from their books. People are gathering and taking seats. I go over to see what's up.

The friendly bearded guy who owns the bookstore introduces the author, Marina Dandridge, making a point of saying she lives here in our town. She is tall and around fifty, a pretty blonde who takes good care of herself. Her clothes look like Nordstrom head to foot—tailored trousers, expensive shoes, silk blouse, cashmere cardigan, matching necklace and rings. (And I'm not talking about Nordstrom Rack either, where I got my Trisha Vanessa espadrilles for a song—a mark down on a mark down on a mark down.)

"Can you hear me all right?" she asks in a clear, strong voice. The fifteen or so of us in the folding chairs let her know we can. "I'm here to talk about my book, *Dancing on the Edge: My Alien Abduction Saga*."

Whoa. Did not see that coming. Not a single thing about her says wackadoo. She begins by telling us that late one night while she and her husband Damian were asleep in their bed, she awoke with a feeling that someone was in their room. In the shadows, she could just barely see the outlines of something, a being of some kind, as small as a child. Without speaking, this being communicated to her not to worry, he had come on a mission of peace. His name was Mr. Captain.

Fully awake but paralyzed, she levitated out of her bed and in a blinding flash of light was transported inside a spaceship where every surface was gleaming white glass. Accompanied by two beings she called the *helpers*, she floated down a long hallway to a room where Mr. Captain awaited—though now he had taken on a different form and was more than eight feet tall, his thin body draped in a flowing gown. She came to rest on a table where the helpers undressed her and assisted Mr. Captain as he gave her a thorough medical examination that included much prodding, probing, and the drawing of her blood. She believed she was under the effects of some sort of drug because during the exam she was not only free of all fear but deliriously happy.

Mr. Captain communicated that she was a very healthy woman and asked if she would like to remember her experiences or forget them. Marina said she wanted to remember, which seemed to please Mr. Captain. Another flash of light and she was back in her bed, with Damian lying beside her. The last thing Mr. Captain communicated before she fell into a deep sleep was that he would visit again. In the morning, she tried to dismiss her memories as just a vivid dream, but then she noticed in the crook of her elbow the small red mark from where her abductor had taken her blood.

She finishes telling her story, and we applaud. She takes a seat at a table next to stacks of her book. People line up to buy a copy and have her sign it.

One heavyset man in a too-tight black T-shirt asks if she might have been examined at a base on the dark side of the moon. No, she's quite certain, it was on a spacecraft, not at a base.

"I see," he says, disappointed. "I'm gathering evidence about the alien moon base and had hoped you could add an eyewitness account."

"Sorry, wish I could help," she says with a genial smile.

A nervous and pale young woman is next in line—probably just twenty or so, maybe five years younger than me. "Did they harvest your eggs?" she asks.

Marina looks at the girl compassionately. "No," she says, as if speaking to a troubled daughter. "I don't believe they did."

"They took mine," the young woman says, twirling her finger around a strand of her stringy hair. "They're making an imposter race." She glances uncomfortably at the book-buyers around her.

It goes on like this with one question after another, and to each one Marina responds like Martha Stewart in complete and effortless control of a dinner party at the loony bin. Then it is just the two of us. She blinks her blue eyes at me, perky as an April daffodil.

"Are you giving a lot of these talks?" I ask.

"I'm on a small book tour." She tries to sound humble about it, but I can tell she's pretty darn pleased. "Tomorrow afternoon I'll be at High Desert Books over in Rampton—even though my husband's not thrilled about the drive. Oh, here he is."

Damian walks up, a good-looking guy with dark wavy hair, dressed out of the same Nordstrom catalog she is—right down to the tassels on his loafers. He plants a peck on her cheek, gives me a cordial smile, and starts loading the stack of unsold books into a cardboard box.

Marina says to him, "I was just telling . . ."

"Rita," I say.

"Rita—that you'd rather be playing golf than driving me to Rampton tomorrow."

"It's a big day for you," he says with a supportive smile—the wife needs a lift, and, by God, he's going to be a gentleman about it. I like him right off. I wonder why she can't drive herself, then an idea pops into my head.

"I don't have anything going on tomorrow," I say to him and notice what pretty green eyes he has. "I'd be happy to drive."

He straightens right up and rests his hands on the book box. They exchange a quick glance and she gives him a nod.

"Awfully generous of you," Damian says. "We live in the south hills." He picks up one of her books and writes the address on the title page. "And let me give you something for the gas—the least I can do." He fishes a bill from his wallet, slips it into the book and holds it out.

"Say, ten o' clock?"

I take the book. "Ten's great."

"Oh, there's this wun-derful little Thai place over there," says Marina. "We'll have an adventure."

They walk off together, the perfect couple. Inside the book I find a hundred-dollar bill.

I drive, she talks—and talks and talks and talks. By the time we return late in the afternoon I'm certain that if I were a contestant on Jeopardy! and the category was Marina Dandridge, I could run the board.

I'll take Marina for $200, Alex.

And Alex would say, "The answer is: 'Ophelia's understudy.'"

And I'd bang the buzzer before the other two contestants and ask: What role did Marina have in a college theater production when she met Damian?

Marina for $400.

The answer is: "Cessna."

In what kind of airplane did Damian fly Marina to his parents' 10,000-acre Montana ranch on their second date?

Marina for $600.

The answer is: "Dizzy spells brought on by medication."

Why doesn't Marina drive?

Marina for $800.

The answer is: "By arranging the ghostwriting, the publication, and the tour."

Alex, I'm going to go with: How did Damian help Marina with her book?

Marina for $1,000.

The answer is: "There's more to this world than meets the eye."

What did Marina learn from her abduction?

And now for today's Final Jeopardy answer: "Puerto Luna, Spain."

Well Alex, I'm betting everything on this one, so I hope I get it right. My question is: Where does Marina want to visit more than any other place on Earth?

The first time Marina mentions the idea of me accompanying her to Europe I think, yeah, right, like that's really going to happen. But as we spend more time together over the following weeks, I learn that even though she's a little loopy, the woman gets things done. With Damian's encouragement and support, all the arrangements soon fall into place. I gloat to everybody at the day care where I work that I'm going all-expenses-paid and promise I'll send a postcard.

That's when I got the call from Damian wanting to make sure I knew what I was getting myself into.

"She has some . . . conditions," he said. "She obsesses about things. At first it was acid rain, then the ozone hole—for a year or so it was a meteor impact. Now it's global warming. I try to keep her away from the news—every sad polar bear story twists her up another notch. I guess the good news is she's sure we'll survive in the end."

He assured me she was getting first-class medical care and that her medications have really helped.

"Has she been like this for long?"

"Since right after we married." Oh, the poor guy. I wasn't sure what to say.

The last thing he said was, "You're an absolute angel for doing this."

I remember him telling me that as he drives us to the airport in his big black Mercedes and parks in the loading and unloading zone. An attendant hefts out of the trunk my two black wheelie bags—one borrowed—and Marina's matched set of four fuchsia-colored suitcases.

At the security gate they hug and kiss and say their good-byes. He opens his arms to me, and we hug too. As we embrace, he whispers, "Take good care of her."

We board the plane and hardly have a chance to get settled into our first-class seats before the flight attendant brings us glasses of champagne—on the house. The jet takes off and Marina starts reading a book titled *Judgment Day Visions: The Four Horsemen, the Whore of Babylon, and the Beast of the Sea.* She offers me a sleeping pill, but I don't want to miss a second.

She pops one and soon conks out, looking as innocent and helpless as one of my day care kids. I carefully lift the book that has fallen to her lap. It has two places marked with yellow stickie notes—one flags a couple of pages about the altarpiece we are going to see in France; the other, a whole chapter on the fresco she's been so excited about seeing in Puerto Luna.

In London we stay four nights at the super-swanky Mayfair Savoy Arms. We race around the city shopping and seeing the sights and even venture out one night to the West End to see a musical. The weather is cool and rainy.

"I thought with global warming it would be so much . . . warmer," Marina says. She can be such a ditz.

We leave for France on a train that goes under the English Channel at a hundred miles an hour. Halfway across, she looks up from her book.

"Listen to this," she says. "The word apocalypse comes from Greek—it means an unveiling."

"Huh," I say. "Interesting." It's what she wants, what she needs. As we've traveled together, I've seen how lonely she is, how she craves attention. I wonder if Damian is there for her when she reads some oddball fact and wants to share.

Paris is like one of those dreams I have where I'm flying and can't possibly feel any happier. We visit the Eiffel Tower and the Louvre and take taxis and metro trains and riverboats and walk our legs off and eat food I've never heard of in one amazing restaurant after another.

The day before we leave Paris, we go shopping at a boutique with prices that have my eyes popping out. An impeccably dressed saleswoman who speaks good English ushers Marina around, helping her pick out enough clothes to last ten years. The more she shops, the more hyper she gets—talking fast, eyes jittery. The saleswoman gives me a worried glance. I do what I can to bring the spree to an end—it feels like trying to get a drunk friend out of a bar. Marina hands the cashier her credit card and signs the slip without even looking it over.

We take a bullet train from Paris to Dijon where we eat a long lunch over a bottle of wine, then board another train. The morning clouds have burned off, and the sun is streaming in, making our car a little stuffy. The countryside speeds by outside the window in a green blur. In the guidebook, I read about our destination.

"It says here that Berbertville is the heart of the Burgundy wine growing region. Maybe tonight we should try—"

But before I can finish playing tour guide, I see that her eyes are closed, her head tilted to one side. I too feel drowsy and spent. All our traveling is catching up. I think about London and Paris and how grateful I am to Damian for urging Marina to add those cities to our trip. It's easy to understand why he was ready for some extended alone time. The sun is warm on my cheek, and the train sways in a relaxing rhythmic rocking. Marina, Damian . . . and me. Such a perfect match. Like in a fairytale. Off to Rome we'll go. Or maybe an around-the-world cruise.

In Berbertville, our hotel is on a winding cobblestone street in the medieval part of town. We try a delicious burgundy with dinner then turn in early.

The next morning is bright and warm, and we get to the art museum just as it is opening. Marina marches right past all the other paintings and sculptures on display, making a beeline to the main gallery, a big high-ceilinged room with one entire wall dominated by the museum's famous Renaissance altarpiece. Painted in the late-1400s by a Flemish artist named Jacob de Wildt, the painting's nine panels depict the Last Judgment, with Christ atop a heavenly throne weighing the souls of the dead on a scale. Those found worthy are guided by Michael the Archangel to the golden gates of paradise in the picture's leftmost panel, while to the right, the unrepentant are banished to eternal punishment, their faces wracked with pain as their twisted bodies tumble into the gaping pit of a fiery hell.

Marina stands back, takes in the whole painting, then rushes up close to its left side, as close as she can get, leaning against the railing that keeps visitors a few feet away. She reaches out, her fingers quiver just inches from Michael.

"There were pictures in my books, but I had to see for myself," she says, her voice breathy with excitement. "It's him."

I draw near to her and follow her gaze to the merciful archangel with great wings and flowing robes. "Who?" I ask.

Cheeks flushed, she says, "Mr. Captain."

Her eyes kind of wobble and I am afraid she might faint. I take her by the arm and hustle her toward the exit.

Looking back over her shoulder at the painting, she whispers, "Fire came down from heaven and devoured them all."

She is limp and sweaty in the cab we take back to the hotel.
I give the girl at the desk an anxious look to let her know
something isn't right in case later on we need a doctor.

"Here we are," I say, closing the door to her room behind us. I
get her a glass of water.

She lies on the bed and sips. "Sometimes I just get these
dizzy spells."

We agree she should rest and make a vague plan for getting
together for dinner.

Returning to my room, I keep thinking about how tomorrow
we'll be off to Spain. I open the guidebook and look at the map
of our route. It won't be easy—train tickets to buy, transfers
to navigate, and a whole new language to deal with. I can't find
Puerto Luna in the guidebook's table of contents, so I flip to
the index. It has just one listing, and when I turn to that page,
there is only one short paragraph, which surprises me—the de
Wildt altarpiece by itself got half a page plus a photo. The text
describes Puerto Luna as "a pleasant boat ride from Boca del
Rio." On the guidebook's four-star scale, the island's monastery
receives only half a star, "a minor curiosity sure to please those
interested in crypts, catacombs, and the macabre." The book
says not a single thing about the fresco that brought us halfway
around the world.

When I knock at her door that evening, she's a mess—bad
bed-head hair and the same clothes as earlier, only even more
wrinkled now.

"I found a cute café down by the canal," I say. "Wanna give it
a try?"

She agrees but seems like she'd just as soon crawl into a hole
and turn off the lights. At the café she helps me with the French
on the menu, further draining what little energy she has.

She orders a small salad and just picks at it.

"About tomorrow, I was just thinking," I say, "what if something happens—an accident, a broken leg maybe—and me not speaking a word of Spanish."

She stares at her salad and says flatly, "I'll hablo from the wheelchair."

"I have an idea. What if we don't go to Puerto Luna."

She frowns. "You want to stay here?"

"No. We could just go straight to Barcelona and fly home."

She glares at me. "We're on a pilgrimage. Don't you see? The road to Jerusalem—there's no stopping now."

Marina is icy in the taxi as we drive to the station and once aboard the train, she doesn't say a word, keeping her nose in a book or scribbling frantically in her journal. We travel west and south, on three different trains.

Finally, we arrive hot and tired in the coastal town of Boca del Rio then take a cab to the dock and catch the ferry to Puerto Luna. It's a smooth passage, and we pull into a broad crescent-shaped harbor lined with quaint hotels and restaurants. A friendly teenage boy with a cart carries our luggage to the hotel and up to our rooms. I help Marina get her clothes unpacked. She's no longer angry, just exhausted.

"Would you like some food?" I ask.

She shakes her head slowly and, it seems to me, sadly.

I sit beside her on the bed and put my arm around her. "Maybe you just need a good night's sleep."

She nods like an invalid agreeing with her nurse. I get her undressed and under the covers.

In the morning, she opens the door looking pale, eyes puffy, her hair a disaster. She climbs right back into the tangle of her bedsheets. I go to her, stroke her face, and do my best to keep my worry hidden.

"Best time to see the fresco is around six," she says weakly. "When the monks sing."

"You think you are going to be okay for that?"

She thinks for a moment then gives a brave little nod. "If I rest."

I bring her some breakfast and get her to eat a few bites and drink some juice. She wants to sleep. When I check in after lunch, she is still in bed, though she seems a bit stronger, or at least pretends to be. I suggest a slow walk along the harbor before it gets too hot, but she says she needs to save her strength.

Her plan works. When the time comes, she has herself put together and is ready to go. We take a cab up a steep and winding one-lane road to a monastery perched on a cliff high above the harbor. A tiny stout monk in a brown robe greets us and guides us to a musty gift shop where he gestures to an inner door.

"Singing soon. You find many seats."

"We've come to see the fresco," Marina says.

"Ah. Is good," he says. "You can read the signs—to the chapel."

We enter the church by a side door as a dozen monks file in through the main entrance and float in a slow procession to the altar. A sign rests on a wooden easel, CAPILLA DE LOS HUESOS/CHAPEL OF BONES.

We follow the arrow to a stone stairway and go carefully down its narrow twisting steps. Far underground, we arrive at a room, a cavern really, shadowy except for an alcove with a kneeling rail before a large crucifix. The air is cool and hangs heavy with sweet-smelling incense. As my eyes adjust to the dim light, I see that the walls all around us are covered with human bones, thousands and thousands of them, gray and white, some simply stacked, some arranged in patterns. I don't much mind the knobby white arm and leg bones—what really gets to me are the hundreds of jawless skulls with their empty black eyes.

Up in the church, the monks start chanting. The sound drifts down the stairs like some ghostly fog, surrounding us, deepening the otherworldly feeling of this eerie place.

Marina spots the FRESCO sign and steps around a corner with me close by her side. Three walls of the small room are made of bones. The fourth is completely covered with the fresco, The Recompense of the Damned by Hector Úbeda. It portrays a huge, almost dinosaur-looking monster with razor-sharp teeth, horns, and wild red eyes, its scaly skin like glowing embers. In the foreground are the damned souls, naked and screaming in agony—gnawed by oversized cockroaches, sawed in half by cackling goat-legged demons, stripped of their flesh by crazy-eyed vultures, and pierced by the stingers of enormous wasps with faces like pigs.

Marina's mouth falls open, her head scans side to side, up and down. I take hold of her arm. "Are you all right?"

"Oh yes," she sighs, kind of swoony. Her lips curl into a weirdly satisfied smile. She murmurs, "For, behold, the Lord will come with fire and render his rebuke with flames."

We stand there for a long time. She stares at the painting. I watch her. The chanting of the monks rises and falls, rises and falls, music from another world.

"I'm ready," she says and abruptly turns and leaves.

I follow her up the stairs. In the garden behind the church, she finds a path to an overlook where, far down the cliff, we see the town hugging the harbor. Everything is awash in the lustrous warmth of the low-angled sun.

"What did you think of the fresco?" she asks, her eyes closed, face thrust out into the caress of the hot wind. Something in her voice sounds better, stronger than it has in days.

"Kind of creepy," I admit, worried I'd offend her.

"That's for sure," she says with a musical little laugh, almost like her old self. "And all those bones—yuck."

She looks like someone coming out of a long illness, still thin and drawn, but the fever has broken.

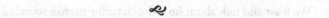

Marina is showered and dressed, her hair brushed, and her make-up fresh and well done.

We stroll to the restaurant and are greeted by our waiter, Ramone, who is almost too good-looking to be real. He leads us through the dining room and outside to the brick-floored patio with small, graceful steps that remind me of a bullfighter. He seats us at a table with a fine view of the lovely pink and orange sunset mirrored on the glassy harbor.

"The tide comes in now," Ramone says. "Is very nice for you."

Marina orders a bottle of rosé and while we sip our first glass in the fading light we ooh and aah over the seafood delicacies pictured on the menu.

Ramone returns, lights the candle on our table, and, while topping off our glasses, asks what we would like.

"El plato de mariscos de la reina," Marina orders. It's the most expensive item on the menu.

"For the queen," he says, smiling. "Is quite beautiful. Enough for two."

95

Our candle fills the oncoming darkness with a merry glow. I listen to the soothing shoosh-shoosh of the harbor ripples lapping onto the beach pebbles. Strands of small outdoor lights strung in pleasing arcs switch on and twinkle soft and golden. I'll sleep well. And tomorrow, Barcelona and home.

Ramone rolls out a cart carrying a huge platter mounded with a bed of ice cubes displaying a spread of seafood like I've never seen: shrimp tails fanned out, crab legs and claws, clams and scallops and mussels and cockles like treasures in their rough shells. The centerpiece, raised above the rest on a jutting platform of ice, is a very large red lobster split in two.

We feast and talk about how the chanting monks sounded like some heavenly chorus, and how freaky it felt in the Chapel of Bones. We finish the bottle of rosé and order two more glasses. The conversation flows easily—maybe it's the wine, or maybe because we've been through so much together and now, having come to the end of our journey, we can relax.

A slushy noise comes from the platter of food—a small avalanche on the mountain of ice. Water from the melted cubes overflows the lip of the platter—drip, drip, drip, drip, drip—forming a puddle on the bricks below.

Marina doesn't notice any of this. She's peering intently out at the harbor. "Something there?" I ask. I can't tell if she hears me. I squint to see what has her attention.

"My god," she gasps.

"What? What is it?"

"Can't you see?" Her excited eyes dart to me then return to the water. "There. Right there." She points. The harbor is completely dark, a black void.

"Surely you can see it. It's glowing, throbbing."

I squint, look all around. "I don't."

"Right there," she says emphatically. "On the bottom of the harbor. A spaceship, fifty yards across. Rainbow colors circling around and around its outside, shimmering up through the water. You hear the hum? Wah-wah-wah. And the dolphins. You see the dolphins, don't you? Ten, twenty, jumping out of the water in unison, twirling, dripping showers of diamonds in the air."

She stares right at me, her eyes ablaze. "He promised to come back. I knew if we saw the fresco, it would be a sign to him." Tears of joy stream down her cheeks. "Our sins like sticks heaped around us," she says, reaching across the table to take my hand. "And Mr. Captain's brought the torch."

I lean in close to get a good look at her. She's lost it, no doubt about that, but how badly? With a reassuring nod, I give her hand a squeeze. I tell her, "There's more to this world than meets the eye."

"That is so true," she says, not recognizing her own words. Who cares—it seems to give her comfort. Her tensed-up shoulders lower, she wipes away the tears and returns to calmly watching her spaceship.

I sip my wine and keep a close watch on how she's doing. This is no mysterious abduction in the night, no dreamy fantasy that could be ghostwritten into a book. She's having a wide-awake la-la-land hallucination. But she isn't out of control. I'll be able to get her to the airport, onto the plane, home. And after that? New psych drugs? Hospitalization?

Then it comes to me. Damian will take care of her like he always has. He and his money. I stab a bit of lobster with my fork, pause, and examine the delicate white morsel. He will need help, a lot of help, and a friend. I'll be there for him. Just for him. I place the rich meat on my tongue.

The Fifty Faces of Albert Einstein

What had brought me to the Bradford Academy was to teach, to inspire the next generation even as I had once been inspired. And to fill the hole left by Jane's death. I had accepted a one-year position and in the first four months I discovered that some holes would never be filled. Likewise, as for my aspirations to prepare students adequately for the estimable challenges of the world they would soon inherit, I was beginning to have my doubts.

But on this particular day the boys were in excellent spirits. And why not? A light snow had fallen overnight on our woodsy New Hampshire campus; outside my classroom's windows the sun now brightly illuminated the chapel and its nineteenth century spire (a century to which I often felt I belonged). It was the Friday before winter holiday and soon the excited boarders would be returning to families across the nation and, in a few cases, around the world. I had purposely concluded my lecture on diplomatic responses to climate change a few minutes early.

"The holiday season brings to mind the subject of giving," I said, looking out over their faces. "I would like to take this occasion to tell you about the most precious gift I ever received."

I was not one given to divulging much about my personal life, so this promise of an unusual intimacy captured the attention of the twenty-two seniors before me.

"My father fought in the Second World War, after which he returned home, married my mother, and some months later I was born—the number of months being greater than nine, I assure you." A few of the boys tittered at the unexpected ribaldry.

"On the very day of my birth, my father left my mother and me at the hospital and gathered with some friends to celebrate at a favorite tavern. After cigars were smoked and many drinks drunk, a small hunched-over man, a stranger, approached my father.

"This man, Lou Delvecchio, said he had overheard the news of the birth and wanted to extend his congratulations. My father was a bricklayer by trade and did not have a great deal of money, but on this night he was feeling expansive and offered to stand Lou a drink.

"Lou declined the offer, attributing his abstinence to a serious war injury. Then he placed in my father's hand this photograph."

With not a little theatricality, I took from my briefcase a photograph in a simple brass frame, my dearest possession, and held it up for all the boys to see—five inches by seven, black and white, the smiling face of Albert Einstein.

"Lou proceeded to tell my father that he worked as a janitor at the Institute for Advanced Studies in Princeton. Part of his responsibility was cleaning Einstein's office—a challenging task given the famed messiness of the world's greatest physicist. One evening Lou entered the office to find Einstein working late, still scribbling at the blackboard. They chatted amiably—call me Albert, and such. The Nobel Prize winner was, as Lou described him, 'like a regular Joe.' This regular Joe thanked Lou for keeping the office clean and in gratitude presented him with this photo.

"And as you can see, here is the signature and an inscription: 'Only a life lived for others is a life worthwhile.'" I pointed to Einstein's cursive scrawl and, holding the photo at arm's length, swept it slowly from side to side for the boys, many of whom were leaning forward in their seats straining to see. "Those words guided me throughout my life, they led me to my career at the Department of State."

"I bet it's worth a lot," one boy said.

"You could put it up on eBay," suggested another, who got a good laugh from his classmates.

"Lou didn't know much about physics," I continued, "but enough to grasp that Einstein, in Lou's inimitable words, 'understood the whole shebang—from the atoms to the stars.' He said it would be a blessing for any child to have a connection to such a genius. With a wink he handed my father the photo and said, 'Keep it. For the kid.'"

The boys were not making jokes now.

"As you head off to your holiday celebrations, I invite you to ponder Mr. Lou Delvecchio. He bestowed his gift not to a family member nor even to a close friend, but to a fellow human being he had never met before. He offered it for the benefit of a child he had never seen—an act of pure, selfless generosity."

A hand shot up. It was Carrara. Carmelo Carrara, a scholarship student. Very bright, but troubled—never quite accepted by the other boys.

"How do you know what Lou said?" he asked with a sincere curiosity. "I mean, you weren't there."

"Ah, the epistemological inquiry. Bravo." Young Carrara blushed. I explained how this was one of my father's pet stories and that, over the years, I had heard him recount it many times.

"Now, before you all dash off, one last thing. During the recess, I will be taking a short trip to visit Mr. Delvecchio. Using Google, I recently discovered his whereabouts. He is a very old man now—in his mid-nineties. My surprise visit will, I hope, bring him a little holiday cheer." I had now said my piece, delivered my secular homily. Perhaps it would get through to one or two. "Class dismissed."

The room filled with the noisy hubbub of boys rising and bustling off. I carefully replaced the photo of Einstein in my briefcase.

"Excuse me, sir. I have one more question." It was Carrara.

"Yes."

"Well, sir, I was just wondering . . . did your father ever explain why this fellow Lou was in the tavern. I mean, doesn't it seem a little odd, as he wasn't a drinker?"

I was overcome. How had I never noticed this incongruity?

"Another excellent question," I said. "One I shall certainly ask when I see him." "Thank you, sir. Have a wonderful holiday."

I stood for some time waiting at the unattended reception desk of the Colonel Ralph J. Kersey Home for Soldiers and Sailors. When a staff member finally appeared—a large, big-haired woman with tattoos peeking out from under the neckline of her smock—I asked for directions to Lou's room.

She sniffled and clicked on her keyboard and squinted at her monitor. "As of a few days ago he's been reassigned." She tapped her finger on the screen. "Uh-huh, looks like Saturday—transferred to C Ward." Her eyes were on me now. "Hospice."

I followed her directions, and while passing through a succession of hallways filled with pungent smells and the sounds of various blaring televisions I considered Lou's relocation to C Ward. How fortuitous that I had come now.

Once on the C Ward, I presented myself to a nurse who guided me to Lou's room. She stopped just outside his door.

"It will do him good to see you," she said. "Go easy. He puts on a good show, but he's quite weak."

Inside the room I saw two beds, one empty, one containing a slight, white-haired man, withered and ashen, staring at the ceiling.

"Lou," I said softly.

He blinked and looked my way, then grasped a small device and pushed a button on it, causing the mechanical bed to clank and hum and raise him to a sitting position. His tongue moved over dry lips.

A cup stood among a few personal items on his nightstand. "Would you like a drink?"

He nodded. I handed him the cup, rolled the portable tray table over the bed, and moved a chair close to him.

He drank from the straw then set the cup down and brushed a crooked finger across his lip. "Thanks," he said in a raspy whisper.

"Whitney Eggleston," I said, extending my hand to shake. His grip had no strength, though his eyes, while slow in their movement, were focused and alert. I took the framed picture from the pocket of my coat and handed it to him. "You gave this to my father."

He studied the photo intently, every corner of it, squinting to read the inscription, moving his lips as he read the words. His face lit up, as if recognizing a long-lost friend.

Almost coyly, he asked, "Remind me . . ."

Poor old fellow—at his age, whose memory wouldn't be failing? I reprised the story.

"Oh, sure, sure. I remember." Using the leg on the back of the picture frame, he stood the photograph on the tray table. Now it was the three of us—Lou, Albert, and Whitney.

"By the way," I said, "I've told the story of your gift many times, but only recently did I ask myself how it was that you came to be in that tavern—you, a non-drinker?"

"That's right, no booze for old Lou," he said, gently patting his midsection. "Only got a sliver of a liver. Doc said one drop could do me in." Suddenly he had the energy of man ten years younger.

He saw something in my face and asked, "What?"

"I'm just a little surprised. You seem so healthy and . . ." I looked around the room.

"And I'm on C Ward?" I tilted my head. "Usually it's for last gaspers, all right. But the B Ward got full up and they had plenty of room over here." He bobbed his chin at the empty bed.

"So, it was just a matter of . . ."

"Yep, that, and on account of now they tell me I got some cancer. Don't feel any different, but all them tests don't lie."

"Are you getting some treatment?"

"Gonna be ninety-six in two months." He winked and reached for his cup. After a pull on the straw, he said, "Now how I wound up in the beer joint, I remember that very clearly. Back then I smoked—used to love my ciggies—and I was buying a pack when your pop comes into the store. He gets a handful of cheapo cigars, and the cashier asks him, 'Boy or girl?' Grinning ear to ear, your pop says it's a boy, his first.

"He was proud as a peacock—proud and a little scared maybe. A kid's a big responsibility." Lou took another drink. "So I followed him over to the tavern, saw him drinking with his friends, and I went and got the picture." He gave a little shrug. "Now you know."

"Everything should make so much sense," I chuckled. "We kept Mr. Einstein in a place of honor, on the mantel right next to the photos of my grandparents. In grade school, I'd bring home a report card and my father would point to the picture and say, 'The professor would be very proud of you.'

"On the day my parents dropped me off at college, my father handed me the photo. 'This is yours,' he said. 'Always do your best. Never forget what's worthwhile.'

"Over the years, I've come to appreciate more and more what you did, your generosity. I've grown to think of you as something of a—"

He held up his hand and waved me off. Humble, he was. Or shy. Not one to seek the spotlight.

"You retired?" Lou asked, his eyes lively. The nurse had been right; having a visitor was doing him good.

"Was. When Jane, my wife, and I finished our careers, we bought a place in Connecticut. That same year she got a very aggressive cancer and—" I cleared my throat to stop the quiver in my voice. "When she passed, friends told me I needed to get out, do something." Lou nodded. "I took a teaching position at a boy's prep school—tweeds and bow tie."

"What do you teach?"

"The curriculum now includes a required three-course sequence, Addressing Climate Change. I'm overqualified—

thirty-five years with the State Department. But the students seem to like me well enough," I said, setting up a line that usually got a laugh. "They've taken to calling me Mr. Egg."

Lou wasn't listening, or, if he was, he didn't deem my quip worth even a perfunctory smile. "On the news, they're always talking about climate this and climate that. What do you tell your kids about it?"

"Well, we cover the science, of course—a bit grim. I try to focus on remedies. I worked on arms treaties—nuclear, chemical, biological—so I have a familiarity with multilateralism."

"I worry sometimes if we're killing ourselves like they say."

"We may eventually establish some equilibrium with the climate, but in how long, fifty years, a hundred? In the meantime, I fear we may see some very dark days."

His bristly eyebrows pinched over his downcast eyes. Regretful for saying glum words that a man in his condition did not need to hear, I changed the subject. "What about you? Something I've always wanted to know, how did you end up at Princeton."

"During the war—island-hopping—I caught one in the gut. Six months in four different hospitals. When I got out, they set me up with the job at the university."

"Quite a stroke of luck," I said.

This brought a smile to his face, and what started as a happy little laugh built into an intense attack of coughing. He turned deep red as he strained for breath. I feared the worst, but the fit subsided. He sipped water and brushed away the strands of snow-white hair that had fallen in front of his eyes.

The nurse appeared in the doorway, her stern face a reprimand for my getting the old boy too excited. She glanced at her watch. "Probably best to wrap things up."

He frowned at her as she departed, then sipped again from the straw in his cup. "I don't know how to put this," he said in a sheepish voice, "but uh, what I told your old man about the photo and all, it wasn't quite a hundred percent true. This picture you brought," he ran his finger lightly along the side of the frame, "it isn't the exact one—it's not from Albert."

"I'm not sure I . . ."

"It's a copy."

"Oh." I struggled to revise a lifetime's belief to conform with this news. "I see, well . . . a copy's nearly the same, isn't it? I mean, nobody would really expect you to part with the original." I forced a smile. "All in all, still quite remarkable. I mean, Einstein reached out to you and of all the people on Earth you reached out to my father."

Lou winced and shook his head. "Nah, it wasn't like that. I worked at the Institute, sure, but I didn't clean his office, never talked to him—he never told me to call him Albert. I only seen him one time, walking with some old professor-looking guy. They were on the other side of a parking lot."

My face was suddenly hot. What a gullible rube, gushing on about Einstein's blessing, the beacon that launched and inspired my career. The godlike man who I had always imagined watching over me was what, a fraud? A janitor's prank? And I was a fool. An old fool. And my father . . . telling the story over and over so proudly. The great boon to the Eggleston household, an utter fabrication.

"But why my father, of all people? You didn't even know him."

"That's right, I didn't," Lou agreed uneasily. "And the truth is, he wasn't the only one." Now I was even more confused.

"It's like at the track, you don't put all your money on one horse to win—you spread it around. If my only bet was your pop, one guy . . . not such good odds, right? But if I gave pictures to a bunch of people, the odds of a payoff go way up. With your old man, on your birthday, hell, the timing was just too good. He was ripe. Look, I didn't mean no harm."

I saw the embarrassment on his face. He must have seen the desolation on mine.

"Maybe I shouldn't have said. You came to visit—I figured I'd be square with you. After all this time . . . you know, the truth. Please, don't take it personal."

I laughed nervously and muttered, "I can't believe it," even as something inside me was tearing apart.

"Believe, believe," Lou said. "Look over there." He pointed to the night table where a tattered manila envelope peeked out from under a magazine. I reached for it, looked inside, and fanned through a stack of pristine copies of the Einstein photo, each inscribed and signed.

"I got fifty of them printed up. Practiced his signature until it looked right. Gave them out over the years, a couple dozen, now and then when the time seemed right. Last year on the B Ward the guy in the bed next to mine, Artie, I gave him one. Nobody ever came to see Artie, but he had the picture thumbtacked to the wall and any time he wanted, there was old Einstein, smiling away, Artie's best buddy."

To hell with Artie. I stood and snatched the framed picture and slid it into my coat pocket.

"Wait," he said, raising his bony hand. "Could you do me one favor?"

Even through my resentment, I recognized his words for what they were, a dying man's request. I found a gentle voice to ask, "What can I do?"

"Would you take the packet with you?" My eyes went to the envelope.

"One less thing for the nurses to take care of," he said. "You know, after."

He was thin, so very thin, and frail and helpless. Through the blanket, I patted his knobby knee. "Of course, Lou."

The day classes resumed following the holiday break, a heavy rain fell from leaden clouds onto the packed snow outside. The boys chittered and bounced in their seats having much to catch up on since last seeing one another.

I lectured on the mass trauma resulting from cataclysmic climate change—drought, floods, forced migration, disease, starvation. When I finished, there remained a little time before the end of the period.

A boy in the first row raised his hand. "You told us you were going to see that old guy, the one with the Einstein picture."

All their eyes were upon me. I had anticipated the question and was ready with a reply.

"I arrived too late," I said. "Mr. Delvecchio was on the hospice ward, hours from death, unable to communicate." They were silent, unmoving, shocked. Then, in a voice I hoped combined professorial reserve with avuncular solicitude, I said, "In conducting one's affairs with other people, the fact is that they will not always be there. Mindful of this hard truth, the philosophers implore us to be present to the possibilities of every moment." I scanned their disconcerted faces. "That's all. You may go."

Chairs scratched across the floor, muted conversations began, students jostled toward the door. "Mr. Carrara," I called out.

He stopped and turned. "Yes, sir?"

"I trust you enjoyed your holiday?"

Carrara approached my desk as the last few boys filed out. "It was . . . quiet, sir."

"Oh?"

"I stayed here," he said. "Long way to go home. And my job—I helped Mr. Hobson repair the boiler."

"Good old Hobson," I said, trying to picture how a boy as scrawny as Carrara could be of much help to the lumbering old goat of a handyman who somehow kept the venerable campus from falling down on itself.

"I'm sorry you didn't get to talk with Mr. Delvecchio, sir. I'm sure he would have liked that. And you too."

This thoughtful boy would be in my care for only a few more months, then off to the university, hurtling with the impetuous confidence of youth into a future I trembled to imagine. I shot the latches of my briefcase and reached inside. It had taken some doing, but I had found a near-exact copy of the brass picture frame. I handed it to Carrara.

"For you."

He held the photo in his hands like some holy relic, staring at it wide-eyed, receiving Einstein's blessing. He thanked me repeatedly until I reminded him of the time. He hurried out the door, thanking me again, beaming. Watching him go, I decided I would agree to teach at the Academy for a second year. There would be a new cohort of students, perhaps a few I would in some small way affect—though who can say for certain how anything will turn out.

The Real Manhattan

On assignment for *Greener World* magazine, I flew to Los Angeles last night to spend a week traveling with climate crusader Tillie McBivens on her twenty-six-city One Degree Fahrenheit Tour. She was a hero to millions— me among them—a sixty-year-old woman driven by her passion to make a difference. She led protest marches, made media appearances, wrote *New Yorker* articles and *Washington Post* op-eds. Last year she delivered one hundred and fifty speeches on six continents; now she was a sure contender for *Time* magazine's 2017 Person of the Year.

Ten of us journalists stood outside the Airporter Fiesta Hotel drinking our morning coffees, awaiting our ride to San Diego. I glanced at the other reporters' credentials hanging from lanyards around their necks and recognized several of their names from bylines. At twenty-six I was by far the youngest and least accomplished in the group. My ID picture was a disaster. I looked like Tina Fey on the worst hair day of her life.

We climbed aboard a large white van while the driver hefted our small mountain of luggage into the back. I took a seat and who should plop down next to me but Laura Chatham from CBS—she and her flowing blonde locks. She talked away on her cell phone while I savored the moment; three years out of J-school at a mediocre state university, and here I was shoulder to shoulder with network news.

Our van took its place at the rear of a small convoy of vehicles. A gleaming black limo led the procession carrying Tillie McBivens, her chief of staff Sigrid Neff, and media relations director Les Hannifin. Behind them was a silver Suburban loaded with luggage and members of the entourage I would get to know in the coming days: Tillie's tour manager/handler, her personal assistant/dresser; and a security guy/driver/gofer whose size made me think he might have once played pro football.

The southbound freeway traffic chugged across the endless splay of Los Angeles; eventually we made a rest stop at a Denny's. I set my sights on Les Hannifin—the man who could get me what I wanted—as he ambled around the parking lot talking into his cell phone. He was plump and energetic, as if so busy managing Tillie's media relations he didn't have time for the gym. When he finished the call, I approached with a little wave.

"Abbie Dial, what can I do for you?" He hadn't read the name on my lanyard. Of course a pro like Les Hannifin would know the names of all the tour's journalists; still, it felt good to be recognized.

With all the self-assurance I could muster, I said, "I'd like to schedule a one-on-one with Tillie."

"Sure, sure, great idea." He checked his wristwatch and held up a finger. "Just one sec." He used that same finger to count the passengers clustering near the van then called out, "Okay everybody, let's get back on board." We queued up, and when I filed past him, he mouthed the word later and gave a smile that I took as assurance he had not forgotten.

I climbed past Laura Chatham to get to my seat, a huge grin on my face.

"Win the lottery?" she asked.

"I just talked to Les—scored a sit-down with Tillie."

"Oh really?" Her voice was tinged with what might have been envy. "Is this your first . . ." she said, making a small circle with her beautifully manicured index finger.

"Embed?" I said, thrilled to be talking shop with a reporter I'd seen file stories from Afghanistan and North Korea. But in mid-thrill I was frozen by a horrifying thought: while I was saying embed, she was thinking rodeo.

"Les is great," she said with a kind look in her impossibly blue eyes. "But sometimes what he promises and what he delivers are two different things."

Her cell rang and pulled her into a conversation that lasted for the next twenty miles. I stared out the window, ego-dinged, my face hot with embarrassment. She hadn't been envying me, she'd been pitying the wide-eyed rookie.

That evening in the hotel ballroom Tillie headlined a fundraiser for the San Diego chapter of Californians for Climate Sanity. I arrived early and took a seat in the reporters' bull pen. The audience got louder and ever more excited as the room filled to overflowing. When Tillie stepped into the spotlight, the crowd went crazy. I'd watched dozens of videos of her speaking, but they didn't capture how thrilling it was to see her live. I jotted in my notebook, "Tiny, grandmotherly woman explodes room with energy of a rock band."

"A fight is before us," she said in her rousing finale. "We must overcome anything and everything that would stop us. And we will win. For Earth's sake, we will win." It was her tagline, and they ate it up, chanting back at her while she pounded out the three beats with her fist. "For Earth's sake. For Earth's sake."

The mantra melted into cheers and wild clapping, as if she had already saved the world. A hundred audience members mobbed the stage. Tillie gave them what they wanted: autographs, a touch of her hand, a listening ear, nods of understanding, a big smile for their photos.

The schmoozing went on for quite a while with Les Hannifin standing just behind Tillie and, next to him, Sigrid Neff—dark-haired and hawk-faced with her arms folded over her precisely pressed chief-of-staff blazer. Les said something to Sigrid, who passed it to Tillie, whispering in her ear.

Tillie immediately pulled away from her supporters and said to everyone within earshot, "I love you all. I'm off to a meeting with your mayor." She and her entourage bustled away.

I followed but got only as far as a security guard blocking a backstage doorway. A flash of my lanyard had no effect. I peeked around the guard and called to Les.

He turned, shrugged, and said, "Private reception." Like that explained everything. I stared at him with what I hoped was a not too subtle, what-the-hell raise of my eyebrows. He said, "Maybe tomorrow," and threw me a quick thumbs-up gesture. They left. I stayed. It sucked.

Someone tapped my shoulder—Laura Chatham. "We're going to the bar," she said, tilting her head toward a clump of our van mates. "Care to join us?"

"So that's how it goes?" I groused. "Tillie's off to another event and we're stuck here?"

"It's a marathon not a sprint," she said with a laugh as charming as everything else about her. "I was on the bus for three weeks with Hillary in '08—heard her stump speech so many times I could lip-sync it." She gave a playful shudder. "C'mon, a drink'll do you good."

❧

Late the next morning the van delivered us to Waterfront Park for the Climate Action Now rally. Conditions were perfect for the Earth Day celebration with a warm sun cooled by a gentle onshore breeze. The park's soccer-sized field was a colorful sea of faces, balloons, placards, and lofted beachballs arcing against the cloudless blue sky. I asked a cop to estimate the size of the gathering. "On the record, no idea," he said. "Off the record, I heard fifteen thousand."

Our group joined dozens of other journalists in the press pit just to the left of the speaking platform. For more than an hour lesser luminaries speechified, a folkie trio strummed guitars and harmonized, and introducers introduced introducers. When Tillie finally took the stage, the audience let loose for more than a minute.

She raised her hands to quiet the roar then leaned toward the microphone and started doing what Tillie does like no one else. She expertly sliced the Earth into climate zones—polar, tundra, boreal, temperate, subtropical, and tropical—and detailed how each is careening toward eco-holocaust beset by melting ice sheets, cataclysmic fires, hurricanes, spreading deserts, crop failures, and famine.

"With negative feedback loops accelerating the rate of devastation," she warned, "the planet grows hotter and hotter—until we hit a tipping point beyond which there is no return from mass death, an Earth made uninhabitable."

The way she delivered the speech—the pacing, the cadence—reminded me of something, but I couldn't quite identify what. Then, during one of the long intervals of applause that punctuated her talk, I remembered. When I was in kindergarten, my Aunt Alma would babysit me while Uncle Vince sat in his big chair watching an evangelist on TV. Vince was almost deaf, and he cranked up the volume so high the whole house rattled with the preacher's threats about Judgment Day and the fiery furnace of God's wrath. I was scared and hid under the dining room table with my fingers in my ears.

"The only hope for any of us," Tillie said, her words rising to a crescendo, "is the political will and focused effort of people the world over demanding what's right, demanding change. This is our calling, our fight, our future. Our future to win or lose."

The audience clapped, hooted, whistled, waved their placards, ululated. Some wept. Tillie stood at the podium, radiant, staring out at the mass of adoring disciples. A chant arose: "For Earth's sake. For Earth's sake." Tillie joined in, her amplified voice reverberating over the multitude. "For Earth's sake. For Earth's sake."

Prompted by the stage manager's nudge, a little girl marched across the platform and presented Tillie with an arrangement of flowers nearly as large as the kid herself. Tillie accepted the bouquet and raised it above her head, beaming like an Olympic champion. More kids came, a small parade, each carrying another bouquet, stacking them in a large pile next to the podium.

The applause faded; the crowd dispersed. We trooped out of the press pit and made our way through security to the backstage area. Among the reporters and jostling camera crews, Les Hannifin played air traffic controller, taking interview requests and doling out precious access to Tillie.

"You've got four minutes," he said to the crew from CNN.

They aimed their camera, positioned their microphone, and asked the same questions she'd been asked a hundred times before. Why couldn't they be a little more original, a little more creative? When I got my chance, would I do any better?

Our van pulled up and my colleagues climbed in. I hung back, watching Tillie. Her hulk of a driver held open the limo door, but before getting in she paused and asked no one in particular, "What happened to all those lovely flowers?"

"Still on the stage," Sigrid said. Tillie frowned.

"I'll get them," I called out. Then, not sure if I had overstepped some boundary, added, "If that's all right."

Tillie smiled at me—our first eye-to-eye contact. Sigrid made a pair of approving nods, one to me, another to the stage manager, then eased Tillie into the limo.

The manager and I gathered up armload after armload of the bouquets in their clear cellophane wrappers and toted them to a nearby curb. I ordered a rideshare, but they were in such high demand following the rally—go figure—that I had to wait nearly an hour. When the car arrived, I stuffed the back with heaps of blooms and wedged myself into the front seat hugging as many more as I could hold, my nose an inch from an overwhelmingly fragrant tiger lily.

At the hotel, I commandeered a luggage cart, piled it high with flowers, rolled it into the elevator, and rode to the twenty-fifth floor's penthouse suite. I knocked and Tillie's driver opened the door. He eyed me and my cargo skeptically while I tried to explain.

"She's okay, let her in," Les Hannifin's voice called out from somewhere within.

I pushed the cart across the threshold, spotted Les, and smiled gratefully. The sprawling suite hummed with activity—much more than I expected. Joining Tillie's team were a dozen activists, organizers, and politicians I recognized from the rally; they scurried about, talked into their phones, thumbed messages, scribbled notes, handed each other pieces of paper, clicked away at laptops.

I parked the cart behind the sofa and asked Les, "What's up? Something happen?"

"Tillie's speech is blowing up—TV, radio, white hot on social media."

I was a little perplexed. It had been an inspiring talk and all, but—

"Trump fired off two angry tweets—called her willy-nilly Tillie," he said with a jackpot-winner's grin. "Now everyone wants a piece of her."

His phone rang and he read the caller ID. "Meet the Press."

I scanned what I could see of the suite and couldn't find Tillie, so I crossed to the far side and entered a hallway. On the left was a bedroom, its door open—two staffers talking on phones. The second room had a closed door, and I raised my hand to knock but heard muffled talking within. I leaned closer, listened.

Sigrid: . . . just got a call from Nagel's people. He wants to see you in Aspen—tomorrow. He's sending his jet.

Tillie: Trump's tweets must have gotten their attention. Thank you, Mr. President. [laughs]

Sigrid: What do we tell the teachers? [pause]

Tillie: My niece was in a car wreck a few days ago in Denver. Nothing serious, but we could play it that way—family emergency.

Sigird: Perfect. I'll take care of it.

Nagel? I knew the name, but from where? The door suddenly opened. Sigrid gazed at me, surprised at first, then worried—confirming my suspicion that what I'd overheard was definitely not meant for public consumption.

"Where do you want the flowers?" I asked, feeling like a sneaky teenager pretending I hadn't heard a thing.

Sigrid made a sweeping motion with the single appendage that was her hand/phone. "Anywhere's fine." She squeezed past me in the doorway and walked down the hallway calling back over her shoulder, "Thank you—about the flowers—that's very—" Someone took her by the elbow and waived a phone's screen emphatically in her face.

I turned back and noticed that the room was not a bedroom at all, but an office set up with all the amenities—phone, computer, large monitor, printer, shredder. Behind the desk sat Tillie, regal in the leather swivel chair.

"I just love flowers," she said, smiling, inscrutable.

"They're out there, by the sofa. On a cart." I pointed vaguely. "Les said I could get you for a one-on-one. Could we—"

"Impossible right now with our dear president taking potshots," she said, her hand dismissively sweeping my interview away. "But I will tell you one thing." She looked me full in the face, eyebrows arched, as if in anticipation of bestowing some incredibly valuable gift. "It was men who went to the moon . . . but it's women who will save the Earth."

The oracular pronouncement was as enigmatic as her Sphinx-like countenance. Was there more to come? Apparently not. Without speaking a word, she communicated that my audience had come to its close. I felt the impulse to press her again for the one-on-one, but knew it was hopeless and backed out the door.

Two hours later Les Hannifin sent a group text message to all the journalists on the tour:

"Due to a family emergency, Tillie will be canceling her appearance tomorrow night with the American Education Association in Las Vegas. She will rejoin us Monday in San Jose."

Another announcement soon went out to all of Tillie's Twitter followers: a link to a dramatic narrative of her niece's accident, injuries, and prognosis, a few heartwarming anecdotes illustrating their close lifelong relationship, and an old snapshot of a much younger Tillie and a gleeful five-year-old girl clutching a puppy.

I checked the detailed tour itinerary: Tillie had been scheduled to participate via Zoom at the Better Future Foundation conference at the Aspen Enterprise Institute. A few quick Google searches revealed that an enormous amount of PR ink had been spilled advertising the attendance at that conference of one Eric Nagel, founder and CEO of CyberChip. Now, it seemed, Tillie would be there in person, transported on Nagel's private jet, cloaked with a cover story that had the stink of a blatant lie. It was all I needed.

At 6:30 the next morning the long hallway outside Les Hannifin's room was empty and quiet. I paced around, leaned impatiently against the wall until room service finally arrived with his breakfast tray. The server took it inside and I marched in right behind. When we were alone, Les stood there barefoot, his hands shoved into the pockets of one of the hotel's terry cloth robes, staring at me with a confused look on his bristly face.

"I need to see her. This morning. Before she leaves."

He rubbed at his eye and poured a cup of coffee. "Do you have any idea how busy she is? With Trump firing salvos—"

"She needs to talk with me." I wouldn't be brushed off this time. He peered over the brim of his coffee cup. "Needs to talk to you, huh?" I nodded.

"And I'm supposed to shoehorn you into her schedule between, let me see," he tapped his phone, squinted at the screen, "The *Wall Street Journal* and Anderson Cooper?" I repeated my resolute nod.

"You're putting on a good show there, Abbie, but I can't—"

"I overheard something, Les. Between Tillie and Sigrid. Something Tillie needs to explain." I suddenly understood the dynamics of this conversation. "Or there could be consequences."

An hour later I stood outside Tillie's suite. I had my list of questions and I'd double-checked that my phone was fully charged and ready to record.

My knock brought Sigrid to the door, her face tight and wary. She escorted me through the suite and out a set of French doors onto a huge penthouse balcony. The view was incredible: the early morning sun lit the sailboats in the harbor, the blue Pacific extended to the line where it met the equally blue sky. I expected Sigrid to stay for the meeting, but she went back inside, the door closed behind her with a click.

Tillie stood in the shadows, leaning stiffly against the railing, small, almost frail in an everyday blouse, a light sweater draped over her shoulders.

"I guess we need to do this, don't we?" She spoke so softly I could barely hear.

I held out my phone. "Do you mind if I record?"

"Not just yet," she said, a pained look in her eyes. "Later, I suppose, if necessary, but for now, I think what's most important is that we understand each other."

"Sure," I said, but I wasn't leaving without getting my questions answered—on the record.

She needed to know what I knew, so I reviewed the basic facts. She listened to every word, her brows pinched together.

"The change of plans is not the issue," I said. "But what you told us, what you tweeted to hundreds of thousands of your followers—using your niece's accident as an excuse." I so wanted to bust her, to say I caught you red-handed. You lied. You let us down—everybody, all of us who believe in you. Instead, I softened my voice and said, "You can see how this is a problem."

She scanned the horizon, as if searching for someone or something to get her out of the mess she'd made.

"It's chilly," she said, rubbing her hands over her thin upper arms. "Let's go sit in the sun."

We walked the length of the balcony to where some patio furniture was arranged around a low table. She took the rattan peacock chair, its high back flared out in the shape of a lightbulb. The sun fell directly on Tillie, warm and golden, giving the tan wickerwork that circled her head a radiant glow. I sat in a smaller chair, my back to the sun. A feeling of sympathy overcame me. I was going to get her answer, yes, but I didn't have to be a hard-ass about it. After all the good work she'd done, I could cut her a little slack.

"This bus trip you are on with us—it's quite out of the ordinary," she said, her voice stronger now. "We're doing it for show. Sigrid likes the optics."

She said it with an edge, almost like a taunt.

"I usually fly from city to city, continent to continent. First class. No other form of transportation releases as much greenhouse gas, the very thing I denounce so vehemently from the podium only hours after touchdown."

No doubt about it. Her brazen words were intended to rattle. They succeeded. "The way you see it, there are rules, a proper way I should comport myself. You're wrong. I'm in a different orbit now. Those rules simply don't apply. If that sounds outrageous, it's your problem—your ethics, prim and hidebound, pinching like a pair of too-tight shoes. Get over it."

Suddenly she was formidable, frightening.

"Eric Nagel has just thrown open a door we've been knocking on for two years. We need him—his name, power, money, entrée to his influential friends."

"What's in it for him?" I asked.

"Congress is working on a bill, an export ban of his company's hi-tech chips—billions would be lost. To stop it, he needs to swing nine votes. He's flooding them with PAC money, but they also need ideological cover. So he's rebranding himself—green, green, green."

"And no better place to play the eco-warrior than at the Aspen conference," I said.

"A first step. Then we form some kind of alliance. Maybe he writes us the big check, or maybe he wants to fund an institute or give seed money for a green Peace Corps. It could change everything."

I felt hot and looked away, buying myself a moment to think.

"The export ban," I said, "there must be a good reason—"

She slapped the arms of her chair. "Who cares if he sends his goddam chips to China. We're talking about millions of people's lives." She leaned forward, pinned me in her gaze, daring me to say another word. "The important question is not my behavior, but yours," she said, jabbing her finger toward me. "You do not want to put yourself on the wrong side of the greatest moral divide in human history."

❧

The hotel's swimming pool was just outside my room, and I tried not to let the kids squealing and splashing distract me while I worked at my laptop with ferocious energy. This was it, this story, my big break. I couldn't screw it up.

After checkout from the hotel, we had a twelve-hour van ride to the Bay Area. The next day, Monday, we crisscrossed San Jose and Oakland from one event to another, morning to night.

Tuesday the same thing, only in San Francisco. Late Wednesday morning, we got to Sacramento just in time for the president pro tem of the California State Senate to present Tillie with a Generational Icon award. A lunch with the governor followed. That night in the city's largest hotel ballroom, Tillie delivered the keynote address at the Tech and Transformation Conference.

Afterward, the ten of us milled around the hotel lobby waiting for the van. I looked at the colleagues I had gotten to know during the past week. Tomorrow morning, they would head north to the California redwoods, visiting a protest group's blockade of a logging operation. Tillie would use the opportunity to . . . well, suffice it to say, the McBivens juggernaut would roll on and on and on. But for me, Sacramento was the end of the line.

I made a visit to the lobby restroom and stood at the sink when the door pushed open and in walked Tillie and Sigrid. I hadn't been this close to Tillie since she went all alpha dog on me in San Diego.

A big smile on her face, she stopped to talk. "Les told me you'll be leaving us."

"Tomorrow." I tossed the paper towel into the receptacle. "How was your time in Aspen with Mr. Big?"

"Well," she said with a sly smile, "he asked me to join him for a planning session at his ranch in New Mexico."

"Sounds promising."

"I have high hopes," she said with a merry roll of her eyes.

Sigrid cut in, "It's been a pleasure getting to know you, Abbie. Good luck." She put her palm on Tillie's back, the way a chief of staff does when it's time for a conversation to end.

Tillie took my hand and held it. "Any time you want an interview," she said, giving me a friendly wink, "just give a call."

The van pulled up; we loaded up and rode back to our hotel. In the lobby, I approached Laura Chatham, her blonde locks somehow still in place at the end of a fourteen-hour day. It was probably the last time I would ever see her—so why not.

"Are you headed for the bar?" I said.

"I wasn't. But if you'd like to, sure, let's."

We rode the elevator up to the top floor, ordered glasses of wine, and found a table with a view of the city's twinkling lights. We chatted, sipped, talked about the day's news, decompressed.

"Where are you based?" she asked.

"Manhattan," I said causally, as if I might have added, I work mostly out of the Hong Kong office, but spend a lot of time in Geneva and Istanbul.

She nodded. "Nice."

Now, with perfect timing I delivered the punchline. "Manhattan, Kansas." She laughed as if I was joking, then saw I wasn't.

"Oh. Well, God bless the hinterlands," she said, laughing again, but this time at the situation, at herself. "You're looking at an Iowa girl—did four years at WTHI in Terre Haute."

She raised her wine in a mock toast.

"To good old Midwestern values," I said, and we clinked glasses.

"Salt of the earth."

"Great place to raise a family." We were cracking up. She was so easy to talk to, like we'd been friends for ages.

"I've seen *Greener World*," she said, "but not sure I've ever read a copy."

"Progressive, social justice, eco-positive," I said. "Love their politics, hate the crappy pay."

"You must have done something splashy to have snagged a seat on the bus."

I felt a blush rising in my cheeks. "What?" she asked.

"Our senior writer got the spot," I admitted. "Last minute, he came down with the flu."

"Well, lucky you," she said. 'Embedded journalist' looks good on the résumé."

"Maybe my ticket to the real Manhattan."

Our glasses were empty—it had been too long of a day to have another. She said she'd buy the drinks, and after she signed the credit card slip, she scribbled a quick note on a cocktail napkin.

We got in the elevator and punched the button for her floor. I hadn't gotten around to the question I'd been planning to ask, so now or never.

"Have you ever had a story that would hurt something you believed in? Greenpeace in bed with a gun runner maybe, or Doctors Without Borders smuggling drugs."

She looked above the door at the floor numbers blinking lower and lower and gave a little shrug. "Stuff happens."

"And when it does?"

"You go after the cancer. That's the job."

The elevator shook to a stop at her floor. I didn't want our time together to end so soon. The doors parted.

"Maybe we'll see each other on another tour," I said.

She wrapped her arms around me, patted my back, and whispered, "Time for the baby bird to fly." She gave me her thousand-watt smile, stroked my cheek, and slipped the napkin into my hand. Blurred by the tears in my eyes, she receded down the long hotel hallway. Such a pro.

Nothing would ever faze her. Plague, revolution, World War Three—Laura Chatham's hair would always be perfect.

Back in my room, I unfolded the napkin, read it, read it again. Just what I needed.

I fired up my laptop and opened the story I had finished late last night. I skimmed the pages: incisive, punchy, the best thing I had ever written. Way too good for *Greener World*. I would write them another piece—I owed them that much—but they wouldn't get this one. No, I could publish this story someplace better, maybe a lot better. I had been worrying that I didn't have the right contacts to make that happen, but now I knew someone who did.

Laura Chatham answered my call. No, she hadn't been asleep, and yes, she'd be happy to help. Almost immediately I got a message from her with the personal email address of a guy she used to work with, the editor in charge of national news at *Greener World*'s far larger competitor *Climate Strike*—based in New York City, New York.

I composed the email, dropping Laura's name and sending her warmest regards. I checked three times to make certain the note was clever, professional, error free, and that the story was properly attached. On my laptop's screen the cursor hovered above the send button. I paused and read again the message on the napkin: News is the water we paddle through to get where we're going.

I tapped the button and off went my words under the headline "Tillie McBivens—Pants on Fire."

Untellable Tales, Chapter XXXVII

Within the soundproof walls of The Company few arts are so useful as the ability to identify and cultivate raw talent. Never did I practice this vital bit of the craft as successfully as in the case to be discussed presently. In previous chapters I have changed the names of various players even though all of them will be dead by the time this memoir is published fifty years hence (for details of the security agreement, see the Introduction). Protecting sources and key assets is foundational to the success of the operations we run out of Langley. In this case, however, my intention is quite the opposite: to make known the contribution of a heretofore unsung hero, Aldous Pritzker. His name is likely unfamiliar to readers though, without doubt, he is the individual whose contribution most significantly improved global ecological and geopolitical dynamics in the first third of the twenty-first century.

Pritzker first came to my attention when I reviewed his application for an entry-level analyst position; many of the brightest prospects enter the Agency through the Analysis Directorate, and I have made it a habit to extend my tentacles to new hires who might offer some valuable future utility.

THE FRAGILE BLUE DOT

Of the materials he submitted what caught my eye was his undergraduate thesis, which, with remarkable depth and nuanced understanding, unveiled the role exogenous currency manipulation played in destabilizing multiple combatant governments during the war in Bosnia-Herzegovina (1992–95).

I arranged a lunch meeting to size up the Brown-educated wunderkind, all six-feet-seven of him, skinny as a rail, nervous as a deer in hunting season. He demonstrated an almost frighteningly incisive intellect and a keen interest in anything I was willing to share with him about the Company and my experiences in the Ops Directorate. A sponge. Full of promise, lacking only polish.

Over the next seven years Pritzker wrote a series of increasingly consequential briefing papers, distinguishing himself as a truly gifted researcher and analyst, a powerful and original thinker.

An interagency loan program then attached him to the State Department for a two-year hitch. State needed some new blood, and his Company superiors hoped it might burnish his somewhat unkempt professional mien to be exposed to the well-dressed, well-spoken, and wellgroomed careerists at State.

A year into this assignment we met in a quiet Foggy Bottom restaurant for dinner. He talked ebulliently about a plan he had been working on in his spare time, a political initiative. His modest proposal would do no less than halt and eventually reverse planetary ecological degradation and climate change. Nations would agree to pay one percent of their military budgets into a multifaceted UN-coordinated effort. The contribution would stairstep annually by one percent increments until stabilizing at ten percent. This $300 billion generated annually

would disincentivize arms and armed conflict while focusing significant funding on our most pressing ecological needs.

He laid out his vision excitedly and in detail. "Unfortunately," he said, the enthusiasm and idealism suddenly draining from his face, "when I presented the plan to my immediate boss at State, halfway through my deck she had her arms folded across her chest and began shaking her head.

"She said the plan failed to offer sufficient near-term advantage to garner support from the US or other G-26 countries. I tried to walk her through my Appendix B, which refutes her contention at every point, but I might as well have been talking to a brick."

I liked him. I liked his plan. And if there is one thing I find most repellant in the quaggy environs of the Beltway, it is seeing initiative and innovative thinking stymied by a hidebound mid-level bureaucrat. In a city full of pathological self-promoters, Pritzker was a far-fringe outlier, seemingly without personal ambition. Still, he needed to learn to stick with an idea worth championing—and if ever there was an idea worth championing, his viable model for funding the resolution of a planetary ecological crisis was it.

I gave a little push. "Go over her head. Straight to her boss."

"To Carter Jepperson? You're joking."

I regaled him with a few tales from my days in Moscow (see Chapters IV–XI, XV, XXI) to drive the point home. It wasn't the first time I sought to inspire a desk jockey to action with tales of field ops derring-do. Three weeks later he called to report on the meeting.

"Jepperson listened intently."

"No head wagging?"

"None. So, emboldened by hope, I asked him, 'Can I infer from what you've said, that you'll back my proposal?'

"'Good god no,' the great Jepperson snorted, 'I have other dragons to slay. Your problem, Pritzker, is that you fail to recognize certain immutable facts of the known universe, certain political realities.'

"I stood there in a daze, uncertain if he'd finished his thought. Finally, I choked out, 'Is that all?'

"He patted my shoulder. 'You are building an impressive body of work—aside from this . . . folly. Let it go. Eyes on the prize. And remember the best piece of advice I was ever given by a sitting Cabinet member: Don't make waves.'"

I knew from bitter experience the tone in which these soul-destroying words had been delivered—had myself been warned off several times from promising gambits by similar strings of platitudes that pass in DC for wisdom. I tested Pritzker's resolve. "Do you agree with Jepperson's analysis?"

He laughed. "I concur that I'm way out on a limb at State, and if I don't want to hear the branch crack, I need to rethink my strategy."

Something about the word strategy has always aroused in me a feeling akin to what a cheetah must feel upon spotting a Thomson's gazelle. "Your plan is too important to die in the bowels of State," I said. "Have you thought about going public?"

"Not exactly my métier," he said with a modest smile. He sipped his wine, napkinned his lip. "But if I were to . . . how would it be done?"

How would it be done? There often comes a point in a negotiation where non-Ops people ask Ops people this very question. The answer might be delivered with a coy smile, maybe even a wink, but the words are always pretty much what I told Pritzker that evening. "I have my ways."

I marshalled the needed expertise from the team that I assembled for Operation Fish Net (see Chapter XXVI). Soon thereafter an anonymous version of Pritzker's plan appeared widely on the internet, and within hours it was attracting attention among, as I like to put it, the "Right People." The media couldn't resist the intriguing mystery of the plan's anonymity, further hastening and broadening dissemination.

An unlikely coalition of estimable clout soon coalesced: labor, libertarians, and the Left; veterans and doves; urban and rural; Gen X, Y, and Z; scientists and social justice warriors and, of course, ecos of every stripe. The tech sector championed Pritzker's idea as a path to their envisioned peaceful *Star Trek* future. Perhaps the strongest testament to the plan's appeal was how it fractured the traditionally conservative senior bloc. While many of the gray cohort stuck with their dogged dedication to protecting themselves and their progeny with a strong national defense, two-thirds agreed that a degraded and contaminated planet was not the inheritance they wanted to bestow.

This populist amalgam took to the streets of cities not only in America but around the world in ever larger shows of support. One can easily imagine the flurry of calls among various agencies and staffers in DC, frantic not to be blindsided or left in the dust by the rapidly developing juggernaut. Pritzker found himself in constant demand, delivering scores of high level briefings on both sides of the Potomac—seemingly no analyst understood the anonymous plan quite like he did.

We met in a Georgetown pub where a fifty slipped into the bartender's hand got the television tuned to C-Span's coverage of the Rose Garden ceremony at which the President, with the enthusiasm of John Kennedy promising to put a man on the moon, unveiled his Green Earth Doctrine, based squarely on Pritzker's idea. The President appointed a czar to oversee the effort—Carter Jepperson, who spoke passionately about the need for the world-changing effort he had been entrusted to lead.

Jepperson was smart enough to avail himself of Pritzker's talent and appointed him as his number two. My unassuming young friend had Jepperson's back from that day forward, deftly guiding the plan and its czar all the way to a unanimous vote of support at the UN. Passage of this Green World Agenda was hailed widely as the tipping point in global commitment to ecological protection. When the Nobel committee contemplated how to commemorate the plan, it was said that Jeppeson's name appeared on the short list of candidates. In the end, the Peace Prize was awarded to the UN itself.

All by Herself

She makes the call. He picks up. Hello. Hey, Gerald. Well, Suze. To what do I owe—

Have you seen your daughter's social media today?

Kali's social—no, not really. Ellen follows that stuff more than I do. Sort of a division of labor. Is she up to something?

Why do you think I'm calling?

Just a sec. He covers the telephone with his hand. It's Suzanne. About Kali. Have you looked at her social media lately? Okay, I'm back. Ellen says she hasn't seen anything. So what's up? She posted something on social media and you're worried.

Who says I'm worried?

Your voice.

Well, yeah, I am. I was just down at City Hall—

City Hall? Oh-kay.

After school today Kali went down to City Hall Plaza and set herself up for a three-day hunger strike.

What? Why? Wait—for what?

Climate change, global warming—whatever the hell they're calling it now.

So she's at City—

City Hall Plaza. Hunger strike. Starting this afternoon.

Is she okay?

She's okay. But I'm wor—

She's not eating?

No she's not eating—it's a hunger strike. Jesus, Gerald, will you shut up and listen.

Okay.

For once. Okay. But why—

Global warming.

No, I mean—

Do you know this Greta Thunberg kid over in Sweden or wherever? She's only like thirteen, fourteen, but she's, I don't know, for some reason she's the spokesperson for climate change.

She's for it?

Nobody's for climate change. She's like the leader—hundreds of thousands of people, millions—it's crazy.

And she's a kid?

I just said she's a kid.

Okay. And?

And Kali's completely into her—videos, magazines. You haven't noticed the T-shirt she never takes off? Greta, Greta, Greta.

I—no, sorry. Maybe I saw the T-shirt. If I did, I probably thought Greta was a band. We're so busy with the twins, they're walking now. And Kali only here twice a month. But go back to what you said—she's on a hunger strike for global—against global warming—and she's down at City Hall.

She wants to be the American Greta.

Silence.

Gerald?

Uh.

You there?

135

Just thinking. She's always been kind of idealistic. I mean, is there really a problem? You said she's okay, right?

For now.

But?

I went down there a little while ago to see how she was doing. Out of nowhere she just casually mentioned extending her hunger strike to a week.

Oh crap.

When she first came up with the idea, I googled about what happens when you don't eat. The first three days it's not much, but then problems start—serious health stuff. So I laid down the law. Three days max. She agreed.

But then today?

She was talking about making sacrifices to save the world.

Oh Christ, Suze. Was she serious?

After three days the body starts like, eating itself. And in a fifteen-year-old, I don't think—

No, definitely. Jesus. Well . . . a week? What about school?

Exactly. It's not normal—healthy. All she ever talks about is millions of people dying, the whole planet dying. It's like she's—

You were the one who thought it was so great when she dyed her hair blue. All about expressing her—

What if she digs in? She could hurt herself—starve to death.

I doubt very much—

You know how stubborn she gets.

So this was her own idea? You didn't—

Priorities Gerald. Your daughter. She's down there right now not eating.

Okay, okay. When you saw her, how did she seem?

Like she could do something stupid.

Is her boyfriend in on this? What's-his-name, Ben, Carl?

Caleb. They broke up.

When?

A couple weeks ago.

Why did they—

Like she really tells me. And there's another thing—the TV news is going to interview her tomorrow.

Huh.

Yeah, huh.

Well, maybe that'll give her a sense of, you know, mission accomplished. Make her feel like she got her point across.

Or maybe she starts thinking, Ooh, ooh, I'm on TV, I'm a big star. It could give her ideas.

Ideas like what?

She snorts.

Have you talked to her teacher?

She has like six teachers.

Oh, right. Well—

One of them showed a video of this Greta kid addressing the United Nations—I think that's what set her off. But she's not on school grounds, it's the long weekend, so it's not really their jurisdiction or whatever.

Do you want me to go talk to her?

She laughs. No, I do not want you to go talk to her.

What then? Maybe just ride it out? See what happens tomorrow after the TV people?

She's posting to social media like every five minutes. Little selfie videos of her sitting there all bundled up, holding the sign she made—Hunger Strike to Stop Climate Change. She's all, The future is totally screwed up. Adults are greedy and stupid and wrecked the planet. I mean it, what she's doing could go so bad in fifty different ways.

You don't think I should go talk to her?

She sighs.

Well, then maybe you should just tell her straight out, Your father and I love you, we support you, but you've gotta stick to three days—no ifs, ands, or buts. How about that?

I keep wondering if she just wants attention. It's always been like we dodged the bullet with her and the divorce. Maybe now it's coming home to roost.

What about her girlfriends? Could you talk to some of them? The tall one, Laura, the volleyball player.

Her family moved back east—Ohio, somewhere like that.

Other friends?

They wouldn't tell me anything I don't already know.

You said three days—does that mean she's going to stay down there at night, alone?

I told her she should get some other kids, make it like a sleepover. She got all huffy.

Greta started all by herself. She didn't need anybody.

So you're telling me she's going to be alone, downtown, all night?

The police station is right there on the plaza. There's a cop sitting at the front desk around the clock. He can literally see her. I talked to him—floodlights stay on all night, there's four security cameras. He said it's probably the safest place in town.

Hmm. Well . . .

What if this is one of those Ys in the road. She starts down one path—

That's something, I guess.

What? What is?

That the plaza's safe.

Silence.

If she starts down the wrong path and gets sucked into—

Suze, I tell you what, I'll drive down there and have a look—after we get the twins down.

Other than that, is there anything else you think I should—

She is not going to make herself sick with this thing. That is not gonna happen.

I'll look at her social media stuff. Maybe I haven't been paying enough attention. I could take her to—spend more time with her. I don't know. I think the thing to hold onto is that this is a very limited thing. Maybe a problem, but ... limited.

And if it's not?

You can only control what you can control, right?

I just decided. I'm gonna get my sleeping bag, make up a thermos of cocoa. I won't say anything, just ... show up.

Huh. That's not a bad idea.

If I wait until ten, ten-thirty, she'll be getting bored, cold. Maybe she won't be so pissy about wanting to be alone.

The forecast is for the low thirties. Not a hard freeze, but—

She doesn't really want to be down there all night by herself.

We don't want to overthink this. It's probably just a phase. She'll grow out of it—like her Barbies. She'll be fine.

Yeah, well, hope so.

Stuff always seems earth-shaking at the time. I can't even remember the things that had me going out of my mind a week ago, let alone a month. You know what I mean?

I don't know—maybe.

Call me later. From down there. When you're with her.

Yeah.

And give her the phone so I can talk to her. Hey kiddo, howya doin'? Make her feel like both of us are on top of this.

Yeah, okay.

Does that sound like a plan?

Silence.

Is there something else?

Silence.

Suze?

They were American Girl.

What?

The dolls.

What dolls?

Not Barbies, American Girl.

Oh, right.

I still have them. In a cardboard box. Up in the attic.

Look, going down there and being with Kal is a really great idea. You do that. See what's up and we'll go from there. Okay?

I go up there sometimes. All our old stuff, packed away in boxes—cobwebs. Your mother's dishes. The pictures from the wedding.

Give me a call later, Suze, okay?

Silence.

Really, I should go—the twins are melting down. Are we good?

She sighs. I guess.

We'll make it, okay? Everything'll be fine.

Mmm.

Alright, bye-bye. Talk in a while.

Yeah, okay. In a while.

Click.

Tool

I was there when it started. And by there I don't just mean
that I was at the Egret Lake Conference Center on the
fateful weekend; two hundred artists, arts teachers, and arts
administrators can all make that same claim. No, by the luck of
the draw, I was assigned to share a room with Larson Teague and
was not ten feet from him when he worked out his idea that, I
think it's safe to say, changed the world.

The timely theme of the Arts Leadership XVII conference
was "The Arts Respond to the Climate Crisis." We heard
presentations and panel discussions and took part in workshops,
Q&As, and brainstorming sessions. On Saturday afternoon we
had several hours of free time before the weekend's biggest event,
the banquet and talent show. I stood next to Larson when he
added his name to the sign-up sheet.

"What's your act?" I asked.

"Not exactly sure," he said with a laugh. "Something kind of .
. . different."

Back in our room I lay on my bed with my laptop and caught
up on some email. Larson was hunched over the little desk and
wrote in a notebook, his forehead furrowed in a look of deepest
concentration.

"What are you working on?"

"Getting my ideas straight," he said. "For tonight."

I fell asleep and when I awoke an hour later, he was still scribbling away. I don't think either of us had the slightest idea what was being born.

The banquet room, full to capacity, clanked with silverware and buzzed with the conversations and laughter of diners. The wine flowed at the round table Larson and I shared with six others. When the waiters took away our dessert dishes, it was time for the talent show.

The MC, a pro with an easygoing persona and a cordless mic, climbed the three stairsteps to the stage that shined under the bright lights. He cracked a few jokes and then did a nice job of introducing the night's acts—talented singers and musicians, a guy who made balloon animals, a juggler, an actor who performed a monologue, a couple of stand-up comics.

I leaned close to Larson and said something about it getting late and that surely it would be his turn soon. He whispered back that he'd chatted with the MC before dinner and suggested his performance might be a suitable way to end the show.

After the applause died down for a tipsy woman who made soap bubbles as big as beachballs, the MC said, "And now for our final performer. Please give a big hand to Larson Teague."

Larson took the cordless mic from the MC and faced the darkened ballroom from the middle of the stage.

"Late last night I walked down to the bench that looks out over the lake." He held the mic close to his mouth, his amplified words breathy, as if he were whispering intimately into every ear. "And sitting there I thought about what we've been focused on all weekend, what we've done to the planet."

We had no idea where he was going with this and hung on his every word.

"I remembered when I was a kid," he said. "I came to a place like this for summer camp. Riding a horse, paddling a canoe—never happier. But what if it all falls apart, withers away? Everything we love, all the great stuff we created, generation after generation. Gone. The party's over. I cried so hard I couldn't see through the tears. Sorrow and grief and guilt and shame.

"What I was feeling—" his voice trembled, and he paused to gather himself. "It's a sickness, a soul sickness. Psychologists probably have a name for it—despondency, desolation, hopelessness. Or maybe it's the jumble of emotions any sane person would feel looking at the mess we've made. Am I the only one, or have you felt this way too?"

His eyes moved from table to table, where heads nodded and soft voices murmured in assent. "So I invite you to try something with me. To give voice to those feelings. All together. To sing."

He walked to the bench at the piano and sat down. After slowly pulling in a deep breath, he started to sing a single note, a simple aaaaah sound. At first there was only his solitary drone, booming over the PA system, but others joined in, then more and more, and soon it was all of us like a great wind swirling around the ballroom, coming from everywhere and nowhere. Larson took the microphone away from his mouth; the amplified sound faded, his own voice melted into the vast, pure, amorphous tone. Unguided by the hand of a choirmaster, our wordless song took flight, swelling upward and falling to the darkest and most sorrowful depths, the harmony of deeply damaged souls, a spontaneous lamentation.

The woman to my left started making a sort of huffing sound and raised her napkin to dab at her eyes. She wasn't alone. How long the singing continued I can't say for sure, ten minutes at least, maybe twenty. Nor can I put into words what I was feeling or what unified spirit seemed to have taken over that room. Something was happening, a purging, a catharsis.

Like the slow decay of a thunderous chord played on a grand piano, our song subsided. Eventually we sat in the cavernous ballroom surrounded by silence. For minutes more no one moved. Then people rose reverently and drifted off.

Back in our room, Larson and I agreed that neither of us had ever experienced anything like that before. I asked him where the idea had come from.

"Last month I was in Japan. Hiroshima," he said. "I toured the atomic bomb museum. Afterward, outside in the Peace Park, I stared blankly at the memorial sculptures—overwhelmed, numb, unable to grasp the incomprehensible suffering, the absolute horror of the bombing. Just then a street performer came up, a butoh dancer in tattered rags, her body covered in mud and ashes. She started to perform, her slow jerky movements were, I don't know, terror-stricken, tormented—the way she held out one gnarled, trembling hand. Her eyes squinted closed, her mouth gaping in a silent shriek—she held all the world's pain. I thought nothing could express what was eating at my soul after seeing the horrors I saw in the museum, but she did."

Soon after the conference ended, Earth chants (as they were soon dubbed) started springing up and, with startling rapidity, became a global phenomenon. Millions of people. Hundreds of millions of hours of mourning song. A secular sacrament.

Chanters appreciated and protected the purity, the no-frills, no-leaders structure of their gatherings—no hucksters, no sponsorships, no tie-in deals allowed. In interviews, Larson often talked about adopting what he called the Craigslist ethos: do a simple and useful thing. Do it well. Don't screw it up.

Journalists seemed almost constitutionally unable to keep themselves from making comparisons between Earth chanting and the spread of COVID-19. "While a vaccine stopped COVID," one of them gushed, "nothing seems likely to stem the spread of Larson Teague's highly contagious response to the dispirited melancholy we suffer from the creeping cataclysm of climate change." Others called it an anti-pandemic, a pandemic of healing.

My favorite place to join in this rite is back on the shores of Egret Lake, where the conference center's owners have shown the generosity to keep a small lakeside field open to the public. There at the water's edge is the bench where the idea for Earth chanting first entered human consciousness.

The last time I met with Larson we sat on that bench. I asked him what he thought, looking back, about his gift to the world.

"What we want, what we absolutely must have, is reconciliation," he said, his eyes squinting as he looked out over the water. "With the planet, with other people, with ourselves."

He shrugged and laughed and looked at me. "We just needed a tool."

Boiling Alive

Why? Because a hundred million people are going to die. A billion people. Ten billion. How's that for a reason?
—Fight for Earth

I'm sitting in a window booth at an all-night coffee shop with a perfect view of a huge warehouse just half a block up the street. The Target Corporation uses the warehouse to stock the shelves of its Oregon, Washington, and Idaho stores with plastic shit from China. In two minutes it's going to burst into flames. That should be pretty cool.

The waitress is carrying a coffee pot around to her customers. One of them is hunched over at the counter, scruffy looking, wearing an old army jacket. The other two are eating 3:00 a.m. eggs and pancakes. Could be lunch on their graveyard shift.

She asks—Refill, hon? I put down the pen on the pad of paper where I'm doodling and pretending to be an eighteen-year-old Shakespeare or whatever and give her a drowsy night owl smile—Yeah sure.

She fills my cup. Gray-blue eyes, light, like Jillian's but without the gold flecks that made J's eyes look like opals. I dump a bunch of sugar and cream into my coffee and think about Jillian for a while, then try not to.

One minute.

I pick up the pen and stare out the window like I've been staring for half an hour, looking for inspiration I guess.

Thirty seconds.

I check my phone, making sure for the third time it's set up to shoot video. I don't want to miss anything good. They told me they wanted it all.

Over the middle of the block-long building comes a wisp of smoke that looks like a ghost in the light of the giant red and white Target sign on the warehouse roof. Nobody else in the diner has noticed. I keep my hand away from the phone.

Then BANG, an explosion and a bright flash.

Everybody in the coffee shop turns to see. There's noise and hubbub and the cook sticks his head out from the back and says—What happened?

The waitress has her hand on the glass door. She yells—Somebody call 911.

I grab my phone and start shooting. The little screen is filled with a rolling billow of smoke, then the first fingertips of flame wiggle up over the rooftop. I zoom in. The fire is spreading fast. In just a couple of minutes the whole side of the building is going up, flames roaring higher and higher in a tall orange triangle. I stare, hypnotized.

Sirens start up and get louder and soon two fire engines come screaming up the street, their jittery lights flickering everywhere, blue and red and white. A bunch of other emergency vehicles show up, so many colored lights strobing on and off it's like some nightmare disco. The firefighters hustle around with oxygen tanks on their backs, the reflective bands on their jackets and pants give off a weird silvery glow. A big extension ladder is silhouetted against the flames, a heavy stream spraying from its top. More trucks show up and more and more. Arcs of water are pouring in from all sides.

They don't have a chance.

Your moral duty is to quit servicing and enabling the Death Machine— resist, destroy, sabotage the apparatus. Until YOU act, the boxcars will keep rolling to Auschwitz.
—Fight for Earth

It's after six and I'm pedaling fast, the chilly early-fall wind in my face, my fingers cold on the handlebars. Everything is tuned up, brighter and sharper and more colorful than usual. A bakery has its morning loaves in the oven and the smell is so intense it's like I'm chewing the bread. I lock my bike to a parking meter a block from where I'm to meet up with the NDF guys.

I find an alley and dig out a cigarette and my lighter. The little flame reminds me of Mom telling me I should quit. A hundred times she told me, and I never will.

She says—I gotta go, sweetie. When I get settled you can come visit.

I need to circle the block, on the opposite side of the street from where the NDF hangs out. They told me to act like I'm out for a leisurely stroll, looking in shop windows, killing time. The cops or the feds might be watching for anything or anybody that seems even a little out of place.

They kept telling me and telling me—This isn't playing around. And even though they said that, it still felt like we were all in a movie or something. Until this morning, watching that warehouse burn.

I toss the cigarette and pull my knit cap down low on my forehead, cover it with the hood of my sweatshirt and start walking down the gray street. It looks like any other shitty block of downtown Portland this early in the morning—papers blowing down the sidewalk, parked cars and delivery vans, a trash truck rumbling its way from dumpster to dumpster.

I was part of it, The Great NDF Target Action of 2019. Maybe I wasn't exactly in the thick of it, but I played my part, shot video like a motherfucker.

I turn the corner and up ahead there's a beat-up white van. Right across the street from where it shouldn't be, the old brick building with the ROOMS sign. I get closer and kneel down, pretending to tie my kick. The back windows are papered over, just like a cop van might be. It rocks just a little. I stand up and get closer, walk along its side. As I'm passing the driver's window something big and angry lunges at me—BARK BARK BARK—a crazy-eyed pit bull, teeth snapping, slobber on the window. I jump back like three feet and hear a voice inside yelling—Bucky, Bucky. Shut the fuck up.

Through the windshield I can see the dog jumping around and a bushy-haired guy sitting up in a sleeping bag. I take some breaths, try to get my heart to slow down, light another cigarette and take one pull after another.

It coulda been a cop van. They coulda stopped me, coulda found the video. I flick the butt and duck in the door under the rooms sign and climb up the four flights of creaky stairs.

When they asked me to shoot the fire, Denver said some guys are cut out for this kind of resistance, some guys aren't. Like he wasn't sure about me. But now he'll know who he's dealing with.

And he's gonna say—We got another plan, another NDF action all set up.

And we'll do it, all of us together. I'll be the one with the bolt cutters snipping the lock on the chain-link fence. I'll lead the way in, a five-gallon can of gas in each hand. I'll be the one lighting the match.

From the fourth-floor landing, I look back down the stairs to make sure nobody's following me, then give the door two shorts and a long—BOP-BOP BOP.

The door cracks and there's Denver, big and bulging with muscles like some superhero. He peeks his shaved head out into the hall and looks around then waves me in and locks the door.

The place is a shithole, just like the other times I was here. Crap all over, mattresses on the floor and empties and wadded up cigarette packs and books and magazines and stacks of Fight for Earth. Except for a halfway decent big-screen TV, the furniture looks like junk you couldn't give away to Goodwill. Five guys are sitting around, mostly in their late twenties and looking about as wrung out as you'd expect after the night they've had. Five guys with vision and commitment and guts. I know four of them.

Chattanooga is sitting on a mattress barefoot and leaning against the wall smoking. He raises his cigarette at me and in his heavy southern accent says—If it ain't our combat photographer. Denver—Did you get it?

I wave my phone around and hear cheers from SeaTac and Homer slumped on the pukey-looking couch. Homer comes off like a pudgy, red-cheeked gnome, but Denver called him a crazy-ass bomb maker. Pretty cool. The guy I don't know is sitting farthest away on a metal folding chair, his arms crossed on his chest. He's got a bushy beard and is sizing me up from behind little wire-rimmed glasses.

Denver—That's Boise. Boise, Phoenix.

I bob my chin and Boise cracks a little bullshit smile like he isn't so sure he's happy to see me. Whatever.

I move a couple of old pizza boxes off a milk crate and sit down.

SeaTac, staring at the laptop on his knees—The fire's trending big.

He reads a news report from his screen, diddles with his keyboard, starts reading social media posts. Next to me SeaTac's the youngest and kind of a geekpimple, but a hacker and a really good computer guy.

I try to look like I'm listening to him, but I was there, genius. I'm the one who saw it.

Another track in my brain is thinking my name is as good as SeaTac's. Or any of the rest of them. Maybe better. Denver asked where I'm from and I sure as shit wasn't about to tell him Tinkle Valley in the middle of bumfuck nowhere, so I said—Arizona. And he said—Phoenix?

He told me the dorky fake names are for security, which these guys are super paranoid about. Maybe that's why Boise's being such a dickweed iceberg.

SeaTac finally finishes up with the Mr. Newsman routine and pushes his long hair behind his ear.

Homer, who's been listening, says—Burned that sumbitch … to … the … ground.

He's slurring his words pretty good and has a half-empty tequila bottle pinned between his muddy boots.

Boise, pushing his glasses higher up on his nose—You gonna show us what you got? I hit the play button on my phone and hand it to Chattanooga.

SeaTac is craning his neck—Is it going? Is it burning?

Chattanooga—Just smoke.

—In a second there's a bigass explosion that got it going.

Homer, a proud grin on his face—Ooh, I bet there was.

SeaTac—I wanna see.

Denver is leaning against the wall with his tattooed arms folded over his black T-shirt. He says—Can we put it on the screen?

SeaTac takes the phone and diddles with it. When should I post the video?

Denver's hand shoots out, palm facing me—No!

Chattanooga shakes his head like posting is the worst idea ever.

Well what the fuck did I get it for?

Chattanooga—The cops would be all over it with a fine-tooth fuckin' … y'know?

Denver sees the look on my face and tells me—What you took'll help us, a lot, with planning, other actions … the next one.

Chattanooga—They'll know who did it when we post our manifesto.

You didn't post it yet?

A lot of squirmy looks go around the room.

SeaTac gets the video on the TV—Check this out.

The fire is starting to get going real good and it looks even more ferocious on the big screen than it did on the phone. Boise moves his chair around so he can see. All we need is popcorn.

Homer—Whoa, look at that.

He takes a slug of tequila and passes it to Chattanooga, who drinks and passes it to me.

The shit burns and I take a second swig. The bottle goes around and around, and we drain it while watching the fire grow.

But what Chattanooga said keeps eating at me.

I can't hold back—What do you mean when you post the manifesto? What's wrong with now? Wasn't that the plan? You said you were gonna—

Denver—Shit changes.

You told me this like three days ago. What shit has changed in three days?

Denver, looks away—We didn't quite finish it yet.

What?

Chattanooga—We thought we'd get it done before last night, but we had a few other things on our mind, okay? Don't worry, we'll take care of it. The longer we wait the more—

Wait? What are you talking about, wait? We're not writing the fucking Declaration of Independence. Can't we just copy something out of Fight for Earth, sign it NDF and call it good?

Homer—How 'bout if we just watch this, huh? Look at them flames.

He's rolling a joint, lights it, stares at it while letting smoke curl out of his nostrils, hits again and passes it to me. I get a lungful, hold it. What is up with these guys?

Denver—We need our own manifesto. Articulate our own identity. We agreed on that.

Exhaling—I didn't.

Chattanooga—You weren't around when we decided.

What's the hold up? We all know what we gotta say. They're killing the planet. We're doing something because if we don't, they'll keep doing exactly what they've been doing for a hundred years, driving the car over the fucking cliff.

Chattanooga, like he hasn't heard anything I said—What if we leave it a big mystery? Give the media stooges something to speculate about. Save the manifesto for next time.

On the screen the fire's become a hell-roaring monster. We can't take our eyes off it.

SeaTac—But if we don't say something nobody's gonna know it was us who did it.

Everybody starts arguing. Yack, yack, yack. Jesus Christ.

Look, it's the actions that matter. Let's do another warehouse. That'll get their attention. How about tomorrow?

Denver sneers at me—It took us three weeks to plan this one.

Fuck you, Denver. Snotty and sarcastic as I can be—Well maybe we oughta speed things up a little, huh?

They look at me like, who is this guy?

Boise—You got a problem, Phoenix?

Denver—Hey, let's all take it down a notch. It's been a long night. We can talk about it later.

Like he's the big boss and that's the end of it. Bullshit.

How much time do you think we have? Millions of people are dying. Sitting around with our thumbs up our asses isn't gonna get it done.

That sounded good. And it felt good too, having something to say. Them looking at me, listening, like they're expecting something more. Out of nowhere I have a thought and blurt it.

I can get a gun.

Nobody moves a muscle.

Boise—A gun ... like for doing what?

I have no idea. But getting it would at least be doing something, you lazy-ass bitches.

No comment. Security first, right? You'll hear all about it after it's over.

Denver—Hey, settle down. We gotta stick together.

Chattanooga—You can't—

The hell I can't. I stand up and get my phone and I'm at the door and just because it feels right, I give it a hard slam.

Clomping down the staircase two steps at a time it hits me, this shit just got real.

&

Breaking things is far easier than building them or protecting them once they're built. Attack the infrastructure, the institutions, the pipelines, the trucks. Watch the flowers of destruction bloom.
—Fight for Earth

Outside, the sun is bright, the air has warmed up. I know exactly what I need to do.

Pedaling through downtown I go past the turn I used to take to Joey's apartment, my only real friend since I left Arizona. I'm remembering the time the two of us drove to San Francisco to hear Tillie "One Degree Fahrenheit" McBivens give a speech. All the way down we talked about how she was like Martin Luther King, but for the whole planet. The huge auditorium was packed, and she was on the stage going all fire-and-brimstone about how bad things are and how much worse they're getting. All those people cheering at everything she said, it was like a school pep rally only I actually gave a shit about what she was saying.

Then she tells us her best shot for how we're going to stop planetary incineration—sign the petitions out in the lobby, write our representatives, read her book and her blog, join her organization, and send her a bunch of money so she can keep up the fight.

Joey and I looked at each other like WTF?

As she wrapped up her talk, McBivens bragged about how she'd given more than three thousand speeches on six continents, at a UN conference in Japan, to villagers on a beach in Sri Lanka, before a gathering of CEOs in Switzerland. And she swore that nothing could stop her from giving thousands more.

I tilted my head toward Joey and whispered—That's a lot of fuckin' jet fuel.

Afterwards, just outside the auditorium, a woman in long blonde dreads was yelling—McBivens is a sellout! Resist or die!

She handed me a little newspaper, my first ever copy of Fight for Earth.

The drive back to Oregon sucked. We were tired and totally let down by McBivens and her hypocritical bullshit. At around three in the morning we passed Mount Shasta, huge, covered in snow and glowing bluish-white in the light of the full moon. Joey sparked a joint to enhance the view and we handed it back and forth. That's when the trouble started. We talked about what we could do to make a better world. Joey said that for him it was writing songs about animals going extinct.

I started laughing at his dumbshit idea and said—Yeah, right, let's all strum along, like that's really gonna make a difference.

This got him pissed, pissed like I'd never seen him. When we stopped for gas I stayed in the car while Joey scrubbed bugs off the windshield, glaring at me through the glass, giving me the stink eye. We didn't say one word for the rest of the long drive home.

Once I hooked up with the NDF, Denver told me that guys like Joey are called reactionary gradualists. And that was the end of Joey.

The road I'm pedaling on takes me out of town, gets me into trees and farm fields. I head up a little rise into a ritzy residential area and there's Uncle Carl's McMansion, in all its mock Tudor glory, with his big shiny Winnebago, my former home, parked in the driveway. His BMW is gone. Maybe he's on one of his business trips to Hong Kong or maybe just doing a local errand.

I park my bike in the side yard, get the spare key and let myself in the back door. The keypad for the home security system starts blinking. It's been a couple of months since I moved out and I freeze up, then the alarm code pops into my head and I punch it in. Nobody's home, but I'm still creeping like a burglar, walking on tiptoe and listening at every corner. Down the hallway and up the stairs to Uncle Carl's office. As soon as I'm inside I feel eyes staring at me and look up at the mounted head of the rhino he shot in Africa. Right below the rhino is the big metal safe with the guns.

From the top drawer in his desk I get the key, unlock the safe, and swing open its heavy doors. I look through the rifles until I find the one Carl taught me to shoot, the Remington. It's heavy and solid and I put it to my shoulder, whip around, take up a firing position. On the far wall above the leather sofa is the head of an antelope with long corkscrew horns. I aim. Yeah, got you, sucker. Pow.

I take a box of cartridges from the safe then close the doors and turn the key. Carl probably won't realize anything's missing for months. I set the rifle and ammunition on the desk and am putting the key back in the drawer when I notice an envelope propped against the telephone. It's torn open. Sticking out is a fancy invitation.

Golf tournament

Fair Oaks Country Club fundraiser for Friends of Kelso County LNG opening remarks by Opportunity Oil CEO Gerald X. O'Toole

There's a small photo of O'Toole, the piece of crap who wants to build a pipeline and shipping terminal so he can make money exporting tankers full of death. He looks sort of like Clint Eastwood, a squinty-eyed relic from another time.

The invitation says O'Toole will speak at noon today. The clock on the desk reads 10:51. Fair Oaks is just a couple of miles away.

As I shove the invitation in my pocket there's a mob yelling in my head, and everybody has ten different ideas for what to do and how to do it. One of the voices outshouts the rest—I can't ride my bike down the street holding a damn deer rifle.

I wrap up the gun with an Indian blanket from the sofa and go to the kitchen where there's a hook holding the keys for the Winnebago. It takes a while to work the key into the RV's door lock with my shaking hand, but I get inside and sit behind the wheel and lay the gun on the floor beside me.

That's when the smell hits me, the unmistakable stuffy Winnebago smell of plywood and new carpet. The dashboard has knobs and dials and switches like a jet plane's cockpit. I've watched Uncle Carl drive it plenty, how hard could it be? I get the big bus rolling, and it bucks and weaves a little until the controls start to make sense.

If Carl's in Asia, great, but what if he's not? He comes home, sees the Winnie gone, and maybe notices about the gun. He calls the cops and I'm driving around in a 38-foot-long billboard that screams—I'M THE GUY YOU'RE LOOKING FOR.

*Stopping any one of us is stopping one molecule in a tsunami, for we
are vast and rising and soon we will tumble forth with the power of
a redemptive flood. We will come at you, wave after wave, a storm
surge, a hard rain, the deluge.*
—Fight for Earth

I drive carefully, keeping an eye out for cops, and just before the
bridge that leads to the country club over on the north side of
the river, I turn west on South Bank Lane. It meanders through
the dense forest that starts at the river's edge. While living with
Uncle Carl I spent a lot of time alone out here, smoking weed,
roaming around and imagining I was in Jurassic Park hiding
from a T-Rex.

I spot the trailhead that leads down to the river across from
Fair Oaks and park the RV. From the closet I grab the jacket
of Carl's camo hunting suit, put it on, and shove the cartridge
box in the pocket. Rifle in hand, I descend the zigzag path to
the riverbank. I keep back in the trees and see the country club
buildings a hundred yards upstream. Working my way through
the dense brush parallel to the bank, I get closer.

Across the river, everything is happening on a big grassy
lawn between the main clubhouse and the water. To the right an
outdoor stage, an elevated platform with a podium and flags and
big arrangements of flowers and stands holding a couple of good-
sized PA speakers. Facing the stage are rows and rows of chairs
and behind the chairs, way over to the side, are big white tents
where some of the early arrivers are loading up on drinks.

I find a little clearing that's sheltered from the river by a
couple of boulders. A log is laying on the ground and I drag it a
couple of feet to make a place to sit.

From here to the podium is about seventy-five yards give or take. Unobstructed. With a scoped hunting rifle. Piece of cake.

It's turned into a warm sunny day and I'm hot in the camo jacket, but I don't want to be seen. The jacket has the Winnebago smell. I remember how that smell got stronger and stronger as the summer temperatures got hotter and hotter. And how after the fire, after there was no more apartment or town or Tinkle Valley High School or much of anything else, Uncle Carl gave us a place to stay. Mom in the guest room, me in the Winnie. The hours I spent lying on that bed talking on the phone with Jillian in fucking Florida, trying to cheer each other up about our stolen senior year, talking dreamy shit about how we could be together again. A couple of weeks later she tells me about the fuck she met playing tennis. After that I didn't have much reason for getting out of bed. That was my life, laid out in the heat and that plywood and new carpet stink, reading everything I could find about the Tinkle Valley Fire, the 726 homes burned, the three people and six smoke jumpers who died, and the thousand fingers pointing to one cause, global warming.

If the judge asks me why I shot Gerald X. O'Toole I'll say— Because I'm part of something bigger than you and your laws, more important than anything that has ever happened before. I'm just one guy and look what I accomplished. And there are lots of others just like me all over the world. Maybe they'll follow my trial. Maybe for them I'll be some kind of hero. Or maybe they won't give a shit because they're too busy doing their own actions. What do you think of that, Mr. Judge Man?

More people have arrived and filled in all the seats. A fat bald guy in a dark suit waddles up to the podium.

I shoulder the rifle and look through the scope. Definitely not Clint Eastwood. Probably some jerkoff introducer. I check the magnification indicator on the scope. The power ring is set at ten and I dial it up to eighteen and look back into the eyepiece. Oh yeah. Mr. Introducer's blurry image now fills the view and I adjust the focus and sharpen him up to where I can see the little American flag on his lapel. He's saying something into the microphone, but at this distance, drifting on the wind, the amplified words are just bits and pieces, distorted mumbles like in some weird underwater dream.

My boy G.X. O'Toole must be on deck. I dig a cartridge out of the box and cup it in my palm. Long, cold and heavy. For some reason this makes me happy. No, not just happy, a jolt of electricity crackles up and down my chest. I kiss the bullet then slide it into the magazine. Then two more, not sure why, one's more than enough. Uncle Carl used this rifle to drop a 700-pound bull elk. I open the breech and shove the bolt forward to chamber the round.

Mr. Introducer finishes talking and . . . fuck. Some white-haired lady is now blabbing at the mike. Get out of there grandma, nobody wants to listen to you. I try to hear what she's saying but her words are faint and garbled, America . . . economy . . . jobs . . . greatest in the world.

A bead of sweat rolls down my forehead and I wipe it on my sleeve. Another whiff of plywood and new carpet. I wish I had some water.

The memories come streaming back in a rush and I pinch my eyes shut.

Mom is yelling at me—Come on, come on! We gotta go. Right now!

I'm standing in the living room looking at my aquarium— But what about my fish? We have to save them.

Mom yanks me out the door and we get into the car and drive through a tornado of smoke and ash and embers and fire.

We leave behind everything, all our stuff, and all my fish. But I can't get the picture out of my head, the blazes blasting through our front door and into the living room, lighting the drapes and table and the sofa. The fire gets higher and higher, closing in on my aquarium and Pinky and Elmer and Speckles and Fat Charlie and Skidmarks and Brainiac. They see the shimmering flames, feel the water getting hotter. They're scared, swimming faster and faster, they can feel the heat but there's no place to hide. They're boiling alive.

I hear what sounds like applause. At the podium, grandma sweeps her hand toward the clubhouse and out he comes. Yeah, that's him. Here comes the birthday boy. He bounces up the little staircase onto the stage with a springy step and the old lady presents him with a trophy. Probably an Academy Award in the category of biggest earth-killing douchebag. He's tall and bends the microphone holder upwards and starts giving his speech.

The great O'Toole is centered in my scope, crosshairs on his forehead. I thumb the switch on the safety, click, ready to fire. A few deep breaths and I move my finger to the trigger.

He's mouthing away, face all stern. Now he's smiling, his eyes all twinkle-twinkle and he's looking around the audience like he just got off a good joke.

The breeze carries an echoing ha ha ha.

You're so funny. Let's put in an LNG terminal. Why not just strangle the whole fucking planet? You're evil, you pig. Pure fucking evil. And I'm gonna do this. I'm really gonna. I'm gonna put a bullet right in your ugly fucking pig fucking head. I'm gonna—Wait. Something's happening.

The fat bald guy, cell phone jammed to his ear, is at O'Toole's side, grabbing him by the upper arm, pulling him close and saying something. Then bug-eyed fatso leans close to the mike and the word EVACUATE explodes like a clap of thunder. I take my eye away from the scope to see everybody in the audience walking, jogging, running toward the clubhouse.

The sound of a faraway siren drifts across the river.

They must know. Fucking Uncle Carl.

I whip the scope back over to O'Toole just as he takes a look this way, scanning the tree line through his squinty eyes, like he's wondering if I'm out here, some crazy fuck with a rifle, ready to drop him where he stands.

My last chance. Aim. Breathe. Feel the trigger.

The fat guy jerks O'Toole from the podium and hustles him off the stage.

Two or three sirens are now whining, getting louder.

Everyone is inside the clubhouse ballroom, but I can't find O'Toole among them. Milling around like they're safe. Hey dumbasses, the whole wall along the river is windows.

I could shoot up the glass and give the TV news a couple of bullet holes to gawk at.

But I didn't come to assassinate a window.

I stand up and start to go but pause to look back across the river. Chairs, stage, flags and flowers, podium and microphone. Deserted. Empty. All set up for something that never happened. But something could have happened. Something important. I could have fired the first shot in the war.

Crouching low, I trot along the bank and back up the trail to the Winnebago. I turn it around and tear off, a straightaway then around a bend and—shit! A cop car is stopping traffic at the intersection by the bridge. I brake hard, shift into reverse. The road isn't wide and I back up into the bushes and CRASH the back bumper rams into something that shakes me in my seat. I crank the wheel fast and complete the 180 and stomp on the gas pedal. The Winnie flies through a couple of turns and groans up an incline and at the top I slam on the breaks. Another cop car, parked diagonally across the intersection below, lights flashing.

They won't find anybody. Then probably search parties, helicopters, dogs.

To my left, the forest goes all the way up and over the ridge and down to the north side of town. My only way out. I turn the rig around and backtrack until I see a gravel road leading up a hollow. I cut the sharp turn too tight and take out a row of posts holding mailboxes. The RV bounces over potholes along the twisting lane, low tree branches rake the roof screeching.

At the dead end an overgrown trail takes off into the forest. I grab the rifle and start running up the hill. The trail is good for about a hundred yards then narrows and becomes harder to follow. Soon it's gone altogether and I'm busting through bushes and ferns and branches, climbing over fallen limbs and trees. The rifle gets tangled in a vine and I yank hard to get it free.

A thorny stem slices across the back of my hand like a red-hot knife and I'm bleeding like crazy. I lick at the deep cut and have never tasted so much blood. I start to gag and spit and wipe my tongue on the sleeve of the jacket.

The slope eases up for a while and I try to cover it quickly. My foot lands in a hole, the ankle folds sharply to the side and I fall to the ground clutching it. When I can get back on my feet, there's a jolt of pain with every other step. I use the rifle as a cane, clutching the barrel, and limp on. No time to stop.

A half hour of this and I'm bent over, panting, and still nowhere near the top. My ankle is swollen over the top of my shoe and I'm dying for some water.

Just ahead there's a huge tree and I hobble over and lean against its thick dark trunk.

Dripping with sweat, I try to control my gasping so I can listen. Nothing.

Two minutes of rest, that's all. Breathe. Breathe.

I stare at the gash across my hand, the dried cake of blood, the shiny dark steel of the rifle barrel.

I feel it all washing away, everything, my whole life. It's gone. Everything and everybody I've known, gone. There's nowhere to go back to.

My gut feels sick and watery. The ferns and bushes and trees around me don't look real. They don't know I exist, don't care. I want to lay down, just lay down right here and think.

No time for that. Gotta get over the ridge. I push off from the tree and my ankle screams with the first few steps. Keep going. No other option.

Another quarter mile and I come to a clearing, pause, look at the terrain and try to see my best path forward. A bird hidden high in a nearby tree shrieks. It shrieks again and flies out from cover and with a few powerful strokes of its big black wings flies straight up the slope, weightless, soaring above the very highest of the trees, to the top of the ridge, and over. I stare at the jagged line where the black forest rips into the blazing afternoon sky. I am floating. I am at peace. I am protected. I have nothing to fear. Everything in the past is gone, peeled away, meaningless. I know exactly what is going to happen. It is all inevitable now, gears in motion, click click click.

I will hide the rifle out here.

I will make it back to town, to my comrades, the NDF.
They'll help me.
They need me.
I'm ready to pull the trigger.
And next time I will.

Endgame

The air in my library is still, the soft light filters in through the tall windows, falls gently on the books I have collected, read, been guided by; the rugs, furnishings, art, and mementoes I have gathered in a lifetime of world travel; the photographs of the people I have loved. Dear memories. I look across the desk to the clock on the mantelpiece—11:58. Jon-Anders will arrive any minute from New Haven. Our fates to be decided.

He will be expecting our ordinary routine, will appear as usual with his satchel and briefcase, his scholarly tools—laptop, well-organized binders, microphone and recorder, his ever-present thermos of green tea—eager to add still more to his doctoral research, to delve further into my life and work.

He says the thesis will be complete in the fall. Will I be alive to read it? Such a worthy Boswell. And for all the impressive encyclopedic knowledge he gained at Brown, Oxford, and now Yale, Jon-Anders is also blessed with a charming sense of humor: The good laugh we had when he told me the working title for his thesis, Steadman Compazzo: The Man Who Almost Saved the World.

It had seemed so amusing at the time. Then an hour later, when he had gone and I sat alone in this study, I thought again of the title and wept.

The clock chimes twelve and returns to its metronomic march.

I hear his car crunching up the long gravel driveway, coming to a stop near the garage. Door slam, chirp of electronic lock, the opening and closing of my front door as he lets himself in, the tap-tap of his footsteps on the hall's marble floor. He pauses in the doorway—tall, thin, tieless in a blazer and buttoned-down shirt. His gray-blue eyes inspect me, as if searching for visible signs of my condition.

"Come on in, my boy. Have a seat." He is far from being a boy, but with nearly five decades on him I can allow myself certain liberties—and now is not the time to withhold affection.

He settles into the chair opposite my desk. "So, you met with the oncologist—what did the tests say?"

"The treatments aren't working—additional organs affected. Despite my doctor's gentle delivery, the prognosis remains hospice, morphine, and an all too quick departure from this mortal coil."

"I'm so sorry," he says, his eyes full of compassion. He waits for me to say more, offering a listening ear, perhaps a shoulder to cry on.

"I will not be so trite as to talk about silver linings, but," I say and pass him a thick folder of documents, "those papers, signed and legally binding, will liquidate my assets, including the family money, and establish and endow a research institute. You will be director, compensated at double a professor's salary." This should be especially persuasive as Jon-Anders has told me numerous times of his career goal of joining the Harvard faculty.

"The pay package may seem overly generous, but you will earn every penny.

Maintaining the Shrink the Pop website is no mean task—
citations in *Foreign Affairs* and *The Economist* do not come
without effort. You will also have speeches to deliver, conferences
to attend, panels and committees and commissions on which to
serve, articles to write, alliances to forge, negotiations to broker.
Because of your singular grasp of population dynamics—
political, historical, economic, ecological—you had no rivals for
the position."

He glances up from the folder, smiles at the compliment,
then continues paging through the documents. I speak the line
I hope will result in a handshake. "I had imagined us working
together with you gradually taking on more responsibilities as
the cancer slowly progressed. But yesterday's diagnosis demands
we accelerate the transition."

He raises and lowers the folder as if estimating its heft.
"Surely you didn't put all this together since yesterday."

"No." I chuckle at the notion of my lawyers and accountants
producing in a day what they labored over for weeks. "I had the
papers prepared for . . . a variety of scenarios."

His eyes return to the folder. "This is remarkable. I mean,
truly." But he says it with a nervous laugh, a forced smile.

What could possibly be keeping him from an immediate and
enthusiastic acceptance? Ah, now I understand. "I appreciate
how much the thesis means to you. So, yes, your magnum opus,
finish it up, of course, with all my blessings."

His face is pained, his lips a tight line. "I'm speechless, Stead,
really I am." He clears his throat. "But, as I've told you, I have
very specific goals. All my efforts have been aimed toward—"

"I am offering the keys to the kingdom. Surely you see that."

He looks away, pondering, then nods, as if surer of his
position. "Steve Jobs said focusing is about saying no."

"This is the opportunity of a hundred lifetimes."

"And one I might someday regret not taking. I'm flattered, I am. But I'm going to have to pass. My path is set."

"For the love of God," I bellow, "don't be a damn fool!"

He jumps in his chair—reacting to my vehemence, but with no clue what impels it. And no idea where his idiot miscalculation is taking us.

About the Shrink the Pop website: I was there. I watched it happen. As head of the UN Special Directorate for Environmental Crisis Response, my job—my responsibility— was to oversee the crafting of what would become the Grand Omnibus Declaration on the Environment, the UN's comprehensive policy document responding to the climate crisis. My group, a small army of lawyers, scholars, scientists, and diplomats, labored for seven years; and indeed, we produced the document eventually ratified by every member state.

The tragedy is that while the Secretary General hailed the Declaration as "the foundation of a future where humanity lives in harmony with the Earth," it is in fact an abject failure.

I had been determined that the final draft of the Declaration include provisions to sharply decrease the Earth's population through natural mortality and diminished birth rates, thereby lowering resource consumption, energy and agricultural demand, and most pressingly, greenhouse gas emissions. With a global population lowered from eight billion to four billion, we would have a fighting chance to deal with climate change; conversely, with growth to eleven, twelve, thirteen billion, a holocaust vastly more devastating than anything previously suffered would be unavoidable.

Various ideological camps within our group coalesced into a bloc fiercely opposed to reversing population growth. The rift grew so contentious that we decided to settle it by a simple ballot: Would a coordinated population reduction program become a cornerstone of the most significant global agreement in human history—yes or no?

The contest could not have been closer; a single vote determined its outcome. A single no vote. We had bowed down once again to the same myopic, self-seeking, tribal impulses that had brought us to the brink of annihilation.

I resigned in protest—very publicly, very vocally. I gave what felt like a thousand speeches and interviews, wrote a hundred think pieces decrying the UN's cataclysmic mistake. Magazines around the world put me on their covers; *The Atlantic* accompanied my image with the headline "The Population Prophet."

I came to believe that since the UN had not adequately addressed our existential crisis, it was now up the world's citizens to demand action. Such a populist movement would require an easily accessible resource for theory, analysis, discussion, organization—a tool, a clearinghouse. Creating such a platform would become my work. And thus was this website born.

Jon-Anders sits before me chastised by my outburst, his eyes moving back and forth between my glaring face and the thick folder in his hand.

"I regret it has come to this," I say, opening the desk drawer and pulling out my pistol. He recoils, tenses with animal fear. I raise the gun and make a show of chambering a round. Eyes on the pistol, palms in front of his chest—as if flesh could stop lead—he rises cautiously from his seat until standing in a crouch.

"Sit down or I will shoot you." I take aim just below his knee. "Neither of us wants that."

He sinks back into the chair. I feel ridiculous, the cloak and dagger, but so be it; I am committed to see this through.

"You're threatening me?" he asks, utterly bewildered. "With a gun . . . so I'll work for you? It doesn't make sense."

"I am appropriating your career. Relieving you, let us say, of the burden of its guidance."

No sane person would believe Jon-Anders or anyone else could singlehandedly stave off global catastrophe. But the stakes are so astronomically high that if there is a chance, any chance at all, that his actions might make a difference, might even fractionally lessen the extent of the climate apocalypse, then the utilitarian choice must be made: the greatest good for the greatest number.

"The loss of autonomy over your future is . . . painful," I say. "I realize that. I hope you will think differently when you hear the rest of it."

His eyes widen. The presence of the gun has him rattled, but he is not so distracted that he misses the import of these words.

"In a few moments I will give my life in protest of the UN's titanic failure," I take a steadying breath, "with an act of self-immolation."

"My God," he gasps, his face going ashen.

"This . . . event will be live-streamed on the internet. You will serve as the proxy eyewitness for people forced by the extreme nature of the act to consider its message."

"No Stead, it's not worth—"

"An antiwar protester burns himself on the steps of the Pentagon and the story comes and goes in a day. But if the head of the Joint Chiefs were to do the same thing, the world would take notice. That is my wager.

"The media will tell and retell the story of my death for decades, show and reshow the shocking video. They will line up at your door asking for comment, providing you endless opportunities to put forth our message."

"This is madness."

"Precisely. Madness contra madness."

"You don't want to do this," he pleads. "You have other options. You could—" I shake my head.

"No, listen, what you're feeling, it could be just a side effect from your medication, a stress response to your diagnosis. You don't know, and you don't want to make any permanent—"

"This choice is the farthest thing from an impulsive act." My gaze is steady, my voice calm.

"Okay, I'll take the job," he says, his eyes frantic. "I'll work for you—whatever you want. I'll—"

"Unfortunately, your sudden change of heart rings hollow. When you declined the offer, you destroyed my faith that you would willingly carry on my work."

"But I will."

"Right now, you would admit to shooting Kennedy if you thought it would put off the inevitable." I raise my hand. "It is decided."

His brow furrows, his eyes slowly reveal a perplexed comprehension. "You're really doing this." I nod.

For him to be at peace there is one thing about my decision he must understand. "The cancer forced the issue," I say, "but the die was cast in the Sahara."

❧

"Why I Do What I Do," S. Campazzo, Shrink_the_pop.org/ Why_I_do

In the early spring of 1982, I flew to drought-ravaged central Africa and spent a month interviewing technocrats and acquiring data sets quantifying the magnitude of the devastating drought from government hydrologists, meteorologists, and agronomists.

When I ventured upcountry to talk directly with farmers, I saw for myself the effects of the advancing Sahara Desert. I met up with Ibrahim Fofasa, tall and rail thin, whose family had for generations raised sorghum in a productive agricultural lowland. We stood together in the blazing sun, peering out over a tract of what had once been his farm but now looked like an endless expanse of broken pottery.

Local customs dictated that Ibrahim invite me to his home for tea. He guided me through the low doorway of the two-room dirt-floored dwelling where we found little relief from the relentless heat.

When he did not see his wife Kandia, he became a bit flustered but still did his best to be the gracious host, fumbling with the teapot, sputtering something about her tending to their sick child.

Before the water boiled, Kandia entered from the other room, the unmoving baby cradled in her arms, her eyes hollow with abject desolation. Ibrahim rushed to her, but she turned away, rocking the baby in her arms, humming an eerily tuneless lullaby. While stroking the head of her lifeless child her gaze fell on me, bore into me, would not let me go, communicated a grief so deep it had no bottom.

All my work to this point had involved only best-case scenarios: improving crop rotation strategies, better fertilization regimes, increasing per-acre yields. But confronted with Kandia, her child, and the unfathomable emptiness in her eyes, I was forced to consider the worst case, the all too real nightmare result of overburdening the Earth's capacity. Continually increasing food production to feed an everexpanding population was an unsustainable, hubristic delusion. Decreasing the demand for food by lowering population, I suddenly understood, was our best and likely only hope.

All this, of course, was more than four decades ago, when we were hearing only the earliest cries of alarm about anthropogenic climate change and how it would alter weather patterns and water supplies, threaten global food production, spark the food wars devastating the world today.

The population grows day by day. Kandia's suffering will soon be multiplied tens of millions of times—tens of millions of times—as we blithely stoke the fires of the planet's slow-motion incineration.

"Get up," I command, a flick of the gun indicating where Jon-Anders should go. He leads the way down the hallway, out the front door. We step off the porch and follow the flagstones toward the garage. He moves slowly, taking each step with deliberation—perhaps planning some foolish act. The gun is heavy in my sweaty hand.

Up ahead the path diverges, one branch continues to the driveway, the other angles behind the garage to the brick patio overlooking the forest and creek.

"At the fork, go left."

The sacrifice of one is nothing in comparison to the deaths of millions. Think on these things, Stead.

Jon-Anders stops. I pull up, leaving a good distance between us, the pistol aimed to deliver a disabling shot to his calf.

He turns his head to see me over his shoulder. "Someone has to carry on your work—I get that." Without making any sudden moves, he turns to face me. "But what you need is a partisan, a zealot. I chose to study you and the Omnibus Declaration out of academic curiosity, not to rectify the UN's blunder."

"That is all behind you. Today you begin a whole new life."

"Look, Stead," he says, "I'm not who you want for this. We can find someone else. I'll help you."

"You are still thinking in terms of alternatives, possibilities. Those have all been erased. It does not matter if you are a true believer—you will act like one. I have eliminated all other reasonable options."

He ponders this, tilting his head in a gesture I have seen many times during our interviews while he absorbed some subtle point. He casts his gaze about desperately, then stops—a chess player foreseeing his defeat in the inexorable sequence of endgame moves. It could all be an act, a ploy to lull me into inattentiveness. But even as I take a step backward, I sense no guile in my young friend; rather, he appears shaken, emptied. How harrowing to be forced into a fate not of one's choosing.

"You are one royal bastard," he mutters.

I had anticipated such a response. Still, the words sting. "This is really what you want?" he asks.

"I would prefer any other path. But this one is necessary."

He stares into my eyes, taking my measure, seeing what I hope is an unshakable certitude. His face contorts.

I want to comfort him but stop. No more explanation, no more words. It will happen—with his acquiescence or with his blood. Seconds tick by. A bead of sweat rolls down my temple.

In a voice so soft I barely hear it, Jon-Anders says, "I'll keep the cancer quiet." He rubs his forehead. "It'll have to be in the thesis, but I can bury it in a footnote. Makes you the better martyr."

He is engaged. Resentful, but engaged. I nearly double over with relief. The feeling lasts but a moment before I am reminded of one aspect of my plan that has troubled me from the start: the cruelty of forcing him to witness the grisly sight, to endure the smell. When I have imagined him objecting, I've struggled with how I would respond. Without success.

"Are you going to be up to this next bit?" I ask.

He squints and looks across the forest to the far horizon. "Not sure." He returns his eyes to me, stares for a long time. "I'll do what I can." His eyes are kind.

The last eyes I shall ever see.

I bob my chin toward the patio, and we walk. I have removed the picnic table and umbrella, the sunning lounge, the grill, end tables, everything except two heavy wrought iron chairs, the gasoline can and duct tape, the smartphone atop a tripod.

The chairs are positioned safely apart, with both still captured in the camera's frame. He sits and I toss him the roll of duct tape and instruct him to secure one wrist to the chair's arm.

He complies and I immobilize his other wrist, then find his
phone in his jacket pocket and place it in his hand. He looks at it
quizzically.

"To call for help, after." I pat the tape on his arm. "There will
be no questions about your saving me." The words sound strange
in my ear, like I am an actor speaking my lines in an empty
theater.

I drop the gun in the bushes, move to the tripod, begin the
video stream.

Only a small number of tasks remain. On the way to my
chair, I sense the world contracting around me as if I am moving
ever deeper into a tunnel. The life of choice, of endless possibility
recedes behind me; ahead, I see the tiny dot of destiny toward
which my body glides, its movements less and less my own, more
and more a digital document.

I sit. My fingers grasp the handle on the can of gasoline, and
while I raise it to my knee, time slows, takes on the palpable
texture of a warm summer breeze, each moment in tactile
motion, blowing past, gone forever. A profound serenity suffuses
my body, warming and diminishing my awareness like some
potent drug administered before surgery. I drift away, no longer a
participant in these affairs, but an observer, keenly interested yet
detached, viewing as from above events unfolding in the lives of
other people.

The old man looks like me, so small and frail. His shaking
hand fumbles to unscrew the cap on the can of gas. The fuel
splashes and drips and spreads, odorless, weightless, neither hot
nor cold, soaking his clothing, pooling on his lap.

His hands come together before him as if in prayer. He holds
a lighter. With his thumb he flicks its little wheel. There is a
flash.

Smoke, Fire, Ashes

LUCY ANN

The Lake Wontaka Lounge isn't as special as Dad said it would
be, just a noisy bar and a bunch of tables and up at the front
a little platform for the band. A little darker than I imagined.
Mom says they play rockabilly music. I don't even know what
that is. Why did we even come here? They told me like twenty-
seven times how much fun we'd have, a family vacation up at the
lake, how much I would just luuuuuuuv it. Right.

It takes the waitress like nineteen centuries to find us then
she asks what I want and I say fruit juice and I'm thinking about
the vitamins and antioxidants and she looks like a cow and Mom
looks at me even cowier and I can tell she wants to lecture me
about the calories. I know, Mom, I know you think I'm fat, but I
don't care what you think. I'm going to drink what I want, okay?
The waitress tells me what kind of fruit juice they have and it
looks like I'm going to end up with cranberry. Not my favorite. I
ask if it comes in a recyclable container and she says she doesn't
know for sure but thinks maybe it comes in a plastic bottle. Oh
yeah, real great, like I really want to kill the oceans for a sip of
juice. Never mind. I have plain old water and Mom and Dad
have their beer. Then Mom grabs Dad's hand and says, c'mon,
let's dance, and he's like nah, nah, nah, can't we just listen? She
gives him The Look and drags him out right in front of the band
where everybody in the whole place can see.

And they're dancing out there all by themselves. Oh god.

It's just too hideous to watch so I open my book. To read it I have to hold it right next to the tiny little candle on our table. This chapter's horrifying, someplace up in Alaska all the ice is melting and there's this polar bear family starving to death.

I sniff Mom's beer and it smells like aquarium water. The singer up on the stage has a fancy jacket with sequins and embroidered roses and his guitar is yellow with gold sparkles. Dad lifts Mom's hand up and they make a little arch and she spins around under it. More couples are out there now—much better dancers. But look at them, all of them, dancing away la la la like the world isn't on fire. Wake up, dummies, there's no more time.

The singer kicks a bright red cowboy boot way up into the air and the drummer bashes the cymbals to finish the song. Dad comes back over to the table and Mom just stands out there, giving him the stink eye. He asks if I've had enough and I'm like, duh, yeah. Mom finally slinks over and they snap at each other and he tells her he's going to take me back up to the room.

TERRY

I don't want to make a scene, spoil everything, so sure, okay Krys, we'll dance. Whatever Krys wants, Krys gets. The band's good and all—very good, in fact—but dancing swing, with Krys, at this particular time—it's just a little too much to fake. And look at Lucy, she's getting antsy. One song is plenty. One and done.

Lucy says she wants to go back to the room, and I ask Krys if she's ready to go. The music's so loud she can't hear, so I yell, YOU WANNA GO? She takes a good-sized hit off her beer and says she wants to stay and listen some more. Okay, sure, I'll take Lucy and probably come back in a little while. She's still mad about the dancing and makes a face like Whatever. I look around and Lucy's already halfway to the exit.

I catch her at the door and outside where it's quieter I ask if she liked the music. She's her usual self, not saying much but obviously not impressed. At least she's not being openly hostile.

We walk down the hallway to the lobby—where that perky red-headed kid checked us into the resort this morning. He lit right up when I told him we had the Outdoor Fun Package, gave me a big toothy grin—felt like a good omen.

Did you like the kayaking, I ask. She shrugs. Did you get a little scared when the wind came up? Shrug. We made it all the way around the lake, didn't we? No response. She beelines to the elevator and pushes the button. We wait, my mind wanders . . .

Oh Daddy, I'm totally loving this vacation. You drove us over to this fancy resort, carried all our stuff up to the room, got us all geared up for the half-day, lunch-included kayak adventure. The windstorm, yeah, that was a little scary, but you led us to safety—an experience I will never forget. And you took us out for a wonderful Thai dinner where Mom even laughed at one of your jokes. And then we—

The elevator bell goes ding. Lucy zooms inside and parks herself against the back wall, looks straight ahead clutching her book to her chest like a life preserver. When the doors open on our floor, she trots off, getting smaller and smaller as she moves down the long corridor of doors and more doors.

Krys saying, "I'm going over to my sister's—she's got a bad cold or the flu or something."

I feel around in different pockets for the room key.

And the next day Krys, like a goddam Mother Teresa, "Poor Patty"—so innocent, shaking her blonde head. "Whatever she's got, it's really holding on. Don't wait up, I might stay over."

I insert the key card into the little slot—click—and push the door open. The room is pitch black.

And me taking Patty get-well flowers, a surprise. Mr. Nice Guy. She opens her front door—healthy as a horse. Is Krys here? She has no idea what I'm talking about. Everything stops. Everything crumbles. And I'm standing there holding the bouquet, the world's biggest chump.

I flick on the light. Lucy wiggles past me, jumps onto her bed and bounces a couple of times. She says she's going to shower, gets her stuff.

I bunch the pillows against the headboard and check my phone. A message from Amanda. Ooh, now that's a selfie. Skimpy black bra, one hand's holding the camera, the other's cupping the back of her head, elbow high, bedroom eyes, puckered lips.

That first night, Amanda in her kittycat whisper, "I'm here to pamper you . . . anything you want." Her voice breathy and hot, right at my ear, in slips her tongue.

Lucy says something in the bathroom. I turn to listen, about to ask her What? Then I hear a few more chirpy sounds and figure she's just sort of singing or something.

Krys swears it was only once. Oh, only once. Well, that's super great news. I guess everything's just a-okay then, huh? No Krys, everything is not fucking okay.

She's begging—Look, I understand, if you need to get back at me, even things up. Go ahead, find somebody. Do what you want.

I stare at Amanda's picture, spread my finger and thumb on the phone's glass surface, zoom in, remember.

We have a couple of drinks on her sofa and Amanda stands up and unzips the tight little skirt and lets it drop around her bare feet. Looking at me over her shoulder, she thrusts out her hip, rests her hand on the curving haunch—the red thong's thin strap disappears into the crack of her ass.

I get home, Krys looks at me all mad and hurt and she starts right in with how she isn't as cool with the arrangement as she thought she was going to be. She wants to go to counseling.

Typical Krys. First I catch her red handed and she's bawling her eyes out—anything, anything, just don't throw me out—but when I have a little fun she sings a very different tune. Okay fine, we'll go to counseling. But you said that if I wanted to find somebody you'd understand, did you not? Okay. Don't forget that.

I told Krys I'd come back down to the lounge . . . but I don't know, it's been a long day. Tomorrow we're hiking up a mountain. I kick off my shoes and pull the comforter over my legs.

Lucy comes out of the bathroom and crawls into her bed, a small bump under the covers of the queen-size. She asks what I'm doing, and I say, oh, just catching up on my email. She says she's going to sleep, and I ask if she isn't going to read. No, the kayaking tired her out. Did you like being on the lake? She says it was cool then turns off the lamp by her bed. I switch off my lamp too and am lying there in the dark feeling pretty great about the kayaking when she says good night and I say good night Lucy Goosey and then she laughs her funny chipmunk laugh and says good night again and now we're playing the good-night game like we used to when she was little, repeating and repeating good night back and forth until she finally drifts off.

The couples counselor says he believes we can make things work—but only if we want to. He looks a little less certain when Krys tells him about the blank check she wrote me as far as other relationships and how she wants to take it back. Then she tries to make me the bad guy for not dropping my extracurricular the second she felt a hundredth as bad as I felt when I found out about hers. The counselor doesn't buy her bait-and-switch bullshit, says he can't exactly bless my affair, but we should look at it as an intermediate hurdle on the way to better days.

At the second session the counselor suggests we reboot the relationship, take a test run as a happy family, go on a vacation. And don't just gut it out, make a good-faith effort to have fun.

If you're not having fun, together, as a family, what's the point? He reminds us of the alternative, a divorce and shared custody of Lucy.

I look back at my phone and think maybe I'll just write Amanda a quick message to keep things bubbling along—maybe we could get together after work on Thursday. I see her picture with those luscious lips and I hear the counselor say good-faith effort. I look over where Lucy is sleeping and can just hear her soft little breaths. I scan around in the darkness, and I guess there must be a mirror on the opposite wall because there's my own face, illuminated in the bluish light of my phone, floating there like a ghost, unconnected to anything.

LUCAS

What's left of my whiskey is rolling around in the bottom of my glass. Goddamn Mercer. Stopped at his trailer. Coupla belts, shot the shit. Tells me his new idea. Gonna fill the tank of his windshield wipers with vodka and run a tube up through the dash so he can flick on his washer and squirt himself all he wants and the cops looking for an open container can go fuck themselves. I told him there's live music up at the resort, let's go. No, he's got some new twitch coming over, a dancer from the titty bar out on the highway. Fuck you, Mercer.

The band sounds good and I turn around to check out the dance floor. Well lookie there, Blondie and some geeze in a Stetson. She got the moves, yes she do. Hello darlin'. Go change your diapers, grandpa, you ain't got a chance tonight. Oh, now he's walking her to her seat, holding her hand up between them like some English fairy. Tips his goddam hat and leaves her all by her lonesome.

The band starts up. I shuffle on over. Evening. This is a real good song, good beat, and you're a helluva dancer.

She takes one look and she's up and rarin' to go. Her hand is small and warm and real soft. I give her a turn, spin, over, hop. My hand slides down her back and around her hip. Give her the lasso, the dirty move, down, up, and down, my hand on her nice soft belly. Spin her around, lean left into a dip, twirl her right and another dip. She likes that. Tornado. Spin cycle. Slide. Slide. Jump rope. Side lean. That's it darlin', over my leg like you're humping it. Let's try that again. Stroll left and stroll right. Our cheeks are close and I feel her heat. The band's working it up to a finish and I reel her in tight. The final note goes WHAM. My arm's around her waist, her face right next to mine. She's got a little sweat on her upper lip like we been bangin' on a hot afternoon.

I ask if she wants a fresh one and she says yeah. I go get us a couple, come back, hand her one. Lucas, I say. Krystal. That's a real pretty name, but not half as pretty as you.

She laughs and pushes aside some of her hair. Ain't twenty, but she ain't bad. She takes a big swallow of her beer like what's next big boy? They're a good band, I tell her. I'd like to dance with you some more.

She looks down and little dimples come out when she smiles. Yeah, she'd like that too. But first it's off to the ladies. She's up and walking, puts a little extra sway in the caboose just for me.

Out in the truck I got a fifth of Jack near full, the bud I got from that prick over in Riverton, and what's left of the crank. Yes, ma'am, I hope you're ready for a night to remember.

And even if you ain't . . .

KRYSTAL

I want to dance, okay? Don't make me beg, Terry, for Chrissake, don't make me. Do you even remember what the counselor said? What we're supposed to be doing here? What you agreed to?

With him it's rock step, rock step, one, two. Always has been. At least we're out here and dancing. Stop thinking, just go with it. Rock step, rock step.

Lucy's watching. Got her mouth all pinched up, nose crinkled . . . like we're disgusting. Oh, now she's gonna hide in her book. Used to be Taylor Swift, morning, noon, and night, now it's Greta what's-her-name . . . Thumb-something . . . Thumbelina. Oh my gawd, she's so cooool. She talked at the UN and she's just a kid and she's gonna save the world. Yeah, well, don't hold your breath.

Now where is he going? Terry, one dance, are you kidding me? No, I'm not mad, I tell him. Yeah, take her back to the room, good idea. Okay, see you back here later. Night-night bunny. I give her a smile and a little wave.

She was about two minutes from a meltdown. What happens when she's fifteen? Ninth grade, tenth? What was I like? "Jagged Little Pill" in my head, sneaking out, smoking pot. Just three years from now. Jesus. We'll make it . . . right? No good reason we can't.

If he'd just let it go. But no, not Terry. Stomps around the house like he's wearing army boots—clomp, clomp, clomp. Gotta let me know, gotta remind me . . . what I did to him, always what I did to him. Clomp, clomp, clomp. Yeah you're mad and yeah it's my fault, all my fault, okay, but you're no angel either.

The old guy standing up at the table over there, with the big white Stetson and a snow-white Hulk Hogan moustache . . . a boot-scooter from way back. Is he coming this way?

All duded up—the hat and leather vest, the bolo tie with a big hunk of turquoise and silver caps on the danglies. Well, yes, I would like to dance.

He takes me out onto the floor and we flow right into it. Spin and turn and forward and under and reverse and back and under and turn and spin. He knows what he's doing. A firm lead, steady, right on the beat . . . a partner you can trust, you always know what's coming next. I relax into the music, the singer's voice. We swirl and twirl and glide. The song finishes and we smile at each other, both knowing we're good together.

Another dance? Yes I would.

The band guys fiddle with their amplifiers and sip their beers then count off and start into a Mexican ballad with a nice medium tempo. Dapper Dan leads us into an easy samba and our footwork couldn't be smoother. I love that about dancing, the way the two of you figure out what you can do together and then start moving as one. With some guys it's a battle, a fight every step of the way. But not with this old boy. It's like we've been dancing together for years.

With a light squeeze to my hand, he signals a final turn and a fun little dipsy-do. Looks like he's gonna bust for happy. Walks me to my seat, tips of the hat. Thank you, ma'am, you have a real good night. And he's gone. A real gentleman.

Terry still not back. Is that him coming in the door? Nope. Where the hell is he? This beer could be colder. If that waitress comes around—

Evening.

Huh? Oh my. Mr. Long and Lean. Rodeo shirt, big silver belt buckle. He says, you're a helluva dancer.

Grabs my hand and off we go. Doesn't have the old guy's finesse but he's strong, oh, very strong. Fast twirl. Throws me left, swings me around right. Tornado? Been a while. A little show-offy, but he can dance. Letting his hands roam. He likes that side lean. Gives it an extra something, got me halfway horizontal. Going back to that again on the other side. The band's taking it home. How's he gonna finish up? A walk out and a stroll and a low cheek-to-cheek and he wraps me up in his big arms and lays me out real low, and when the music stops his face is right next to mine and he's burning into me with those green eyes. We're breathing like racehorses and he smells like whiskey.

The singer says they're gonna take a break. Walking to the table, I pat my hair back into place. Well yes, I would like a drink.

Mr. Slim Hips. Mmm-mmm-mmm. If those jeans were any tighter. He's back with the beers, says his name's Lucas. Fits him head to toe. And he tells me I'm pretty. Well here we are, aren't we?

He says he'd like to do some more dancing. What he really wants is written all over his face . . . his very nice-looking face with that strong jaw and those green, green eyes.

Miss Dinkybladder says hey girl, and I tell Lucas, now don't you go anywhere, I'll be back in a flash. Making my way around the tables everything feels so different. Now I'm at a party I want to be at.

There's one woman in a short pink skirt waiting outside the bathroom so I take my place. I should have brought cigarettes. I'd die for a cigarette. Lucas. Going down into the dip, my hand on his strong back. Mmm. Strong like Vic.

A prune-faced woman comes out of the bathroom and pink skirt goes in. Alone in the hallway now ... Vic. Me and Vic ...

I'm taking a quick smoke outside the back door at work—Terry would kill me if he knew—and some guy in white pants is up on the ladder next door painting the outside of the Jiffy Lube, sees me looking.

Hey, sweetheart, you got another one of those? He comes over, him and his big easy smile, and I light him up. Don't you know they'll kill you?

He exhales a cloud and laughs. Least I'll die happy. Funny guy, Vic. That beaded necklace with a cross on it. Never took it off. Our one night.

Pink skirt comes out, squeezes by me and I wonder where Terry is. And what are we doing, huh? I go in, take the open stall. We're trying to make this family thing work ... but he doesn't care, it's all about him, he's off having his little ... payback. We come up here, put on a show, and why? He'll be with her next week. I know he will. Damn you, Terry. God damn you.

Out of the stall, I look at my eyes in the mirror. Skin's getting a little thin. In the bar light, Lucas won't even notice. That's funny. I look good when I laugh. Pretty, he said.

I push open the door and start into the hall, but he's right there in front of me blocking the way. I look up at him and he says, out on the highway there's a place you might like, real good for dancing, The Crossroads.

LUCY ANN

What's that noise? Dark. A blast of light and Mom's creeping in from the hallway, hunched over, holding her shoes. She closes the door all careful and it's black again. The clock says 5:11. I smell cigarettes. She's not supposed to smoke. Dad rolls over. He's gonna be so mega pissed. She goes into the bathroom, the lock clicks. A bar of light comes on under the door.

The shower starts up. They're gonna fight.

I pull the covers over my head and roll up into a ball, small as I can be. I start to shake and squeeze my arms tight against my chest and try not to think about anything and remember that right before I woke up I was dreaming. There was a big horrible forest fire, roaring into a town like that one in California, Paradise. Everybody running and screaming, driving their cars all crazy trying to escape. Smoke and fire and ashes. Every building burning until there wasn't a single thing left. Stupid greedy adults. Greta blames them, says they're the ones who wrecked everything and it's us kids who are gonna pay. You stole our childhood and you stole our future.

How dare you. We'll never forgive you. I will never ever ever forgive you.

The Burning Planet

The forecast was for record heat, so I got on the road ahead of the morning rush hour and drove east out of the L.A. basin toward the desert. The temperature had jumped thirty degrees by the time I steered my old Volvo wagon off the freeway and onto a two-lane county road headed straight into what looked like a thousand square miles of nothing. I felt like some latter-day gold miner off to the wilderness in search of riches—and had a pretty good hunch I was about to get lucky.

On my map Burro Flats looked like a town, but it was not much more than a single crossroads with buildings petering out in each direction after half a block. My destination was the Oasis, an ancient tavern held together by dust and peeling paint. The neon Budweiser and Pabst Blue Ribbon signs in the window were unlit, but the door was propped open with a shovel so I stuck my head in. The place was empty except for a middle-aged, puffy-faced guy behind the bar who was taking inventory notes on a clipboard.

"Can I help you?" he asked, friendly enough.

"I'm looking for an old guy who lives around here, Hollis Tozer. Do you know him?"

He rubbed his chin and looked up at the ceiling in a bad pantomime of searching his memory. "I'm a little thirsty. A beer might jog my memory."

"Sure, yeah, why don't you have one," I said. "On me."

In the time it took him to belt down that beer and a sequel,
I learned quite a lot from my new buddy, Larry. He let Tozer
use the bar as a mailing address ("sumbitch gets more mail than
God almighty"). He hadn't seen Tozer in a while ("the old coot's
probably dead") and a goodsized pile of his mail had built up ("I
ain't the fuckin' Post Office"). Larry suggested I deliver the mail
for him and retrieved from a back room an overflowing pink
plastic laundry basket. "There was probably twice that much, but
I shit-canned the junk mail."

I lugged the basket to my car's back compartment and looked
through its contents: magazines from *The Economist* and *Nature*
to *Asia Week* and *Technology Ate My Brain*, as well as books—
three from Amazon, five from Oxford University Press.

Following Larry's directions, I drove out of town and after a
few miles turned onto a dirt road full of ruts and potholes bad
enough to make me wonder if my car was up to the task. The
road came to a driveway, a long steep incline gouged into the
side of a red limestone hill. Marking it was a tilted post holding
a crooked sign with large-headed nails driven into it that spelled
TOZER. Not far up the slope a metal gate barred my further
progress. I got out and had a look at the No Trespassing sign
attached to the gate with twists of wire—taking special notice
of the three bullet holes precisely placed an inch below each s.
I pushed my little finger into one of the holes and ran my hand
over the hot nails. Not even noon yet and the temperature was
already pushing 100.

A gunshot cracked—unmistakable. I don't remember
running from the gate back to my car, but I know I got there
fast. I crouched behind the front left tire with the engine block
between me and the direction of the shot.

"No trespassin' means no trespassin,'" a raspy voice warned from some distance away. "You don't read English?"

I kept my head down and called back, "I talked to a guy at the tavern. He said you'd be happy to see me."

"Who was that?"

"Larry."

"Larry who?"

"I don't know. He seemed to know you pretty well."

"He's two-thirds piss and half blarney." He paused, then, "Did he get you to buy him a beer?"

"Two."

"Piece of shit."

I couldn't tell if he meant Larry or me.

"He gave me your mail," I yelled. It would have been more persuasive if I could have waved a fistful of letters at him right about then, but the basket seemed very far away, and I wasn't about to move. "He said you still owe him twenty bucks from the Super Bowl."

I listened. No response. Was he moving, changing position, coming closer? "What do you want?" came the voice from the same direction and distance as before.

"I was researching Edward Abbey and came across a couple of references to some ideas you had." It took a lot to get even that out—making it loud enough for him to hear using lungs constricted by my crouching position. Plus, a rock was digging into my knee, my back was beginning to ache, and the sun was frying the skin on my neck. "You think maybe we could just talk, you know, like normal people?"

A drop of sweat ran into my eye. I was blinking away the burn when I heard his reply. "Well . . . get your ass up here and we'll have us a cold one."

He sounded almost neighborly now—but still. "You're not gonna . . ."

"Plunk ya?" he cackled. "Likely not—but there ain't no sure bets in this old world."

I peeked up over the car's hood. There he was—a rifle in one hand, his head protected by a broad conical hat of a kind I'd seen people wear in rice paddies. Small and lean and sinewy, he wore an Earth First! T-shirt and had the leathery skin of a three-pack-a-day smoker, well-suited for survival in this sun-blasted wasteland. He unlatched the gate and swung it open.

Keeping a close eye on him, I stood up and brushed the dust off my pants.

"What's your name?" he said.

"Luke. Mayfield."

"Well alright then, c'mon up," he said, waving me forward. "Sun'll cook your gizzard out here."

I got the laundry basket of mail. Tozer led the way up the steep winding road to a cinderblock house perched atop a mesa. We entered a big front room that smelled like cigarette butts and looked like a combination living room, office, and overstocked used bookstore. Every surface was stacked with paperback and hardback volumes, and strewn with papers, magazines, empties, and overflowing ashtrays. Tozer removed his rice-farmer's hat, freeing a wild mane of wavy, steel-gray hair, and sailed the hat across the room like a frisbee. I set the basket down, and he guided me to one of two ancient leather wingback chairs arranged at a picture window that framed a panoramic view of the pink shimmering desert and a faraway range of blue, snowcapped mountains. He brought two tall cans of beer and handed me one.

"You mentioned something about me and Eddie."

I was used to making elevator pitches and in a few punchy lines laid out the reason for my visit: how I'd come across the letters he'd exchanged with the legendary Edward Abbey during their days studying philosophy together at the University of New Mexico; how the ideas he articulated in those letters about the role of the human population in damaging the earth's ecosystems have become almost prophetic as we've come to understand global warming. I told him I had recently graduated from UCLA film school's documentary track, and I wanted to tape an interview with him.

I sipped my beer. He stubbed out one unfiltered Camel, lit another, and squinted at me through the first-puff haze.

What didn't make it into my pitch was the fact that a few months back *An Inconvenient Truth* had won the 2006 Academy Award for Best Documentary and had so far raked in close to $50 million in global box office.

Tozer picked a fleck of tobacco from his lip. "Where you from?"

"Not far from UCLA."

"And you drove all the way out here."

"I tried to call first."

"I don't have a phone."

"Yeah, I figured that out."

"Don't need one. Don't want one. Aristotle didn't have a phone. Thoreau didn't have a phone. Emerson didn't have a phone. Anybody who wants to can come see me."

I was tempted to remind him of the warm welcome I'd received but held off as I was working my angle.

"Okay," he said.

"Okay what?"

"Okay, let's do her. No time like the now time. And besides," he said with a wink, "I'm sober today."

I hadn't anticipated this, didn't have a crew—no sound or lighting help, no one to operate the camera while I asked the questions. But I did have my gear in the car and didn't want the opportunity to slip away. It took three trips to tote it all up the sun-scorched hill, leaving me sweaty and breathing hard.

"Another?" he offered, standing at the open refrigerator. I declined. He shrugged, cracked one for himself, and drank contentedly while I set up for the interview.

I got rid of the ashtrays and empties and moved one of the wingback chairs in front of a sagging and comically overstuffed bookcase in an arrangement suggesting some eccentric professor's throne. Harsh desert light streamed through the window, and as I didn't have a softbox for fill lighting, I improvised a warm and sufficiently even light field by partially closing the threadbare, cream-colored curtain. I positioned the camera and composed my shot.

Once he was seated, I handed him the mic and he slid it up under his Earth First! T-shirt and clipped it on the collar. The shirt was a perfect visual element: once black but now badly faded and thinned by a thousand washings, it featured the radical environmental group's clenched fist symbol.

I fine-tuned the composition, moving the camera half a foot to the left for an angle that caught a little more of the crazy cascade of Tozer's Einstein hair. The framing was good, suitable for zooming in and out. While adjusting the tilt for proper headroom on the medium shot, I noticed something.

"What's the matter?" he asked.

I pointed at a small hole in his T-shirt, right over his heart, from which sprung some kinky gray chest hairs. Edgy cultural philosopher is a good look, old geezer in a ratty T-shirt isn't. In my gear bag I found a roll of electrical tape, tore off a piece, and stuck it on the inside of the shirt to cover the hole.

Tozer cocked an eyebrow. "So much for telling the unvarnished truth."

I didn't let his jab get to me and was preparing to ask the first question, but before I could, he dove right in like he'd been waiting a long time for someone to aim a camera at him.

"First thing is, nobody wants to feel guilty they're killing the planet. But they don't want to change how they're living either. Stop using so much gas or electricity! Stop eating beef! Stop using plastic! That's gonna fly like a stainless-steel turd.

"Second thing is, the planet isn't dying, what's dying is its capacity to host. And the more people, the more critical that problem gets. We stop the population increase, turn it around, get the numbers into a precipitous decline and in not too long most of our problem goes away. We can live with five billion people, with four billion—three billion and we're back in Eden. But ten, eleven, twelve billion? Twelve billion's a death sentence." He raised his can of beer—his third—and tilted back a large swallow. A talking head swilling beer is not useful video. I could eliminate the beer in editing by cutting away to b-roll, but I'd much prefer making editing decisions by choice rather than necessity.

I paused the recording. "Let's try it without the beer, huh?"

"Eddie used to say I drink like a thirsty horse," he chuckled, surrendering the half-drained can. "I take care of my empties with my guns and drop acid every New Year's Day whether I need to or not. Heh-heh." It could have been Keith Richards laughing.

I set the can on an end table just out of his reach. We resumed shooting, and he picked up right where he had left off.

"People won't do something hard. What they need is something easy, something that allows them to keep doing pretty much what they're already doing and lets them off the hook.

And another thing is," he paused and laughed, "another thing is, I gotta take a leak."

He lit a cigarette while I helped him get free of the microphone wire, then off he went. From the bathroom came the sound of his gravelly voice softly singing, then a fit of hacking so rough it could have been a garbage disposal, then more singing.

"Goddam cigarettes," he grumbled, making his way to the kitchen. "What I need is a phlegm-cutter. Beer just don't do the job." From the cupboard he pulled a bottle of Wild Turkey. "Whiskey on the other hand is a phlegm-cutter of note, a phlegm-cutter extraordinaire, a phlegm-cutter worthy of immortalization in a Petrarchan sonnet." He held up an empty juice glass and while looking my way rocked it side to side—did I care to join him? I shook my head, and he poured the glass half full and threw it down in a gulp, wincing at the burn.

"Ready?" I asked.

Back in the chair and miked up, he lit another cigarette.

"You know about the UN climate change conferences?" he asked, waving his hand to extinguish the match. "They meet every year like clockwork—since '95. Gather in lovely places—Paris, Milan, Sharm El Sheikh. And by gather, I mean fly in from the ends of the earth—twenty, twenty-five thousand of 'em, staying almost two weeks in fine hotels, eating fine food, and talk, talk, talking about how to save the planet. And in twenty-some odd years of all this high-class diplomatic chin-wagging,

you know how many times they've brought up the subject of
population control?"

He paused and pulled on the cigarette. I figured it was a
rhetorical question, but as he exhaled, he fixed me in his gaze.
"Well?"

"I don't know. How many times?"

"Let me put it this way. For each time they broached the
subject I'd be happy to give you my left testicle." This got him
laughing and the laughing set off another hacking spell.

The interview was going beautifully. Tozer's rap poured out
of him like music out of Mozart.

When the coughing stopped, he took up the challenges
and benefits of reducing the population. He described the
thorny political obstacles that would have to be addressed and
detailed practical measures for doing so. It was an impromptu
graduate-level seminar. I had conducted hundreds of interviews
and learned that the ratio of usable to unusable material is
depressingly low. Not so with the silver-tongued Mr. Tozer.

After more than an hour he shifted in his seat, raised his
arms, and had himself a good stretch. "Somebody has to pay
the piper," he said in a tone that suggested he was summing
up. "It's gonna get squeezed out of you and me and the rest of
us alive right now or—or, or, or—or we charge it to people
not born yet. Cutting population is the least painful option.
Sure, we do everything we can to cut back on emissions, add
renewable energy, all that stuff—and lo and behold, the net
effect is multiplied—multiplied—by the amount we decrease
the population. Comprende? It's not only our best hope, but
our simplest." He reflected on what he had just declared and
chuckled. "Remember, I said simple, not easy."

I felt the tingle, the unmistakable thrill of knowing I'd just shot stellar material. In this one session I had gathered the bones of an outstanding documentary. There was no doubt in my mind that Tozer had just given me what would probably be the punchiest lines in the film—and maybe the finale. Even better, I had my title: *Simple, Not Easy.*

That's when things started going downhill fast. After he'd tossed down a second glass of whiskey, Tozer's whole demeanor took on a snarling edge. He drank more beer. He smoked some weed. I tried to keep him in his seat, but he flashed a look that said any attempt to rein him in would be futile, if not dangerous. I'd been around mean drunks before.

When he'd sufficiently fortified himself, he plopped back in the chair and called out, "Roll tape," then broke into a too-hearty laugh, a heavy fog of bong smoke pouring from his nostrils.

I fed him a question. He rambled, boasted, free-associated, slurred his words. His earlier brilliance was now overshadowed, dulled by a bitter cynicism. I tried to keep him on track, asked him to clarify, to amplify, but he could only manage to string together a few trenchant lines or get halfway into a complex thought before losing the thread. Maybe I could use some of it— hope springs ridiculously eternal when a subject is in my frame. Unfortunately, I had broken the most basic rule of production: never lose control.

Enough was enough. I told him we were through. Tozer said he had a few more points he wanted to make. When I held firm, he flew into a rage, ripped off the microphone, stomped into the kitchen, and cursed me as he poured more Wild Turkey. I packed up my gear as fast as I could and got the hell out of there.

On the long drive home through the shimmering desert, I thought about the shoot. What I had in the camera was a decently photographed interview of a colorful, crusty, and highly intelligent desert rat, part Old Testament prophet, part twenty-first century eco-visionary. Plus, he was one of Ed Abbey's cronies from the old days—the value of this connection couldn't be underestimated. In America, fame has long coattails.

But the fact remained: famous or not, Tozer was a jerk. Did I want to associate myself with someone so unstable, a drunk who could embarrass himself in so many ways? And what were the chances he'd hate the documentary or try to control it? I'd heard nightmare stories about disgruntled subjects declaring war on a finished documentary, saying damning things to undermine it or the integrity of the filmmaker or even going so far as to bring a lawsuit.

I didn't need the headache. Some things just don't pan out. Best to cut my losses. Another opportunity would come along. For an angry moment I wanted to trash the Tozer footage, put the whole distasteful experience behind me. But documentary filmmakers are packrats by nature—I've never let go of a single frame I've shot—so I archived the interview, believing that, who knows, someday it just might come in handy.

That day arrived more than ten years after the day I had spent with Hollis Fanshaw Tozer, now long dead from lung cancer.

Following a few lean years in L.A., I had moved to Portland, Oregon, and was working hard on an equally lean career punctuated by a few small successes with documentaries, the work that fed my soul. To pay the rent, I did commercial work out of my one-man video production studio and had a semi-steady gig teaching at a junior college.

On a sunny Saturday morning I got an email from my good friend Kaz Takahashi, a virtuoso musician and terrific composer who I'd collaborated with on many projects, telling me he'd read about a new contest, something called the Pemberton Prizes. "Nice money," he wrote.

"Got anything to enter?"

I poured myself a cup of coffee and clicked on the link Kaz had provided. The contest website described how Portland native A.J. Pemberton had made a pile of money in technology and now wanted to give back, his philanthropy taking the form of twenty-four prizes of $10,000 each to artists coming up with "creative responses to today's changing world." There were four categories for film and video. I lingered over one of these, Problem Solving, and the wheels of my imagination began to turn.

Any other problem would pale in comparison to global warming. And if anybody was offering a creative response, it was Tozer. In the years since our interview, the many threats of climate change had become better understood, the problems it posed were now far more immediate, more frightening, more urgent. Tozer's ideas were more important than ever. Sure, others had laid out many of the ideas in his plan before, but no one else had synthesized them into a coherent whole, a workable strategy that could literally reboot the world. His folksy charisma and deep understanding would appeal as much to eco-warriors and policy wonks as to Joe and Jane Sixpack. And I already had the footage.

What about my competition? Any film addressing a problem other than climate change would be at a distinct disadvantage— what other topic could possibly check the boxes as well?

Would another global warming doc stack up against the one I could create? Surely no other videographer would have anything like a Tozer to spring on the world. And without a Tozer . . . so many other responses to the crisis were long on handwringing and arm-flapping and woefully short on practical remedies. The answers that were offered invariably pointed down a few well-trodden paths: renewable energy, electric vehicles, phasing out coal-fired power plants, planting trees. Yes, Tozer said, of course, do all that, but population control would catalyze, accelerate, and vastly increase the power and effectiveness of every one of those other efforts.

Another cup of coffee was called for. As I poured it, I paused when confronted with the memory of why I had abandoned the Tozer documentary the first time around. Presenting him as a latter-day prophet would be at best a half-truth. Anyone viewing all the raw footage would surely slam the film as an out-and-out misrepresentation. The fact that he was now dead didn't mean that some damning bit might not come to light, some outrageous thing he'd said or written, something that would expose his size-sixteen feet of clay. And if that happened, I'd look like a dupe, or worse, a liar.

With all this this fretting about one small part of Tozer's credibility, reliability, whatever, I wondered if I might be falling prey to what Werner Herzog called the accountant's truth. My crazy patron saint of documentaries railed against the slavish adherence to superficial facts, decried stories so straitjacketed in the accurate, the mundane, the obvious that they had no life. Instead, Herzog used imagination, fabrication, artifice to chase higher, poetic, ecstatic truths. He opened one of his docs with a stirring, tone-setting quotation from Blaise Pascal, "The collapse of the stellar universe will occur—like creation—in grandiose splendor." Only Pascal never said that. In a singular, brilliant, and stupendous act of artistic bravado, Herzog just made it up.

Maybe I too could play a little looser. Why not? No one would see the raw footage of Tozer—I could make sure of that. Plus, winning the Pemberton Prize would give my career a much-needed boost. And then there was the prize money.

Well … good enough for Werner, good enough for me. I chuckled aloud at this, knowing even then that it was something of a rationalization. Still, it got me over the hump. Forget the complications; think about the doors that might fly open.

Dear Mr. Ken Burns, As the recent recipient of the Pemberton Prize for my documentary *Simple, Not Easy*, I was hoping we could meet to discuss … Fantasies aside, I considered the very real challenges of creating the documentary itself.

The through line. The materials I already had and those I would need to gather. A rough production timeline. A ballpark budget. It's easy to make a film that looks like a million bucks if you spend that much. I would need to rely on my ability to make a great looking film on half a shoestring.

It took many months, a swimming pool of strong coffee, long days, and longer nights. The result: *Simple, Not Easy*, which, by attaching a long, slow credit-roll at the end, I was able to stretch to a total running time of 60:07—enough to satisfy the hour-long requirement of the Pemberton competition and give a nod to James Bond.

Yaz Takahashi composed a stunning soundtrack. I used his bass-heavy piece "Dark and Foreboding, Part IV" to rumble ominously beneath the doc's one-shot, 39-second opening sequence—referred to in my shot-sheet shorthand as CUA, for Chinese urban apocalypse. I found the footage on the internet and obtained permission from the Beijing Film Academy student who had photographed and posted it. The beautifully compressed, long-lens image begins with tens of thousands of bustling sweat-soaked Chinese pedestrians on a densely packed sidewalk trudging through hazy, heat-shimmering air, many wearing white surgical masks over their noses and mouths. The camera slowly zooms out, revealing a grand boulevard, six lanes of cars, vans, delivery trucks, and motorbikes idling in fume-belching gridlock. The frame widens still further to take in a sprawling city hellscape baking under a late-afternoon sun. More reversezoom brings in a horizon line of industrial plants boiling smoke and steam into a sick rustcolored sky. Roll title and opening credits.

Having set the dire and portentous mood, I amped the tension even higher with a two minute fright-fest establishing the timeline of doom should global warming continue unabated: hundreds of millions of climate refugees, tens of millions of deaths from droughts, flooding, famine, and other planetary retributions.

Enter Tozer. Following a brief introduction, the remainder of the doc followed point for point the key elements of his arguments, cutting between his analysis, supporting graphics, secondary interviews, and b-roll. One segment drew a brief history of the Chinese single-child experiment. Another raised and addressed ethical issues, ending with an international development guru drawing a stark distinction between old-style eugenics and modern population control measures based on the agency, education, and economic empowerment of women.

A series of graphics illustrated the shocking amount of greenhouse gas generated over the lifetime of a typical American consumer and how it expands exponentially with his or her offspring, their offspring, and each successive generation. This segues into a contrast of the carbon footprint of an urban American child today with that of a kid on a subsistence farm in Bangladesh. Then the payoff: the skyrocketing populations of Africa and Asia, the rapidly rising standards of living in these areas, and the projected alarming consequences for the planet—by themselves and, even more frighteningly, when added to the already staggering and still growing damage inflicted by more developed countries.

Add horrific visual images—melting ice sheets, raging fires, Amazon deforestation, and then-and-now satellite imagery (obtained at zero cost from NASA and NOAA). Blend all ingredients together with Yaz's killer soundtrack. Season with the piquant spice of Tozer's barnyard phrasings and the narrator's this-is-how-millions-will-die voice—et voila.

Tozer was on screen or heard in voiceover for one third of the doc. My film school professors would object to this as overreliance on a single source, but they had never met Tozer. He deserved every second he got, this wild man savant who would eliminate billions of humans and potentially save humanity from planetary holocaust without plague, science fiction miracle, or the shedding of a single drop of blood.

I submitted the completed documentary along with the required mountain of paperwork including artist's statement and photo—me in a leather jacket, long curly hair, aviator sunglasses—to the Pemberton Prize competition a good forty-eight hours before the deadline. Two months later I got a phone call letting me know I had won. It was the call that changed my life.

On the night when *Simple, Not Easy* premiered, a dozen friends and I gathered at an Irish pub in downtown Portland. We drank and laughed. After a few rounds, Yaz clapped his hands to get everyone's attention over the barroom bustle. In his herringbone cabbie hat, he stroked his wispy beard and made a

toast that was, thank God, short and sweet (like Yaz himself).
It was time to go. We got our coats and headed outside into a
gently misting rain.

The bunch of us cheerfully ambled the over wet sidewalks
reflecting light from signs and stores and cars in glowing streaks.
Rounding a corner, we came to the Odeon, a gloriously restored
velvet-and-gilt movie palace from the 1920s. The theater's
marquee was huge and bright and ringed with twinkling bulbs.

ECO FILM FEST

THE COVE - WED

KOYAANISQATSI - THU

AN INCONVENIENT TRUTH - FRI

SIMPLE, NOT EASY - SAT (PREMIER)

My friends gave a little cheer, patted my shoulder, clicked
pictures. I was overcome, humbled to see *Simple, Not Easy* up on
the marquee with Academy Award winners, films I'd studied in
film school and after.

At the ticket booth, the tattooed goth kid behind the glass
told us to go right in and said, "Your seats have little card
thingies that say 'reserved.'"

We made our way through the lobby's overwhelming
popcorn smell and pushed open the big padded doors into the
cavernous auditorium. Our seats were in two rows, one behind
the other. I did what was necessary to be social, smiling, laughing
at jokes, quipping back at quips delivered, but I also kept an eye
on the crowd. The theater was mostly full, and people were still
filing in with a few minutes remaining before showtime.

My eyes ran across the expanse of the blank white screen,
marveling at its size. Over the years, I'd seen hundreds of films
here, retrospectives of auteurs and lesser directors, actors well
known and obscure, genres highbrow and low, foreign films,

festivals of animation, a million documentaries, midnight grindhouse marathons. The toil and sweat of people I considered gods.

The house lights dimmed. Screen black, Kaz's soundtrack booming through the theater's first-class PA system. With the opening visual sequence, I took in a sharp breath. I'd only seen my film on desktop editing monitors, and here it was on a movie palace screen, images towering thirty feet tall.

The perfectionist in me soon became fixated on the film's many flaws, pesky as aggressive hornets. Focus and composition problems, lens flares, mic noise, bits of muddy audio (that we could never clean up no matter how many equalizers Yaz ran it through), TMI graphics, jerky animations—the sickening parade of technical errors that had bedeviled me during production and forced one distasteful compromise after another.

At each cringeworthy glitch I braced myself for the laughter, sniggers, hoots, or derisive comments from the crowd. None came. I looked around and much to my surprise saw all eyes focused intently on the screen. I let out a sigh of relief.

Now relaxed, I was able to dispassionately observe the hundreds of discrete elements I had created and collected and edited together into a unified whole. I felt like one magician watching another's performance, analyzing how the tricks are constructed, the artistry of the illusion. When the closing credits rolled, all I could think was, How did I make it all work? The thought was interrupted when the clapping started, then the whistles, the stomping, the cheers.

Afterward, in the lobby, I was briefly mobbed. People wanted to congratulate me, shake my hand, say nice things about my film. I noticed someone waiting patiently at the periphery of the small crowd, a tall skinny-necked young guy, maybe twenty-three or twenty-four. As the well-wishers thinned out, he stepped forward.

"Clifford," he said, extending his hand. We shook. "I'm a volunteer for Mim Donahoe."

I couldn't imagine even the slightest connection between me and Mim Donahoe, a candidate in the upcoming US presidential election.

"Your movie, which I thought was awesome, is perfectly in sync with Mim—she's totally progressive, all about new ideas," he said in a rush. "Would you mind if I passed your name along to my coordinator at the campaign office? I mean, well, unless— you're not like voting for the other candidate or anything, are you?"

I told him to pass my name along to anybody he wanted and assured him that I'd be voting his way. A few days later I got a call from Cher Insmoor, a senior staffer with the Oregon Committee to Elect Donahoe.

"We're excited about Mim making a campaign stop in Portland," she said, speaking fast over an echoing cell phone connection that sounded like she was in an airport or a busy restaurant. "At her rallies across the country, Mim celebrates local people doing good work. It's an inclusivity thing—part of her New Ideas platform."

I was beginning to see where this conversation might be headed. "Mim would like to call you out at the rally, congratulate you for winning the Pemberton Prize and hold up your film as an example of the kind of thinking that can lead us into what she calls the Extraordinary Years—another key element of her platform, as you probably know from our ad campaign."

I had some vague memory of seeing an ad touting Donahoe and New Ideas but nothing about extraordinary anything had made its way into my consciousness.

"Is population control part of her platform?" I asked.

"She's very strong on climate change—the need to take meaningful action. What matters here is the optics—roots in the local community, appreciating the hard work of ordinary Americans—all key concepts for Mim."

The night of the rally came. Yaz and I presented ourselves at a special VIP door of the Schnitzer Auditorium, a large downtown performance hall. I flashed my ID and got us through the first and second security perimeters and to yet another staffer who looked over my credentials and tapped keys on her laptop. She passed us to an usher who led us into the auditorium crammed with a sea of boisterous Mim supporters and down to a cordoned-off area of a few hundred seats in the center of the main floor.

We sat and looked at our fellow VIPs. "Fat cat donors and local politicos riding the Mim train," Kaz said.

The night's festivities were pretty much what I expected from a bigtime political rally— music and lights and a couple of lead-in speakers and then the main event.

Mim Donahoe took the stage and basked in a seemingly endless standing ovation. Finally, she held up her hands to quiet the crowd and launched into a rousing speech that kept hitting on her campaign theme. New ideas about the economy and new ideas about health care— the same for gun control, immigration, race relations, international relations, infrastructure, student debt, and on and on. She came across as friendly, smart, and capable.

Her talk changed into more of a pep rally as she built to a crescendo, one I could tell she'd built to many times before. "My opponent is the very face of the status quo. Old, worn out, tired, stale. I am the candidate of new ideas. And these ideas will lead us into extraordinary times, extraordinary years. The choice is yours. The choice is critical. The choice is now. And the choice is up to you."

The audience went nuts. Now that she had the mesmerized masses eating out of her hand, she started giving these little shout-outs to people she said were doing great things—a lot of people, one after another. A rhythm developed, a sort of name-checking call and response between Mim and the audience. She called out a name and that person rose and waved in a spotlight's beam while she highlighted their work. The audience cheered and quickly quieted, allowing Mim to rapidly work through her list of local heroes: an elementary school teacher whose class grew vegetables for a food bank, a guy who built low-cost tiny houses for homeless people, a professor who came up with a way to remove hydroelectric dams without lowering energy production, a businessman who created companies to employ people with disabilities.

"And finally, I'm especially pleased to have filmmaker Luke Mayfield with us tonight," Mim announced. Yaz elbowed me and I stood. It was heady, there with the spotlight and all eyes on me. What she said about the film is a blur, but I do remember the enthusiastic smile on her face as she locked eyes on me and gave me a thumbs up and a "Congratulations, Luke." I thought to myself, holy crap, this is Mim Donahoe, possibly the next president of the United States. Thousands of people cheered and clapped wildly. I'll tell you straight up, it felt good.

After our ride-share Prius dropped off Yaz and rolled toward my apartment, I decided to check my social media. The screen of my phone lit up the back seat's sand-colored upholstery with a soft glow. Three new posts popped up from people I didn't know. The first: "Congrats on yr movie! Sounds brllnt! Cant wait 2 C!!!" The second: "Only New Ideas can get us out of this mess. I'm all in with Mim. Together we can do this." And the third: "You are such a puppet--No climate prob. No population prob. All lies of power elite globalists. Quit carrying their water you sleazoid dirtbag ASSHOL"

Back at my apartment I turned on the TV and toggled between the local eleven o'clock news and CNN. Neither was saying anything about Mim's rally, so I checked my laptop for trending stories. One entry caught my eye, "Ruckelshaus takes swipe at Mim's support of pop. control." A link took me to some shaky cellphone footage of the other party's candidate, Texas Senator Bruce "Bucky" Ruckelshaus, taken as he was stepping up into his campaign bus. Someone in the crowd of reporters shouts out an inaudible question and Ruckelshaus pauses from his elevated perch in the bus's doorway.

"Yes, I just heard about that," he says, a disapproving scowl on his beefy face. "Let me say this: she's endorsing this fringe film that advocates for all sorts of radical nonsense." He shakes his head while more inaudible words come from someone off camera. The comment makes Ruckelshaus smile. "Yes, absolutely. I think it shows clearly just how out of step she is with the American people." He gave a candidate smile and a candidate wave and slipped into the bus.

For the next hour I watched the clip spread like wildfire to national news sites across the internet. A CNN reporter embedded with the Ruckelshaus campaign filed a brief follow-up interview with the candidate on the roaring bus. The camera was shaky, and the audio was so bad it was difficult to hear, but what came through was a withering attack on Mim for endorsing my film, at one point calling it "a downright un-American attempt to undermine our most cherished and hard-fought freedoms."

Donahoe's campaign responded by issuing a short statement that Mim was looking forward to talking about this and all other issues on Friday in Chicago at the debate.

I looked at my social media—147 new comments. Each was heatedly pro or con, the overwhelming majority of the "sleazoid dirtbag ASSHOL" variety, though many were quite a bit more graphic.

While I was reading a post that included the phrase "rip your eyes out," the phone rang and I jumped. I didn't recognize the number or the caller's name and probably shouldn't have answered, but I did.

"Is this Luke Mayfield?"

"Yes," I said, ready to hang up if the insults started to fly.

"Chelsea Zebeida. I'm with Mim Donahoe's national campaign staff in New York." She spoke fast like she might be a native. I hesitated to respond, as she might or might not be who she said she was. "I know you talked with Cher Insmoor out in Oregon."

My tensed muscles relaxed. I looked at the clock—on the East Coast it would be past 3 a.m.

"Did you hear about the Ruckelshaus attack?" she asked.

"Yeah, I saw it. My social media exploded—and not in a good way."

"Getting involved with a campaign can bring . . . unwanted attention."

"Am I involved?"

She laughed like that was a joke. "We really need to be proactive—prepared."

"Right. Sounds good," I said, having no idea what she was talking about.

"We want you to be ready for what might occur—as things move forward. There will be some digging into your background."

"Oh?"

"I could put this more diplomatically, but we really don't have the time, so here's the blunt version: Is there anything in your past we should know about?"

I hadn't expected this and instinctively recoiled, resenting the scrutiny. At the same time,

I understood why she had to ask. "Nothing much."

"No arrests, DUIs, drugs? Girlfriend problems? No nanny you're paying under the table?"

She paused and I felt like I was supposed to blurt out some horrible secret. "A couple of parking tickets. A car accident, but it was the other guy's fault."

"Our people are already checking you out. It would save a lot of time if you told me—"

"No, no skeletons. Is all this really necessary? I just made the film."

"Unfortunately, at this level, it is necessary. Next question: do you have an agent?"

"No, I never really needed one."

She didn't speak for a long time, long enough that I knew I hadn't given the right answer, long enough that I started to think she might be rolling her eyes at the bumpkin lacking in even the most basic understanding of how the game is played.

"You'll be getting calls, I'm telling you—TV, interviews. You need an agent. Get one." She paused again—apparently the conversation wasn't going anywhere until I acknowledged hearing her message loud and clear.

"I can do that."

I felt strangely grateful to her—for calling, for giving me a break from the angry internet trolls, for the advice about the agent. I wanted to give her something in return.

"You know, Chelsea, the responses I'm getting on social media, really ugly—there's a lot of pissed-off people out there. And now with Ruckelshaus making a big deal out of it—have you thought that Mim associating herself with my film might, you know, hurt what she's trying to do?"

"Are you being concerned?" she said. I could almost see her smile, almost hear her say that's so cute.

"We're counting on the controversy," she said. "Our polling ranks climate change as a top-five concern—worth six, maybe seven points among undecided voters. Ruckelshaus is soft on the environment, so we've got ourselves a wedge issue."

"I see."

"We'll take care of the campaign; you just worry about you. We'll be in touch."

She hung up. Off to what, more 3 a.m. campaign calls?

I checked social media again—385 messages.

After making some calls the next morning to people I knew who had agents, I had the name of a guy, Mickey Meyer. He was supposed to be well connected, energetic, and likeable. Along with the usual image, branding, and career development skills, he also had a familiarity with film distribution. And a big plus, he had an office in downtown Portland. If I was going to have an agent, I wanted somebody who I could talk with face to face.

I called Mickey, he said he'd like to meet immediately and asked me to send over some photos of myself. It was just after noon when I found his address at a well-kept 1930s office building dripping with charm. I rode a rickety elevator to the fourth floor.

Mickey was older than the energetic voice I heard on the telephone led me to expect, closer to sixty than fifty. He was a small guy with a head of neatly trimmed graying hair and green-gold eyes that made him look at once kindly and intense. He gestured for me to sit in a chair on the opposite side of his tidy desk and asked a lot of questions rapid-fire—about the film, about my involvement with Mim, my background and career. He made a few notes and seemed satisfied with my responses.

"And just to be explicit," he said, "you have full ownership of all rights related to the film and there are no encumbrances of any kind that would limit my ability to promote it in any way. Is that right?"

"Correct."

He jotted another note. "Good, that's good." He interlaced the fingers of his hands and looked into my eyes. "You're an artist," he said. "And if you are like a lot of artists I know— artists I represent—your top priority might not be putting a lot of effort into your brand."

I laughed. "Packaging myself has definitely not been a top priority."

"Okay, so here's my question to you. In a perfect world, what would you do? With all the money, all the freedom you wanted, what would you do?"

I didn't need a lot of time to think that one out. "I'd make documentaries. That's what

I'm good at, what I love."

"Good, good. That's just where I come in," Mickey said, resting his hand on his heart. "In today's market you can't just sit in your studio and make your movies. I hate to break it to you, but that's ancient history. Now you need to be out there, available to the public, cultivating your followers, communicating with your fans. I'll handle that for you. I'll manage it—your branding, your platforming—the enchilada. I'll push you where you wouldn't push yourself.

Push-push-push, that's Mickey. We make you the biggest success we can, and then," he waved his index finger through the air, "then you'll have the freedom to do what you want."

He took a contract from a folder on his desk and handed it to me. "Here's the paperwork.

Standard stuff, standard percentages—I'm twelve and a half percent. I have an associate, Gretchen Caldwell. A sweetheart. She'll be working with us. She's hourly—but reasonable and worth every penny. You'll like her. Have your lawyer look this over. Get it back to me as soon as you can. Okay?"

"Got it." I expected him to hand me the contract, but he held it just out of my reach.

"Before we get started, I just want to ask, just want to make sure—are you ready for this? I mean the commitment. Because the kind of work I do, it only succeeds if the client—that would be you—is committed."

"Sure. I'm in," I said. What else could I say? No, Mickey, the idea of being promoted like toothpaste makes my stomach churn. Besides, I figured I had already burned about thirteen and a half minutes of my fifteen minutes of fame. "We're a team."

"Okay," he smiled in a way that reminded me of a kid getting a new toy. "Time's too precious to wait on your lawyer. We shake and it's a deal, all right?"

I put out my hand and we shook. "You won't be sorry," he said, passing me the contract. "Now first things first. Today you're hot, but things change. They change fast." He made a knowing shrug as if he'd had the experience before and not much liked it. "So we gotta move faster. You know about Zulu?"

"Sure," I said, surprised and intrigued by the question. "A low-cost pay-per-view service—movies, sports. A couple nights ago I used it to watch a concert."

"Exactly. The beauty of Zulu is that it's basically a buck-a-pop format—with a 70/30 split. A thousand people watch your movie, we're talking seven hundred for you. This is gross.

Remember that and you won't be disappointed. Any objections I give them a call?"

I shook my head, impressed. It would never have occurred to me to hook up with Zulu.

"Good. Everything works out, you'll be getting a call for the digital file of the film."

I was blown away. An hour of talking with Mickey and suddenly I felt like I wasn't in this thing alone anymore. He was now a part of what I was doing. A big part. I had always thought of myself as being above all the brand management bullshit that everyone said was so important. I saw now it was time for me to get past the luxury of disdain, time to roll with it.

But like some law of emotional physics, for every positive feeling there seems to be an equal and opposite pang. Just as I was joyfully shifting the burden of my career's management to Mickey, I had the sudden urge to hold on as tightly as I could to anything I could still control. My mind filled with horror stories of old-time jazz musicians and rock bands getting swindled out of the rights to their music, of studios butchering directors' films.

"One thing, Mickey," I said, "I need to retain final decision-making power about the film.

I need to be in charge. With Zulu, with any deals you cut, I get final say."

He looked at me like he'd never heard such nonsense. "You know that'll cost you." I tried to look resolute.

"Say I'm negotiating," Mickey said, "and I tell the nice lady, 'Oh yeah, Luke Mayfield needs final say, total artistic control.' And what does the nice lady say? She says, 'Sure Mickey, no problem. But that changes things a little, doesn't it? I'll need to knock a couple of points off the split—maybe a lot of points.'" Mickey's face pinched as if watching those points fly out the window. "You see what I'm getting at?"

"I don't care. Call it an insurance policy."

"What are you, Allstate?"

"I just need it."

"There's a lot of things you don't need when you've got money."

I wasn't about to cave. We were arguing over a percentage of money that at this point was purely hypothetical and, as far as I could tell, had little chance of ever materializing. "Just this one thing, that's all I ask."

He shook his head. "I want you to remember this, Mickey does not agree. I want this duly noted."

"Of course."

"If you insist on retaining control, I suppose I can weave that . . . high-mindedness—as much as I might disagree with it—I can weave it into your brand." His head rocked side to side meditatively. "It ups your artistic credibility. You're some kind of purist. Yeah, I can work with that. Sure, I like it. Okay. Done." He made a note on his pad of paper and underlined it.

"Next up: two days from now is the debate. A huge opportunity. I'll book some time at a TV studio for after-debate interviews. There will be plenty of requests—from all over. And we want to give each one its own slot. Make them feel special."

I knew what TV studio time costs and was about to ask if there might be a less expensive alternative.

"Don't even think about Zoom. Mickey will not let you look like garbage and sound like you're in an oil drum. No, no, no." His fingers danced on his keyboard with remarkable speed.

"There," he said, hitting the send command with a flourish. "I just sent you the studio's address. It'll be worth it, trust me. Be there before the debate, we'll watch it together. I'll send you some talking points."

I could tell he was ready for me to leave, but I had one more question. I felt a little embarrassed, but he was now my imagemaker, so I asked. "If I'm going to be interviewed, do you think I should . . . get my hair cut?" The longer it gets the wilder it looks, and it was currently about as long as I ever let it grow.

"Cut?" Mickey said, almost in disbelief. "Are you kidding me? No! Don't touch it. The long hair—and the sunglasses, like in that one picture you sent." He was talking about the pair of goofy aviators that I bought as a joke after seeing Tom Cruise wearing the same ones in *Top Gun*. "It's a good look, casual—like Spielberg." He chuckled. "But the hair? Long hair says artistic genius. And artistic genius I can promote. No, no, no, please, do not cut those beautiful locks. The hair, the glasses—it's you."

It was so cut and dried, so calculating, I had to laugh. "Is that how it works?"

"Image is like the radio," he said. "We send, they receive."

Outside on the downtown sidewalk it was as if I'd just gotten off some dizzying amusement park ride. I adjusted to the flat, stable surface, but something inside me still swirled with the thrill of the speed, the sharp turns, the disorienting loop de loop.

I arrived at the TV studio and the receptionist, a guy with the looks of a *High Fidelity*-era John Cusack, escorted me to a sitting room furnished with a pair of sofas, some chairs, and a large flat screen TV mounted on the wall. I was grateful when young Cusack brought me a paper cup of ginger tea that I sipped while worrying about how the interviews might go and reading and rereading the talking points Mickey and Gretchen had scripted for me.

Mickey burst in. "I got news, news you're going to want to hear." He waved a sheet of paper. "This is the latest from Zulu. And it wasn't easy to get, let me tell you. Our fine partners only post their numbers weekly, Saturday night at midnight. But I was insistent. And when Mickey insists—" He wiggled his eyebrows and laughed. "You don't need the sausage-making but look at this." He handed me the paper, a spreadsheet full of numbers in columns. He snapped his finger against the bottom right side of the page where a figure was circled in neon yellow highlighter: 17,156.38.

I had a guess as to what it might mean but waited for him to explain.

"Yes, dollars," he said, beaming. "Seventeen thousand of them. For you. These are rough figures—subject to some change. And gross. I'm telling you, these are gross figures—don't forget that. But still," he held his hands wide and smiled broadly, "not bad for a day and a half, eh?"

I stared at him, speechless. Kaz and I had watched my film on Zulu the first hour it was available—and turned it off after twenty minutes. Money or no money, seeing it on my studio monitor was a letdown compared to seeing it on the Odeon's monster screen.

"Am I through yet? No, I am not." Mickey was enjoying himself so much I almost expected him to do a happy dance. "As of about forty-five minutes ago we have a deal for showing the film on screens in some towns you might have heard of: New York, Los Angeles, Chicago, Houston, and DC."

I couldn't believe what I was hearing. "In theaters?"

"The box office, meh." He extended his hand and tilted it first left then right. "Five screens is not *Star Wars*. But still, five is five more than we had this morning."

Zulu was one thing, but now Mickey had my doc screening in America's biggest cities where thousands of moviegoers would watch my film. I was searching for words to express my elation when I noticed the candidates on the TV screen, walking across the stage, waving to the audience.

They took their places at a pair of lecterns facing the debate moderator, Jasmine Peliakov of the PBS *News Hour*. Ruckelshaus wore a dark suit with a tasteful but subdued necktie, likely chosen to avoid drawing attention to his overly ample neck—not his most telegenic feature. Mim Donahoe had

on a similarly understated business suit, given a little flair with
a silk blouse of a green shade that brought out the color in her
eyes.

About forty-five minutes into the hour-long event, they
got into a tedious tussle over the Federal Reserve's monetary
policy, surely putting thousands of viewers to sleep. Mickey was
diddling with his phone, uninterested in the candidates dickering
about stimulating the economy through a quarter-point drop in
the interest rate.

That's when the moderator said, "Let's turn now to the
climate crisis."

I nudged Mickey, and he lowered his phone. "Scientists
have warned that we are facing a disaster of unprecedented
magnitude. Please describe your position on this truly global
challenge. Ms. Donahoe, let's begin with you."

"My campaign is based on new ideas leading us forward into
an extraordinary future by addressing the pressing issues of our
time—including climate change." She came out strong on the
issue, made her points smoothly and succinctly—and didn't say a
word about my film.

Mickey frowned. I hadn't spent enough time with him to
know if this expression meant he assessed our exclusion as a
minor setback or if he thought our ship had just rammed into an
iceberg. The camera now focused on Ruckelshaus.

"Climate change is one of the most profoundly important
issues of our time," he said, his Texas accent smoothing the edges
of his words. "My administration will move aggressively on every
front to address this challenge—for our children and for our
future."

Mickey was still looking glum and I thought I might try to cheer him up, so I made a talking-hand gesture and said, "Blah-blah-blah." He forced a smile, but it left as quickly as it came.

Then Ruckelshaus cut loose. "What the American people need to think about is how the two candidates on this stage differ fundamentally in our thinking about climate change. Just a few days ago, my opponent endorsed a remedy for the climate crisis so shockingly outrageous I think we should pause to consider it."

Both of us sat up, eyes fixed on the screen. Ruckelshaus leaned forward with the steely eyes of a predator going in for the kill.

"She wants government dictating limits on the number of children we have. She wants to depopulate the earth. She wants to hand our future to some global government over which we Americans will have little if any control. Euthanasia. Mass abortion. Global redistribution of wealth. And why? All in the service of her fuzzy-headed notion of a better tomorrow. We the people know better than that. We know that lurking behind this radical agenda is a plan for social engineering on a scale never before seen in human history." He shook his head in disgust. "So much for her new ideas."

Mickey leapt to his feet, fingering his telephone as he rose. Mim knew it was coming, was well prepared. In her rebuttal, she sounded moderate and sensible, reviewed the facts, refuted his most egregious misrepresentations. But it didn't matter. Ruckelshaus had landed the zinger. The media couldn't resist a snarling attack, and his would be shown and reshown on a hundred news programs, dissected in thousands of newspaper stories, endlessly analyzed by expert panels on cable news shows. Social media would blow up in a hundred different ways.

My phone vibrated—Chelsea Zebeida.

"The ante just went up," she said. "Way up."

"How bad is it?"

"Ruckelshaus looked at the same wedge issue we did, only he's calculating it will energize his base more than it will cost him swing voters. He's forcing the issue, going all in. Journalists on Twitter are eating up the conflict, playing it up like a high-noon showdown, six guns blazing. So strap in, partner, everything just got real clear."

As soon as the debate ended, Mickey hustled me into the studio. I sat under the hot lights, the little earpiece allowing me to hear the questions from interviewers I couldn't see. What I could see was Mickey in the control booth, pacing back and forth, talking, talking, talking on his phone, his other hand waving in the air. He'd emerge between my interviews, phone still clamped to his ear, making sure my clothes looked right, fixing my hair, offering me a small bottle of water. I went through four of those water bottles during the next few hours without a single trip to the restroom. I lost count of the number of interviews at thirteen and gave many after that. When there were no more reporters, no more questions to answer, Mickey trudged into the studio looking as exhausted and bedraggled as I felt.

We shuffled back to the sitting room and collapsed on the sofa. CNN was on the big screen, muted. A panel of pundits talked with great animation while the video intermittently cut away to Ruckelshaus delivering his carefully scripted beat down.

"You okay?" he asked.

I was too wrung out to know just how wrung out I was, so I just laughed. "You?"

"Oh," he coughed into his hand, "working on a few things. Nothing definite. You'll be the first to hear."

And the next morning while I was still in bed, I did hear. I pawed at my groggy eyes and got the ringing phone from the nightstand. "Yeah, Mickey, what's up?"

"A little movie called *Simple, Not Easy* is now booked to show on 200 screens nationwide."

"You're kidding?"

"International distribution is trickier. Lawyers like you wouldn't believe. I'm working it, but it might take a little time."

The more the candidates ripped and gouged and clawed at each other, the more the media liked it. The cover of *Time* magazine framed the confrontation as "The War Over Warming." The accompanying story read in part: "Never in recent memory has a single issue risen to such prominence and split voters so decisively into opposing camps. It harkens back to the antiwar candidate George McGovern vying against Richard Nixon at the height of the conflict in Vietnam."

Ruckelshaus hammered at Mim's stance on climate change and relentlessly attacked her support of my film. The strategy not only played to his traditional base, but it united them with a variety of special interest groups. For Catholics and the religious right, Mim was pro-abortion and pro-euthanasia; for Wall Street she was anti-business; for labor, she was a killer of American jobs; for seniors, she was a threat to Social Security. "Ronald Reagan described America as the city on the hill," he said, "and now my opponent is doing everything she can to extinguish that beacon light of freedom."

Mim counterpunched, gave as good as she got. In most normal campaigns, the release of a position paper attracts little attention and maybe a few yawns. But when her team rolled out

"Six Steps for Saving Our Burning Planet" they hyped it with the kind of saturation ad campaign you'd expect from a movie studio promoting the hell out of a summer blockbuster.

My own world changed at dizzying speed into something I could barely recognize or understand. Everybody wanted a piece of the film, a piece of me, a piece of anything vaguely related to me. My calendar was always full, an endless list of obligations: newspapers, broadcast and cable media, websites, podcasts. Requests for interviews came in from radio stations in countries I had never heard of. I got used to seeing images of myself. Everywhere, it seemed. Everywhere. In them all, there I was with my mop of curly hair and the aviator shades. Fan mail and hate mail poured in, including death threats credible enough that we informed the police.

I wasn't doing anything except being associated with Mim Donahoe's campaign . . . and that, it turned out, was a full-time job. I bitched about all this to Mickey.

"Being in too much demand is a high-class problem," he said. "Enjoy it while it lasts."

This high-class problem got so bad (or as Mickey would have it, we'd so successfully leveraged my brand recognition) that he arranged for an assistant, Giulietta, to take care of my social media. "To free up your time," he said, but I think he wanted to shelter me from seeing the death threats. I also enlisted the services of an entertainment lawyer, a new tax guy, an investment consultant, and a promotions specialist to enter Simple, Not Easy in film festivals and competitions around the world. I was becoming my own cottage industry.

Way back in the distant past when I was living a completely different and much less complicated life (a few weeks ago) I had believed that success—a few more jobs, a little more money in the bank—would magically make everything easier, relieve me from pressure and worry and the crushing limitations of a tight budget. Hah! Mickey had warned me over and over about fame. Now I understood. I was getting swept up by a tornado, sucked right off the ground by something big and of unimaginable power, moving in a direction I could not control, a direction I doubted anyone could control.

Early one morning I sat at my computer with my coffee and toast, searching to see what film critics were saying about *Simple, Not Easy*. The reviews that treated it as a normal documentary were generally positive (though, to be honest, many were a little tepid). They considered it a timely cultural manifestation—"of the moment" was a phrase more than one reviewer used—and they generally forgave the film its glitches and low-budget imperfections. Other critics treated the film as politics not art, a battleground in the campaign—and often took sides zealously for or against. The more argumentative or even incendiary the language used in the review, the more it got forwarded, reposted, retweeted, commented on, trolled.

I scanned another page of search results and froze when I saw "Fight breaks out at antifilm protest." I read and reread the news article, then did a more targeted search and found other stories that recounted the events with additional information.

At a screening in St. Louis, a small group of people from a Catholic church picketed, carrying placards and candles. They objected to what they believed was the film's support of abortion. The story of their peaceful demonstration made the local newspaper and television stations. The following night, nearly a hundred protesters showed up along with a light police presence. Many joined the Catholics and picketed on the sidewalk in an orderly fashion, their position reflected in the signs they carried:

GOD'S LAWS NOT MAN'S AMERICAN JOBS!!!
NO EUTHANASIA
U.N. OUT OF MY BEDROOM
RUCKELSHAUS NOW!

A counter-protest group gathered at a nearby shopping center
and marched toward the movie house. One news account
estimated their number at fifty, another said between fifty and a
hundred, adding the detail that some of the marchers wore black
ski masks. Whatever their number, they too carried signs:

ITS ABOUT WOMYN!
DOMINION IS DESTRUCTION
RUCKELSHAUS = NAZI
GLOBAL RACIAL EQUITY
MIM NOT HIM

Police called in reinforcements, but too late. A series of clashes.
One guy got a broken nose, several others sustained minor
injuries. In a press photo accompanying one of the stories,
a young man with hate-filled eyes swings a placard like a
broadsword at three other protesters leaping out of the way.

This wasn't random. It had happened because of my
documentary, because of me. Had I not made the film, there
would have been no fight, no broken nose, no blood.

My idea had been to elevate Tozer's ideas into a cultural
meme that might help stave off climate change. But as I read
these news reports, I saw that the meme was not born into this
world alone, it had arrived with a sinister twin.

The violence in St. Louis set the pattern. Another melee
broke out in Madison, Wisconsin, leaving shattered windows
in the business district, a police car burned, six people in the
hospital. In the following nights riots erupted outside theaters

showing my film in city after city. Protest, counterprotest, violent clash. It was a thing.

Mickey called one morning while I was reading about yet another bloody scuffle. "No time for chitchat," he said. "How do you feel about Utah?"

"Beautiful country, I hear."

"I just got a call from Donahoe's people. She's having a big rally in Salt Lake City. They want you to be part of it, give a short talk—two minutes. On the stage, right next to her. And need I mention, this will be in front of the press corps—the national press corps."

"Why Utah?"

"It's a battleground state and it's a dead heat out there. Tozer's papers are housed in the library at the University of Utah. You'll present them with a copy of the film for their collection. The exposure, Luke, think about the exposure." He really wanted this; I could hear it in his voice.

"The head librarian was pushing for you to give them all the raw footage from your interview with Tozer." I gripped the phone tighter. "I don't know how you feel about that, but I'm thinking it might be something to hold in reserve—until we want to make a splash around your next film maybe, or when you publish a book."

"Yeah, good idea. Hold it in reserve," I said, relieved I didn't have to come up with some excuse about the footage. "When's the rally?"

"Thursday."

"This Thursday?"

"Piece of cake. Don't worry—you only talk for two minutes. And what do we get? Unbelievable exposure. I told you I've been working on the Times, right? I dangled this Utah thing in front of them. Now it's all set. You meet with one of their writers, Marla Valentino, tomorrow afternoon. This is exactly what we wanted, trust me."

"The *Times*. Tomorrow. Everything's happening so fast." It didn't seem real.

"Look, Gretchen's here, you need to come over. We'll get you prepped. I hope you fully understand the magnitude of appearing in the Times. And in case you don't understand, let me explain it to you: the magnitude is big. Big-big-big."

Before I left to meet with Mickey and Gretchen, I went online to check out this reporter, Valentino. I had expected to find somebody from the Arts and Entertainment section. Instead, she was from the political team, a seasoned reporter who a colleague described as "a practitioner of the take-no-prisoners school of journalism." She had many notches on her gun. Was this a set up? Could she have found out something about Tozer? A newspaper like the *Times* was not to be trifled with—as crooked politicians, thieving union bosses, defrocked priests, and a thousand others had learned the hard way.

When I got to Mickey's office, he and Gretchen were seated at his desk. I'd talked to her many times over the phone but only met with her twice before. She reminded me of my secondgrade teacher, with her graying hair pulled back and her half-glasses on a chain around her neck.

I liked her a lot, her quiet competence, as reserved as Mickey was boisterous.

"When it rains it pours," Mickey said. "And we're having a cloudburst. Between the time we talked earlier and right now, I made a call. New numbers from Zulu. *Simple, Not Easy* is now the most-watched documentary they've ever shown. Ever."

"Nice work," I said and raised my hand to give him a high five.

But he didn't slap my hand. Instead, he shrugged his shoulders and asked Gretchen, "Did I say I was finished with the good news?"

"Apparently there's more," she said, playing along with Mickey's fun.

"The theaters, all two hundred screens, have extended the run for a second week." Now our hands slapped. He threw out box-office numbers that explained his excitement while he leaned way back in his creaky desk chair, triumphant. "And even now, after all that, am I done, am I done with the good news? I don't think so. But I'll save the last one for later. Never let it be said that Mickey Meyer is not a showman." He rubbed his hands together. "Now, some work to do."

I pulled up a chair next to Gretchen.

Mickey leaned forward, placed his palms down flat on the desktop. "When I talked to the assignment editor at the Times, he says he's interested is the protests outside the theaters—the Sturm und Drang. Well, maybe the Sturm more than the Drang. In any case, he's in love with the angle. The reporter will ask other questions too, but the protests, that's the catnip." He raised his eyebrows as if to make sure I understood what he was saying, and when he was satisfied that I did, he pointed to Gretchen.

"Like Mickey says, what they're going to ask you will likely be something like this: How do you feel about the protests of your film and the violence it seems to be attracting? Do you feel responsible? Have you considered withdrawing the film to avert further violence? Might not the most admirable thing be to, so to speak, pour oil on troubled waters?"

She gazed at me as if she expected an answer. I looked at Mickey and found the same eager stare. It was a trap. If I didn't withdraw the film, I'd be blasted for failing to defuse a violent situation. On the other hand, if I took the ethical high road and stopped all screenings, I'd look like a coward, caving to the demands of extremists and lacking the courage of my artistic convictions.

"To tell you the truth," I said, "I don't like people hitting each other because of my film."

Mickey made a sympathetic face. "Who likes the hitting?"

"It is a tricky question," Gretchen said kindly. She picked up some papers from the desk.

"We've worked up these talking points."

I had the feeling of reinforcements riding over the hill.

"I'll read them to you," she said. "I'm an artist whose job is to ask questions, get people to think. I'm not telling anybody what to think, that is for viewers of the film to decide for themselves."

She looked up from the papers. "So far so good?" I nodded.

"Okay, here's some more. I could not leave important questions unasked, even if they are controversial, even if they make people uncomfortable. We only have one planet and the stakes couldn't possibly be any higher, so we absolutely need to respond as well as we can to the hard choices before us. I created the film to help people make these critical decisions, decisions that might be the most important and consequential in human history."

"We have lots more," Mickey said. "Pages and pages responding to specific questions you might get—but that's the main idea."

"I like it," I said.

"What we want coming out of you," Gretchen said, "is short, punchy, answers that flow and make good sense. Control. No winging it. No wandering off into la-la land." Made perfect sense.

"Okay," Mickey said. "Now the last thing, the news I tantalized you with." He drummed his hands on the desk. "I've been working an angle on *People*—the magazine. The one with a circulation of three-and-a-half million."

Did the guy ever sleep?

"As soon as we got the *Times* interview, I put in a call to an editor I know at *People*. Hook, line, and sinker." Grinning like he'd just won the lottery, Mickey leaned back in his chair, put his feet on the desk.

"A photo in *People*. Maybe more," Gretchen said. "It's huge."

"Wow, that's great. When do we do it?"

"Like I told you, when it rains it pours," Mickey said. "Thursday."

"Same day as the *Times*?"

"*Times* in the afternoon. *People* in the morning. What a life."

"Are you shitting me?"

His shoulders rose and fell while the look on his still-giddy face left no doubt that no, he was not shitting me.

"Relax," he said. "You'll be ready. We'll practice, the three of us. Don't worry about it." I did worry, all the way across town driving back to my studio. *People*. The *Times*. Especially the *Times*, and their pit bull reporter. I had talking points that made me sound like a hero and I was going to put on my hero suit and parade around in front of Valentino telling her how great I was, telling her . . . lies.

The traffic light turned red, and I stopped at a downtown intersection. The fear and shame that had been building in me

for weeks boiled over. How had it all gotten so out of control?
I wanted to confide in Mickey, to hear his take. But telling him
would bring things to a head in a way I wasn't ready to deal with.
The car behind me honked.

I parked in my spot, climbed the stairs, and jammed the key
in the deadbolt. Inside, I plopped into the chair at my editing
bay. I had to watch it again. For the thousandth time. Watch it
and maybe figure a way out. I opened the video clip file. Pressed
play.

Tozer in his faded black Earth First! T-shirt, talking into
my camera. "Cutting population is the least painful option.
Comprende?" he says with a sincerity I knew would grab any
viewer's heart. "It's not only our best hope, but our simplest."
He pauses, laughs self-reflectively. "I said simple, not easy." And
that's where I made my cut, that's what I put in the film. But that
wasn't the end of it, was it Luke?

"I said simple, not easy . . . like levitating a million pounds
of lead. Simple, if you have an anti-gravity device. Bah!" Tozer
makes a sour face and waves his hand in the air. He stretches and
grabs the tall can of beer I thought I had put out of his reach. He
chugs what's left, tosses the empty over his shoulder, and burps.
"The fault, dear Brutus, is not in our stars, but in ourselves.
My plan is so full of shit"—he cackles, and this morphs into a
coughing fit. "So full of shit it would lead to economic disaster,
endless wars, mass starvation, eugenics, religious strife—make
the Counter-Reformation look like a flag football game." He
says it disdainfully, almost spitting the words, then breaks into
a rendition of the lion's song from The Wizard of Oz in his deep
bass voice, "If I were king of the forest." He rubs his face and
mumbles, "We can fix every problem.

Yeah, right—when pigs fly, and snowballs stack up in hell."

Later that afternoon, I was in the kitchen when a text vibrated my phone. The message had a link to information about the flight to Utah that Mickey's people had booked for me.

The event in Salt Lake City would be on Saturday night—in three days. I would fly out early that morning. But before departure I had to take care of a few small items on my to-do list, you know, like back-to-back interviews with one of America's most read magazines and with the newspaper of record for the entire nation. What could possibly go wrong?

I memorized my talking points, and though I practiced my answers for hours with Mickey and Gretchen in his office, I couldn't get it right. My delivery sounded fake, forced, choppy, insincere. Gretchen gave Mickey a worried look.

"You know what, I've always wanted to see Utah," Mickey announced. "I think I'll go out there with you."

I read between the lines. They thought I was terrible.

Back at home I went over the talking points in front of the bathroom mirror, tape-recording my answers and playing them back, cringing at every amateurish uh and um. I practiced for hours, until my delivery began to sound natural.

At 5:00 a.m. on Thursday morning, I paced nervously around my apartment with the allnight classical radio station murmuring away at low volume so as not to wake my neighbors, who were sleeping normal sleep, not yet ready to rise and start their normal day. But not me. The clock was tick-tick-ticking me closer to my interview with the people from *People*. I gave the apartment another lap. *People*. Freaking. *Magazine*. When I was a little kid my mother used to have a subscription, and I would cut out the pictures of the movie stars and paste them on popsicle sticks and use them as puppets.

Just after 9:00 a.m., Mickey called to do some handholding. I asked him what kind of exposure he expected from the interview. "You never know," he said. "With *People* the interest goes up and down. If you aren't staying hot, okay. If some other celebrity is getting hotter . . . maybe you get one small photo and a caption or maybe you get bumped from the issue. But little picture, big picture, it doesn't matter too much. This is *People* don't forget. *People.*"

No, I wasn't in danger of forgetting *People* or the *Times*. My whole career I had struggled to pay the bills while keeping my time and soul free enough to pull ideas out of the ether and turn them into something the world had never seen before. But now, here it was, my big moment, my shot—maybe the only one I would ever get. Your big audition, Luke. Do not blow this.

We had blocked out four hours for the first interview and photo session. The writer, photographer, and lighting guy arrived at my studio just before 10. The tallest of the three, the photographer wore a goatee and a fifty-pocket vest. He ran the show. The short, plump reporter deferred to him, working in his questions while the man of many cameras poked around the studio looking for good backgrounds, talked with the lighting guy, adjusted exposure settings.

For the first series of photos, the shooter had me pose on a stool in front of a brick wall cradling my camera. Next, he had me sit at my editing bay.

While the lighting guy repositioned the flash and fill rigs, the reporter asked, "What are you working on now? Do you have another documentary in the works?"

I had a notebook full of half-baked ideas, but they weren't going anywhere as long as

Simple, Not Easy was, as Mickey liked to say, hot, hot, hot.

"I have a few projects in ... various stages of development," I said in a way that conveyed it was too early to go into any more detail.

He scribbled on his notepad. "It wouldn't be anything to do with Mim Donahoe, would it?"

I laughed and begged off with a wink and a smile—what Mickey called a noncommittal committal.

The big-dog photographer said he wanted to take advantage of the sunny day with some location shots. He and his crew loaded all their gear back into an SUV that I followed across Portland to the Japanese Garden. The photographer posed me with mossy pagodas, Zen boulders and raked sand, and by a twisted maple tree with its autumn leaves blazing red, orange, and gold.

We finished late, and I had to race back to my studio to meet the reporter from the Times. While driving as fast as I could on a bridge across the Willamette River, I thought back over my morning and realized the magazine's writer hadn't asked a single question about the fights outside the theaters. Strange.

There wasn't time for lunch and my stomach was growling when I heard the knock at the door from Marla Valentino. She, too, had a photographer, but there was no question Valentino was the boss. While the shooter positioned me and posed me around some of my studio gear, by a window, beside my framed poster for Vertigo; Valentino scowled with increasing impatience and finally said to the photographer in her thick New York accent, "You're done, right?"

She was barely five feet tall with hair buzzed severely on the sides and bangs hanging down in front of her eyes—her hard, dark, intelligent, and very intimidating eyes.

We took seats in my director's chairs on either side of a little table where she laid her phone and turned on its recording app. She started out with easy background questions, though even these she posed in a fresh way. How many times had other interviewers asked what documentaries had influenced me? What she asked was, "What was the first documentary that changed your life?"

"*Lessons of Darkness*. Definitely," I said, citing Herzog's apocalyptic doc on the oilfield fires that burned out of control in Kuwait after the Gulf War. "He broke all the rules."

This got us going on film school, aesthetics, Herzog. "Is there a Herzog film no one has seen that you loved?" she asked.

"*Even Dwarfs Started Small*. Absurd, anarchic, alive with dark madness. He did it in his twenties." She made me feel comfortable talking about movies.

We were an hour into the interview when her phone rang. She peeked at the screen, shrugged "I got to," and took her phone to a corner of the studio where she could conduct whatever business was more important than talking to me.

So far it had been Journalism 101, with Valentino searching out colorful background material, those little stories and anecdotes that good writers love to recount. That wouldn't last— she'd soon be getting around to the tougher questions about the riots. I was confident I could give smooth responses to any question, but would my carefully spun answers be enough to take in a hardballer like Valentino? What if she came back at me with a follow-up question that I wasn't ready for, a trick that would trip me up, leave me looking like a fool.

Valentino returned to her chair. It was the only time in my life I wished someone on a cell call would have talked longer. She started recording again and asked about Mim and Ruckelshaus, my politics, sudden fame. My answers came easily. It was time for the catnip.

"I want to ask about the violence that's been happening at your screenings," she said. "Have you considered withdrawing the film?"

My answer came out just as I'd practiced. Valentino even nodded along at one point, as if my position made perfect sense. She asked a follow-up, and another, and another, but I handled each of them with ideas from the talking points, if not direct quotations. She seemed satisfied and moved on to other areas.

"So, were there experiences or relationships from your early days that you think of as being especially important—stuff that made you the person who could create your documentary?"

It seemed like a good question, and I launched into a story I thought was amusing and revealing, possibly giving the reader a peek behind the curtain of video production. It was just the kind of anecdote she was looking for, and I had told it enough times to friends or fellow film nerds to know it would fly.

"When I was in film school I took a production class in experimental cinema and our assignment was to create something truly unusual. Over the course of the semester my idea evolved from a film to a film within a film to an almost surreal hall of mirrors where the viewer lost all sense of reality. It was while making this film that I came to understand the modular nature of the elements of production—how they can be moved around, like Legos, snapped in here or there, easily switched to a different position for a different purpose."

Valentino was losing interest fast, looking at first as if she was longing for a cappuccino, but as I blathered on, her face hardened into a scowl of impatient disdain, like I was stealing minutes of her life at gunpoint. Gretchen had said to keep my answers short and punchy—I was doing neither.

I couldn't just stop in the middle of the story, but each additional word made things worse. When Valentino picked up her phone and checked the time, I sputtered a hasty conclusion that made the story even more pointless and incoherent.

She sighed. "Okay, let's talk about Tozer. Tell me about your interview with him." Much to my surprise—and relief—everything she asked about Tozer over the next half hour seemed very straightforward. She was getting the background, making sure she had the facts right, fishing for a sparkly detail. I had followed the exact same play book a million times.

I told her how Tozer often used language so salty I couldn't include it in the film, about the bullet holes in his driveway sign, about the rifle shot fired at our first meeting. But even as I was giving her just what she wanted, I worried I was handing her the rope she'd use to hang me. Were my recorded words going to be contrasted with some damning information that she might have dug up? Tozer was long dead, but that didn't mean he couldn't speak from the other side of the grave. The take-no-prisoners school of journalism.

She pressed the stop button on her phone. Apparently, we were done.

"A fact checker might be calling you," she said, "sooner rather than later. The editor gave me a hurry-up deadline."

"Do you know when it will be published?"

She rose from the director's chair and shrugged, "My guess, a couple of days."

It felt like the moment at the end of a terrifying procedure in a dentist's chair when you realize the drilling is over.

Relieved, but only for a moment. As she walked out the door I saw how it could all go wrong. Her idea of a good time was to blow the lid off corruption, to right an injustice, to expose a person posing as someone they are not. How fucked was I?

Tired and achy, I could barely get out of bed the next morning. Did I have some kind of bug? The interview came back to me in bits and pieces like some half-remembered nightmare. My insecurity said it was a disaster. How did it really go? I didn't trust my judgment. What I knew was that a positive article in the Times could be a huge break for my career—just as much as a negative article could be a death knell. It took a long shower and a couple cups of coffee to get me feeling even a little bit better.

I dressed and drove to the studio for my daily meeting with my assistant, Giulietta. When she arrived, she looked me over and said, "You look ... "

"Like crap?"

"No," she said, "not a bit." If Giulietta was anything she was peppy and eager to see the glass three-quarters full. "You look ready for your trip to Utah." A nice kid.

We took care of the twenty or so most pressing items on the to-do list, a blur of details and trip preparation and phone interviews that took us through the afternoon and into the early evening.

I went home and started to pack for the next morning's flight. With piles of clothes on the bed and the suitcase only halfway full, I was once again bedeviled by thoughts of the interview and the pissed-off look on Valentino's face. To distract myself I recited my Utah speech—two inspiring minutes about the visionary, potentially world-saving ideas of Hollis Fanshaw

Tozer. I practiced in front of the bathroom mirror to make sure I punched up all the right words, made the right gestures.

The flight to Salt Lake City went smoothly, and I got settled into my hotel early Saturday afternoon. The room was on an upper floor with a good view of the jagged and snowcapped Wasatch mountains. The hotel was only three blocks from the big downtown plaza where Mim's rally would take place at 7 p.m.

My phone rang—Mickey.

"I just landed. We're at the gate," he said. "Look, I talked to my guy at the Times. The story will run in the Sunday print edition—biggest circulation of the week. It should post online at around six or so Utah time tonight."

An electrical charge crackled through my body—excitement, fear, both.

"I also wanted to let you know Donahoe's people changed the format a little," he said.

"They added a press availability following the rally." My throat tightened.

"Are you there?" Mickey asked.

"What kind of availability?"

"Q and A. You and Mim and the woman from the university library. No big deal. They'll be focused on Mim, trust me. Look, I gotta go. See you soon."

I imagined myself at the Q and A, standing before the glaring lights of the national press corps. If Valentino trashed me or the film, it would be brutal up there. How does it feel to have the Times say you suck?

When Mickey finally knocked on my hotel room door at 4 o'clock, I was more than ready to see a friendly face. He stepped inside, a garment bag draped over his arm.

"What's that?"

"A little gift," he said, handing it to me. I opened the zipper, pulled out the hanger, and marveled—a sport coat made of shiny gold material.

I gasped. "It's like the one . . ."

"Sure, just like Elvis," Mickey said with a devilish smile. "A copy. Not an original Nudie, not gold lame—but close enough."

I held the coat at arm's length, dazzled—it was every bit as gaudy and glorious as the one Elvis wore on the cover of 50,000,000 Elvis Fans Can't Be Wrong. Then a jolt of panic shot through me. "You're not thinking I'm gonna wear this—"

"She could be president," Mickey said, imploring me with his hands spread wide. "You need to look the part—a little flash, a little camp. Imagine the pictures! The pictures will live forever. If anybody should understand that, it's you."

"I don't know, Mickey. Elvis is . . . Elvis. And I'm about as far as you can get—"

"You don't have to decide right now. Let's get some room service. You hungry? I'm starved."

I shrugged and laid the gleaming jacket carefully on the bed where it rested like a bright angel in repose. While Mickey ordered our dinners, I sat at the table where my laptop was opened to the *Times* website. I hit the refresh button with no luck—and hit it again and did so repeatedly as we waited for room service to knock. When the food arrived, I wasn't the least bit hungry.

"You should eat," Mickey said. "Especially the fruit and vegetables. Nice and light."

Ours was such a strange relationship. One moment strictly professional, with him telling me what opportunities to act on and which to avoid, negotiating contracts, taking care of a thousand business details I didn't even know were there to be handled, showing up with a crazy gold sport coat. At other times it was like he was a doting uncle who had always been there, always looked after my personal well-being. I was never quite sure which was the real Mickey.

I looked at the clock, five past six—we were supposed to check in with Mim's people soon. I hit the refresh button again. We would need to leave in just a few minutes. I went to the closet and got the dark sport coat I had planned to wear.

"I'll make you a deal," I said. "If the *Times* piece is positive, I'll wear the one you brought. But if I get slammed, no way." I laid the coat on the bed, deathly drab and boring beside its radiant gold twin—Elvis's roadie next to Elvis. Leaning over the laptop, I tapped the refresh key once more. "This is like waiting for the jury to come in. Why can't they just—"

Mickey held up his hand, waved for me to stop. "I have a little news. Something we should discuss. Sit down." He was serious and I sat. "I've been making a few calls," he said. "You know me, the last thing I do is overpromise, and I'm not promising you anything here, but like I say, I've been making some calls. There might—might—be some interest in getting you connected to a film. I called; they didn't hang up. In Hollywood this is a big deal." Hollywood.

"And by connected," I asked softly, "you mean?"

"Direct. A picture. Yes. They want the next hot thing—I'm telling them it's you. So far nothing firm, nothing solid. I'm just saying, we play our cards right, maybe we get more than talk."

"My god," I muttered. Suddenly the *Times* story meant even more. I leapt to the laptop and hit refresh. Hit it again. Nothing.

"A million things could be hanging them up," Mickey said. "All out of our control.

There's a good chance we won't see the story before we go."

"I'll have my phone. I can check—"

"Nope." Mickey shook his head. "No distractions." He extended his hand and wiggled his fingers demanding the phone.

I handed it over and he tossed it on the bed.

Refresh. Refresh. "What is wrong with those people?"

Mickey checked his wristwatch. "It's time."

The screen was taking longer than usual to reload, and when it did it looked different.

"There!" I called out. We both bent close to the laptop and read the headline. "Move Over Michael Moore."

Mickey ran his finger over the text and read aloud. "With his controversial documentary, *Simple, Not Easy*, Luke Mayfield takes his rightful place among America's new generation of documentary filmmakers."

He nudged me with his elbow. "They're talking about you, my friend."

I read on. "Mr. Mayfield describes his film as an argument for lowering the earth's population in response to the growing climate crisis. 'That's an important idea,' he says, 'an obvious idea, but somehow, not an idea that is part of our conversation. And given that stakes have never been higher, that omission is troubling if not downright dangerous.'"

I scrolled down farther and read silently until I found what I was looking for. "Here it is," I said, tapping the screen. "In response to the recent spate of protests and street clashes," blahblah-blah, "he says he has a duty as an artist to bring Mr. Tozer's ideas into the world, giving politicians, policy makers, and everyday citizens information to do with as they see fit."

"This wouldn't have happened without you," I said, patting Mickey's shoulder.

"It's a win, I'll give you that," he said modestly, while not doing a good job of hiding his joy. "A very nice win." Breaking into laughter, he added, "A very, very, very nice win." He looked at his watch. "Let's go get another."

From over on the bed, the gleaming coat beckoned. I put it on—heavy and cool, it fit me perfectly. All my fears about the speech and the availability had vanished. I could do this thing. I could do anything.

We were just at the door on our way out of the room when my phone rang. I looked at Mickey who glanced at his watch and nodded. I went to the bed and picked up the phone—

Chelsea Zebeida from Mim's campaign.

"Nice piece in the *Times*," she said. "Congratulations."

"Yeah, thanks." I put the phone on speaker. "I was a little worried."

"I wasn't," she said.

"No?"

"Not in the least."

"Why not?"

"Well, you're Mim's darling and Mim has that newspaper's endorsement. Ipso facto, no surprise. Gotta go. But, again, congratulations, really. I'm happy for you."

We got on the elevator. "I'd call it a rave," Mickey said.

"And the quote, 'my duty as an artist,' just like you scripted it."

"I'm just about positive they read the *Times* in Hollywood," he said as the elevator clunked to a stop. "You had some buzz before. Now you're a beehive."

The doors slid open and I floated across the lobby's polished marble floors like silk over glass. We pushed through the revolving door and out onto the sidewalk. The fall air brushed my face, cool and crisp. I drank it in and felt alive and light on my feet and bounced toward the rally site.

Half a block ahead, the banks of bright artificial lights radiated down from atop tall poles, illuminating the raised platform where Mim would do her Mim thing, and I would play my part in her show.

A mass of people stretched from the stage and spilled out onto the street that the cops had blocked to traffic. Some kind of ruckus was going on. A line of police ready for war in their bulky black riot gear was keeping two large groups of protesters separated behind metal barricades. The crowd on one side chanted, pumping their fists in the air, the others replied with taunts and insults. Angry faces on both sides were contorted into hateful masks. As we drew closer, I read the picket signs waving in the air above the tumult—not pro- and anti-Mim, they were pro- and anti-*Simple, Not Easy*.

Someone tossed a water bottle, eliciting a roar. The crowds moved toward each other with a hundred shoving arms. An officer using a bullhorn blasted, "Disorderly conduct will not be tolerated."

I felt a tug on my elbow. "Come on," Mickey said, pulling me toward the security checkpoint that would admit us to the backstage area. We needed to cross the street, but a delivery van the size of a UPS truck was in our way, its emergency lights flashing. The van's engine roared to life, rattled into gear, and accelerated, picking up speed faster than it should— heading straight for the protesting throng.

When the van crashed through a first line of barricades, the cops and demonstrators tried to run out of the way, but for many there was no escape. The screeching van veered sharply and jerked violently as it bounced over a curb, slammed into several people, then crashed into the base of one of the mobile lighting towers. High above, half the floodlights on the tower blew; the supporting pole tilted and began a slow-motion fall like a lumberjack's tree.

The crowd saw the heavy apparatus arcing toward them and somehow managed to jump away just before the light-panel smacked into the ground with the sound of breaking glass and puffs of smoke. The cable that fed electricity to the tower grew taut, snapped, and lashed in the air like a writhing snake spitting sparks. It came to rest touching one of the metal barricades— two people pressed against the retainer stiffened and fell to the ground. For a fraction of a second the scene froze like paused video, then, as if someone hit play, the action started again— screams, yelling, frenzied movement.

Mickey grabbed me by the lapels of my golden jacket and drew my face close to his. "Go back to your room. I'll call you. Stay put." I stared blankly at him. "Do you hear?" He shook me.

"Go." I must have understood because I stumbled back toward the hotel, through frantic people rushing in every direction. Sirens blared. On the sidewalk outside the lobby a clump of people had formed, even as others emerged from the revolving door, stretching their necks to see, confused looks on their faces.

In the lobby, an old man in a wheelchair asked me, "What happened?" I could only shake my head.

Once in my room, I closed the door and leaned against it as if to keep some evil thing from busting through. I felt sick, weak, my bones had turned to water. I slid to the floor and sat there, eyes staring at the blank wall before me. On this screen I saw a montage going backward in time: the van veering, people screaming, electrocuted people falling; cut to, Mickey smiling, eyes twinkling, telling me he has some good news; cut to, Mim on the stage, pointing at me in the spotlight, thousands cheering; cut to, my eyes getting big as I read the notice about the Pemberton Prize; cut to, Tozer taking a pull from his bong and laughing out a huge cloud of smoke.

The door rattled—a pounding sound close to my ears. "It's Mickey." More hard knocking.

I got to my knees and turned the knob. He burst in. "You alright?"

But before I could answer, he spoke again. "I know it sounds cold, but business is business. With the *Times*, *People*, and this thing tonight, this is a very good place for you." He was at the window, peering out. "I can book you on a late-night in a heartbeat—two million, maybe three million viewers. We show a clip of the movie. You say the right thing, boom, it goes viral."

I got to my feet while he darted around the room. "I know a guy in publishing—you'll do a book. An autobiography, a memoir." He looked my way, seemed to see me for the first time. "What's the matter? Is it the book? Don't worry—I'll get you a ghostwriter. It's easier than you think."

I stared at him. It was Mickey, or at least it looked like Mickey, but he seemed different, spouting crazy ideas, making insane plans. He babbled on—platforms and exposure and synergy.

It wasn't just him; it was the both of us. We needed each other. Me and Mickey, burnishing the brand, skipping down the garden path to hell.

"Kill it," I finally choked out. "Kill it all. I'm done."

He squinted at me, confused, then slowly grasped what I was saying. "I did my part," I said. "Now we're done."

"Think about how big the snowball has gotten—jumping off now, it's a bad idea. Think of all the—Luke, c'mon, this kind of attention, it's once in a lifetime."

I pointed toward the plaza with a shaky finger. "People are out there, probably dead, because of my film."

He looked at me like I was some tantrum-throwing idiot child. I wanted so badly to yell out, It's a fake, Mickey, I fudged the film. What I said was, "Just shut it down. All of it. Pull the plug. We can do that, right?"

"Yes . . . there would be penalties. It would cost you. But that's not the point. You've got to think—"

"No. No thinking. Thinking's over. You hear me?"

I got my suitcase and threw in my clothes, then went into the bathroom for my toiletries. Stuffing my toothpaste and razor into their little bag, I saw myself in the mirror, a golden joke in the stupid Elvis coat. I ripped it off and flung it in the tub.

Mickey leaned against the wall and watched while I zipped the suitcase shut. "Where are you going?"

"Away."

He might have said something more as I left. I wasn't listening.

The scene on the street was less chaotic now. The cops had set up a perimeter a few hundred feet from the hotel. Onlookers gawked, leaned to get better views. Cameras from local TV stations were shooting from an area blocked off for their use.

I went in the opposite direction, turned onto a side street, up a few blocks, and ducked into a diner where I ordered coffee and made some calls. I found a car rental place said they had one left on the lot, and that were about to close but would stay open if I hurried.

It was fifteen blocks and I half-walked, half-jogged until I saw the sign for Deseret Transportation. They set me up with a white Escalade SUV. It was huge and hideous, and I thundered down the main avenues of Salt Lake in an amped-up daze. Driving to drive.

Restaurants and gas stations and neon signs. Green light, yellow light, red light, green light.

I turned onto a side street and got to a residential neighborhood where I pulled to a stop in front of a house with no lights on. A dog barked somewhere up the block. The engine cooled and contracted. I sat in the darkness and squeezed my eyes shut, but I still saw the pictures, the plaza, the van, the falling bodies. Tears pooled in my eyes and rolled down my cheeks. I sobbed and howled and gasped until there was nothing left inside, only a spent numbness.

I don't know how long I sat in this oblivion before I began to feel something, vague at first, then more defined. I needed to go, to get away from Salt Lake, as far and as fast as I could. I cranked the motor and drove west, out of the city and into the nothingness of salt flats and desert.

By midnight I was deep into northern Nevada, past Elko, then Carlin and Primeaux, each smaller, darker, more isolated. When I was too tired to go on, I pulled off on a dirt road and slept. At a quarter to four I needed to pee, got out, and stood in the chill air beneath the Milky Way stretched across the sky as clear as I had ever seen it. Countless dots of light journeying billions of years to arrive on this vast silent wilderness—only here, only now, captured only by the optics of my eye.

In the morning I gassed up at a Chevron station in Winnemucca, found a diner, and called Mickey.

"Did you shut it down?" I asked, smiling a thank you to the waitress who filled my coffee mug.

"Truth is, no, I didn't. You were in bad shape. I didn't want to do something we couldn't undo."

"Hoping I'd come to my senses."

"In a manner of speaking."

"I did," I said flatly, "and I'm out."

"Before we address that—"

"Just shut it down," I said and hung up.

When the waitress brought my bill, I asked if there was a barber shop nearby. She gave me directions and I found the place. The sign on the door said it wouldn't be open until 9. I killed time at a truck-stop minimart across the street, walking among the aisles of stuff. An array of hats caught my eye—one of them was a little less ugly than the others—blue with a Mack truck logo and a bulldog. I took it. Next to the hats was a rotating rack of sunglasses. I found a pair that looked as little as possible like my wireframed aviators—square lenses set in heavy black plastic frames. Purchases in hand, I left the store, put on the new shades, and tossed the aviators in a trash can.

The barber, Cruz, had a thick, dark moustache and smelled of hair tonic. I told him to make me look different.

"A little different or a lot different?"

"Like I'm going into Witness Protection." He nodded like he knew just what to do. My dark curls drifted to the floor as he snipped.

I felt the cool of the air conditioning above my ears. When he was done, Cruz spun me around so I could see his work in the mirror. "There you go."

It took a second for me to recognize myself. Shaggy and flowing was now short and trim. With all the hair gone, my head seemed smaller. Exactly what I wanted.

I holed up a few miles outside of Lovelock at the Shangri-La Motor Court. While the clerk checked me in, I noticed a shelf of well-thumbed paperbacks for guests to borrow. I read three of them over the next two days in my ancient twelve by sixteen cabin kept cool by a gasping air conditioner a few decades older than me. The heat let up around sunset, I hiked each day along a trail that started behind the office and twisted down to a dry creek bed, through the wash, and out into the desert. The place I ended up was barren and peaceful, it could have been a million miles from nowhere except for the hum of the big trucks rolling down the invisible highway.

I drove into Lovelock for lunch the next day, then stopped at a 7-Eleven to replenish my supply of bottled water—what came out of the tap at the Shangri-La smelled like sulfur. Standing there with the twelve-pack in my hand, I noticed a guy restocking the magazine rack. I strolled over and saw the new issue of *People*—with me on its cover, standing between a waterfall and a pagoda, the curly hair wild in the wind, the aviators. The headline read "Luke Mayfield: Terror and Redemption."

I put my water and magazine on the counter, hoping the cashier wouldn't recognize me. When she took the money, our eyes connected for a split second. No recognition at all.

I stowed the water bottles in the back of my great white whale of a car and tossed the magazine on the passenger seat. The cover-boy's smug face, its smirking, king-of-the-world expression was too much to take, so I turned the damn thing over. An ad for a cruise ship company now beckoned me to a faraway blue ocean.

Back at the Shangri-La, I pushed the pillows against the headboard, rested my back against them, and stared and stared at my picture on the magazine cover, brightly lit in a beam of sunlight slanting in the window. I hurled the magazine. Its thin pages fluttered wildly through the air, slapped flat against the wall, slid to the floor.

I cracked one of my water bottles, took a sip, took another, screwed the blue cap back on. Carson City Agua. Sixteen ounces. I squeezed the bottle. Flexible, transparent. Some kind of plastic polymer. A chemist's discovery—experiment number 347. Changed the world.

My call last night to Mickey had confirmed the film was pulled. There would be no more blood. I shook the bottle hard, turning its contents into a thousand shimmering quicksilver orbs. The bubbles wriggled to the top, popped, left no trace. It reminded me of those scenes in Herzog's *Encounters at the End of the World*—scuba divers' bubbles rising—glub, glub—in the eerie blue-green world beneath Antarctic ice, trapped beneath the sheet of frozen seawater, pooling like mercury. End of the world, full of alien sights and sounds, jellyfish ghosts, giant slithering starfish, spiky sea urchins pink and red. Werner said that if the world were ending tomorrow, he would start shooting another film. I shook the bottle hard, again and again and again, recreating the universe in grandiose splendor.

Acknowledgments

This book would not exist without the help and support I received from many dear friends and colleagues. Alice Tallmadge offered unstinting encouragement and talked me through more than one fit of doubt. During the dark days of COVID-19 I workshopped these pieces with my Monday night Zoom writing group (Myrna Daly, Darren Howard, Sandra (Lou) Maenz, Michele Koh Morollo, Joe Stowitschek, and Steve Theme); their invaluable observations helped me shape, sharpen, and trim.

My editorial Baker Street Irregulars were unfathomably generous with time and attention, always willing when asked to have a look at a new story: Greg Hazarabedian, Guy Maynard, Marjory Ramey, Vince Tweddell, and my writing salon coconspirators Anne Dean and Sondra Kelly-Green. I am grateful most of all to my first and best reader and editor, Barbara West.

About the Author

 Ross West earned an MFA
in creative writing from the
University of Oregon. His
fiction, essays, journalism,
and poetry has appeared
in publications from *Orion*
to the *Journal of Recreational Linguistics.* His work has been
anthologized in *Best Essays Northwest, Best of Dark Horse
Presents,* and elsewhere. He wrote and edited the University of
Oregon's research magazine, *Inquiry*; was senior managing editor
at *Oregon Quarterly* magazine; and served as text editor for the
Atlas of Oregon and the *Atlas of Yellowstone.*

Printed in the USA
CPSIA information can be obtained
at www.ICGtesting.com
JSHW031924171123
52029JS00005B/27